THE HAUNTING OF MACNIDER HOSPITAL

"The lonely bird flying in the sky is forced
To fall into a haunted hospital,
Yet is this destiny or a trap?
The lonely bird can't fly with broken wings.
As she heals, she must live within the haunting of
MacNider Hospital."

Ann Marie Ruby

Disclaimer:

This book (*The Haunting Of MacNider Hospital*) in no way represents
or endorses any religious, philosophical, political, or scientific view. It
has been written in good faith for people of all cultures and beliefs.
This book has been written in American English. There may be minor
variations in the spelling of names and dates due to translations from
international dialects, regional languages, or minor discrepancies in
historical records.

This is a work of fiction. Names, characters, places, and incidents are
the product of the author's imagination or are used fictitiously. Any
resemblance to actual persons, living or dead, is purely coincidental.
While the cities, towns, and villages are real, references to historical
events, real people, or real locations are used fictitiously.

Published in the United States of America, 2025.

ISBN-13: 979-8-9917416-4-4

DEDICATION

This book is dedicated to the unwavering determined individuals who strive to end forced marriages and trafficking, as success on these issues is weighed through their sacrifices.

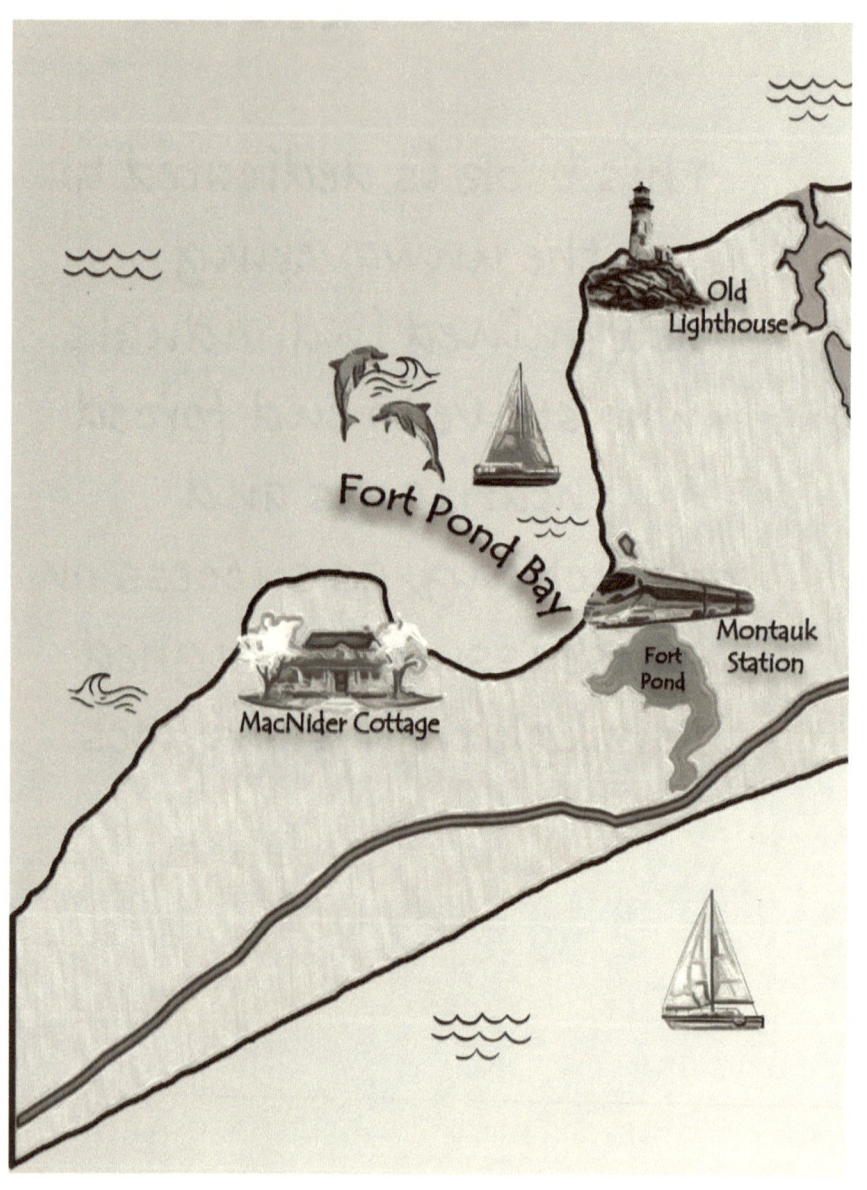

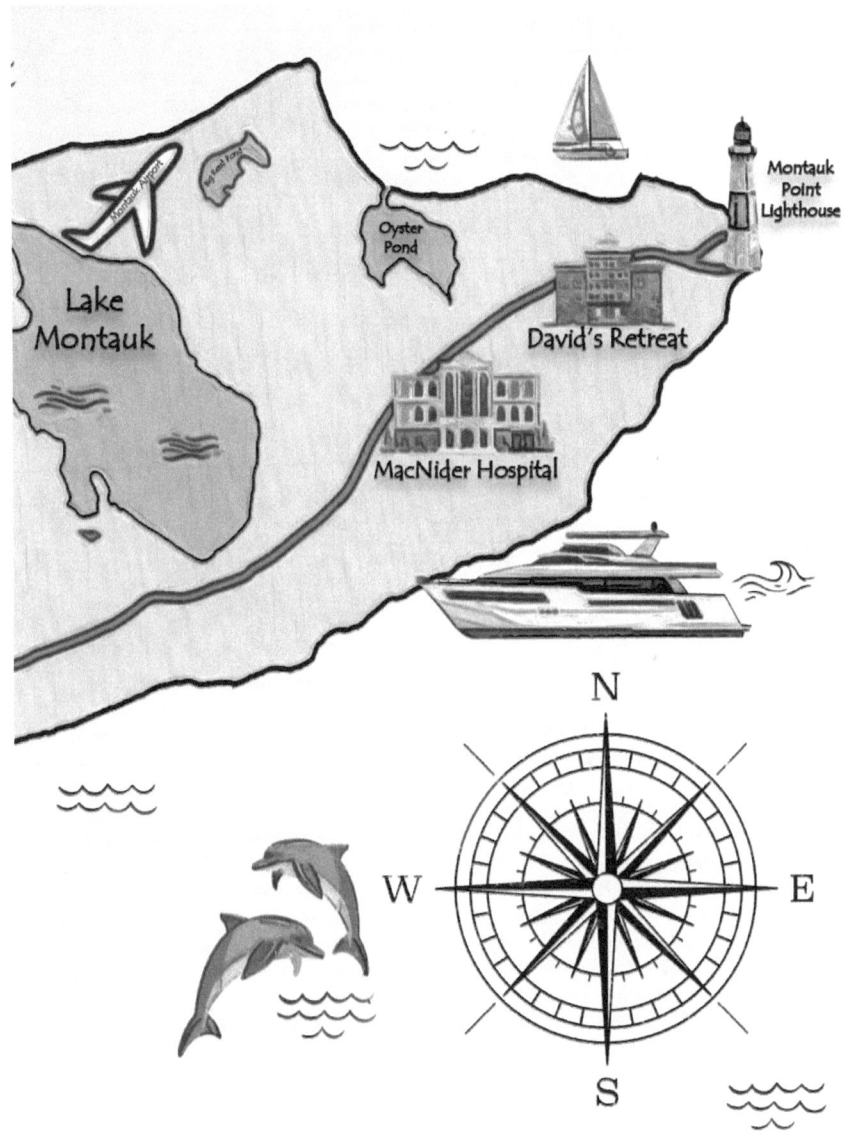

TABLE OF CONTENTS

PROLOGUE:

The Innocent Victim

"Oppressed
Through
The powerful society,
An innocent soul
Can't even
Defend herself
As she becomes
The
Innocent
Victim."

The excruciating and unbearable cries of a woman stabbed through the cold air of Montauk, a small beach town located on the easternmost part of Long Island, in New York. That night, the cries of the crashing Atlantic Ocean waves didn't awaken me, but the cries of a woman did. It's no wonder poets have compared the cries of a woman to the waves of the ocean. I too see the resemblance.

For some reason, the voice sounded so familiar, so close by, yet so far away. I tried to freeze everything around me so I could hear her. I couldn't hold on to her as she faded away and her painful cries kept getting further and further away until they became whispers. I couldn't say who she was. I knew she was in pain and wondered why I felt like she was a prisoner, a secret prisoner hidden away somewhere, waiting for me to rescue her.

The pain and anguish of a broken heart awakened me from the nightmare. I was repeating the name of my beloved wife who was buried under the cold Earth. Our sweet passionate memories live within me forever, even though she is not within my arms. All my life, I will treasure our passionate love, and our two minds, bodies, and souls uniting as one on our wedding night. That one night is enough for me to last not just one but seven lifetimes.

The dream of a woman being tied up and crying kept sneaking back into my head repeatedly. Each time, the dream reminded me of my beloved wife. Maybe my wishful thinking that she was still alive and not buried six feet below somehow gave me multiple nights of dreams. Maybe the Earth would break open and bring my beloved back to me. Maybe she would fill the empty space in my heart and wipe away all my tears. My heartbeats were so loud that I could hear my racing heart. Outside, thunder roared within the night's skies right after a fire broke through from the skies above onto the Earth beneath.

The electrical sizzles caused the trees to dance back and forth as they were swiveling and performing a wild dance concert. It was a miracle the trees didn't fall, nor were they on fire. I wondered whether everything and everyone around them was at risk. Mother Nature was wild as she was performing a destructive dance.

Maybe my inner chaos seeped out from within my heart and was dancing like a mad person who had been cheated on life. I could never blame the love of my life for ripping out my soul as she ripped out her soul first. Sometimes, I do blame her for my solitary life, however, my love for her is greater than my anger toward her.

A woman can take so many different forms such as a sister, a friend, or a mother who provides for her children, her family, her siblings, and her friends. She can become a threat and danger to her enemies. I wondered if the kindest woman imprisoned by society could ever become a warrioress. Yet that night, I watched the mother we all share, the one and only Mother Nature, be assertive not aggressive. While we were all forewarned about a wild stormy night, it was up to all of us to take shelter, not for her to provide. Mother Nature had no boundaries as she set herself free. I enjoyed her enthusiastic dance performance as I knew she was imitating my feelings.

As a lawyer, I must diligently study all the evidence before I argue or represent my clients. My feelings have to be overruled by the profound truth and reality. I see unjust behaviors in the courtroom more often than they should be allowed. As I listened to Mother Nature, I knew she was innocent as her anger was not placed upon us, but rather we were on her path, blocking her concert.

I had upon my mind one such case, a woman whom I would protect and represent in court if I must. She could neither support herself nor could she speak for herself. She was part of a three-strand braided bread which once untied, opened one by one. All around her were not impartial or partial, but just tragedy. Yes, I would speak for and help a woman who never spoke to me. Nor did she ever share her feelings about anything with me as I had held her only once when she was a few hours old.

Her mother had wrapped her in a blanket and given the child to her new husband. I asked the mother of the newborn child, the love of my life, if I could hold her just once. After that, I would forever hold my peace. I was invited to the hospital by the husband of my beloved wife. Yes, it was strange as she was still my wife, yet she wore the ring of another man.

Why I had gone to the hospital, I have no clue. Why he invited me was another question I never asked as I was so greedy to see my sweet innocent child just once. I will treasure and keep that moment alive within my inner chest. No one can ever take that memory away from me.

I prayed my memories stay intact so I could keep that one memory intact within my chest eternally. May the sacred memory stay safely framed in my chest and not fade away like the clouds after the pouring shower of tears. My daughter held my finger with her small, tiny fingers. She had a good grip. I kissed her and prayed she finds all of life's happiness. I prayed for her to give me all of life's sadness and suffering. I prayed for her life be filled with all the happiness and joys from both of our lives combined.

I tried to shield my tears in front of everyone, and I reminded myself who says love lasts forever on both sides? I would keep my love for Viana alive through memories. Promise I had made to myself was I would be there for both if they ever need me. It felt good as I knew my love was innocent and all giving. Nothing needed to be returned.

I only whispered, "May my love and blessings be with both of you eternally. May all the happiness of this world be yours eternally. To respect your wish dear Viana, I shall leave you and never, ever come looking for you. I leave you with my prayers, and even though I shall never be here by your side, may my prayers and love never leave, but always be there with you both eternally."

I saw tears fall from my beloved's eyes as if they were not in her control. She tried to stop them and failed with her effort to hide them. She blinked and tried to hide them, yet they just poured. She bit her lips and was trembling as she kept looking at someone outside of the glass room. My inner heart wanted to see my own child for one reason, just once, as that's all I had to keep my biological child within my heart. No, I did not take anyone to court. I did not complain as I let my love and blessings be my judge. From far away, I would forever be there for both, the mother, and my daughter.

In front of my eyes, another man held my beloved and my daughter in his arms. As he watched me, I saw a single tear drop from his eyes. He tried hard not to show any emotions, but these tears had their own tales to tell. I realized he was a good man, and I prayed may he keep my family safe. Even though my wish was to keep my beloved and our child within my embrace eternally, for them, I would stay far away as that was my beloved's only wish.

Yet dear beloved, may you know I shall always honor your wishes even though they crush mine. May your prayers be answered, and my prayers always protect you. My wedding vows were to keep my promises eternally, so I shall keep this promise. I shall let you go for I love you too much to argue with you even when I know you are wrong. So, my promise to never let you go is now I shall never let you go but I accept your wishes as you let me go.

Viana was the love of my life with whom and for whom I had bought a house with a white picket fence. I had made a porch swing in front of our small cottage home. Being young and madly in love left me with memories, a heart filled with pain, and eyes overfilled with hidden tears. I watched my beloved leave me and get into happily wedded bliss with a man from her own birth country, India. For her, I held my peace forever. Neither did anyone know, nor did I ever tell anyone the child she carried was mine. I gave away my beloved and my newborn child for the sake of my love.

No, true lovers don't always unite and live happily ever after. Some love stories are set in a framework where the lovers say, for you my beloved I shall forever hold my peace. My beloved's parents threatened, or were threatened by someone, to murder their own pregnant child and more family members if I refused to walk out of the picture.

I never wanted any harm on my beloved, our child, or any family members. So not like a quitter, but like a winner, I left so all could live and be happily ever after even though my life would be filled with pouring tear storms. My eternal love story survived in letting go of my beloved. Who says love stories can't continue after separation, for my love story continues with eternal memories. My love story survived because of my sacrifice as I saw my newborn child take birth and take her first breath without any harm.

So, for my unconditional love, I walked away and kept within my heart only memories of my beloved and my newborn daughter whom I had taken courage to visit and lay my eyes upon just once. Forever, her eyes would stay as my heartbeats. My daughter was brought up as an Indian

American who thought she had two biological Indian parents. Never did I speak of this truth to anyone, nor did I ever forget the very blue eyes of my newborn child. No one questioned my daughter's birth as the Indian father who raised her too had very rare blue eyes. No blood test was ever done to confirm the paternity of the child.

This is one such diary, which is written from my perspective through my eyes. So here, you get to witness the story through my eyes only. In this story, I had encountered the very soul of my being, my daughter, under very strange and odd circumstances. Life is a circle, and it's filled with karma.

My child, a newly married Indian woman, with blue eyes, brown skin, silky long black hair, just walked out of her David's Retreat hotel room. She had bags under her eyes. Her hands had bruises that she hid under her silk saree. She had a red dot which I believe Hindu married women wear as a sacred sign of marriage. Her mother had worn one when we had eloped secretly. Yet my marriage never got any recognition as I watched my beloved remarry to please her parents and her society. She didn't think of me and my feelings, or our secret wedding vows I had eternally honored even though she had not. How could she remarry when our marriage was never annulled?

My daughter bumped into me as she was walking obliviously, without blinking or watching where she was going. She had tears pouring from her eyes. It was like a sudden jolt of electrical lightning had struck me and froze me in place. I loved her and always kept an eye out for her from far away.

The promise I made to my then wife was, I would walk away without any harsh feelings, but I would from afar always keep an eye on my daughter. She always thought I was her mother's friend as she had become my student in college. Strangely, she went to medical school and became a doctor, but then went and got her law degree. She called me Professor MacNider.

I held her hands and reminded her to breathe as I said, "Hey Daviana Shaw, right? How are you? I heard you got married as that's what your parents had planned for you. An arranged marriage, right? I honestly hope and wish both of you all my love and blessings. So, tell me, are you back in New York? I assumed you went to India."

She stared at me and was in an oblivious state. I wondered what was wrong with her. It was as if she didn't even recognize me, her favorite teacher. At least, I thought I was her favorite teacher. A cab came, and the driver asked her if she had called him. She said nothing but just stood there. The driver left as there was no communication or words spoken. I knew Daviana was in some kind of shock as she said nothing but just watched me.

The hourly church bell rang. I took her in my embrace and walked to the church that stood in front of us next to MacNider Hospital. We walked in there as she started to cry. I knew she was part Christian and part Hindu. Her Indian father was a devout Hindu. He, as a single dad, had taken care of her since her birth mother, the love of my life, had passed away. My beloved's father had asked me to forever hold my peace and not place shame upon his family or his dead daughter.

With tears hidden and rolled back into my eyes, I held my peace even though this act ripped my inner soul, and I felt like I too had died that day. The only thing that kept me going was the knowledge that I would join her in death or in life as this mind, body, and soul belonged to only one. Until I cross the ocean of life, I will keep my beloved's memories alive within my soul.

I attended the funeral service from far away like a stranger and knew the societal pressure and shame would be something I would not place on my beloved, her parents, or my daughter. The only part of the funeral I didn't understand was why no one ever got to see the face of the dead as it was a closed coffin and burial. It was not a typical Hindu cremation. Nor was it a Christian funeral as my beloved Viana was half Christian and half Hindu. Her mother was a Hindu who too had entered a forced marriage and married a Christian.

Suddenly, Daviana said, "How are you? I hope everything is all right. No, I didn't have a normal arranged marriage. I was forced into a forced marriage, a marriage I tried to avoid at any cost. It robbed me from my life. I breathe today yet my body died at the wedding altar. It was the altar of the dead."

Daviana tried to see if anyone was watching as she looked all around us. She took time and just did her breathing exercise to relieve stress. I wondered what happened and why. I had tried to stay away. I had given her space and privacy thinking that would be better for her. Yet today, I regret my sacrifice might have been a total misfortune. The sounds of cars and people walking outside gave Daviana a panic attack. At the slightest sound, she jumped up and hugged herself as she closed her eyes and clenched her teeth.

Daviana again was absent from everything around her. It was as if she gets in and out of thinking or is on some kind of medication or just absent from everything. I gave her time to recollect herself.

She was inspecting everyone around her and said, "I am on my honeymoon with my husband. A marriage by force, yet I walked into it because I absolutely had no other path to stand upon. I had no other person I could go to for help either. I know you're the best lawyer in this whole world. I need you to help me if you ever hear I did something wrong."

Daviana was crying and praying at the same time, something her mother had also done so many years ago. Viana would walk into temples, churches, mosques, or synagogues, just to pray for our union. She would look at me and wonder why I watched her while she was praying. Maybe I knew our time together was short, so I wanted to keep all our memories intact. All her smiles, worries, and even the weird faces she had made, I wanted to save them in my book of memories. Never did I believe her lifeline was that short. I still don't believe it as I always wonder why I am even alive when she is not.

Daviana was trying to read me as she knew I was so far away, lost in my land of my beloved past. She gave me time. I realized she had a lot of me in her too.

Then she said, "He tried to hurt me with a knife. He said I'm crazy and must say to everyone I hurt myself. He has been doing this to me ever since our wedding night, when he threatened me to hurt myself. When I refused, he did it. He looks so different when he hurts me. Most of the time, I am sleepy or drowsy. We didn't consummate our wedding. I was in the hotel room where he gave me something to drink. I woke up after seven days with bruises all over my body. I don't remember anything that had happened in the past seven days. He kept saying I'm imagining things that are not there."

I touched her hands and tried to talk to my law student who was a doctor and a lawyer herself. Yet she was talking nonstop as if confused. I let her speak when I realized, I must help her, but how? I couldn't call her stepfather nor her grandparents. Who could I call to ask help for her? I watched the child I let go because of love, now on her own grounds come back within my embrace asking for help.

No, I wouldn't be breaking any agreements Viana, as I promised to stay away from our daughter. I did not promise to ignore her when she comes to me for help by herself. The bruises were visible on her hands. Different spots were blue, purple, and red. The red spots were bleeding. Bruises take time to heal, yet I wondered why she was hiding her injuries as if they were nothing.

Daviana was weeping and tried to wipe her tears slowly as she said, "His voice changes like it's not even my husband when he calls me a whore. That's what he said my name is. I am a virgin, and I don't believe in anything before marriage as that's not who I am. He also said I murdered someone. I called the police, and they said he called them and warned them I would call as I'm crazy. My wounds hurt and he said I did them to myself. He brags he will sell me as a sex slave and after I have been used, they will sell my organs. I need you to find out who I killed or why he keeps saying I did. Please represent me."

I didn't know where this conversation was going, but I feared for my child so much that I was shivering. In a church in front of my God, I was holding on to her hands. Her hot and salty tears were falling on my hands and my shirt. Maybe sweetheart today, my soul could have found peace, yet today I feel even more tormented. Why did I let you go?

Daviana wiped her tears with her soft hands as she said, "Even though there were no dead bodies or people, he keeps saying I am mental. I told the police he said I did something wrong. Everyone I try to talk with, he tells them I killed someone. He said he will tell everyone if I don't stay quiet and do as he says. What did I do? He keeps repeating I did something terrible. Why did he tell the police I am mental, and everything is in my head? Please help me. I don't know where to go or who to ask for help. By God, I fear what if bodies surface from somewhere and he says I did it?"

A very tall Indian and European mixed-race man came toward us. I wondered how he knew we were at the church. He bent his head toward one way and waved at Daviana. He walked in like he owned the place. He saw Daviana and held her bleeding bruised hands as he pressed them hard with his nails. More blood was seeping out from her wounded hands.

He smirked and made a hissing sound like a snake as he said, "So is he your elderly lover? Or a sugar daddy? I do wonder how many lovers you have. I should let your father fix you up. I really don't think he would like to find out you kill people and are a whore too! Remember sweetheart, your family basically sold you. They don't care."

The Catholic church we were standing in had a group of people singing Ave Maria. Daviana went and lit a candle.

Daviana then unlike herself, in a full rage with tear-filled eyes said, "I am innocent! No one was murdered! No one was hurt! And I am not a whore! You had planned all of this. Why did you go to India and force my family into deception so you could marry me? You promised me the world. Now, you are saying you will sell me off like a whore and harvest my organs. I can't be your wife as you never touched me, nor did we consummate our marriage. Why is it you call me a whore then? How would you know if I am a virgin or not? Why is this phrase even in your vocabulary? Who are you? I don't even know you. Also, who is the other guy who looks like you? You are trying to make me look crazy, but it won't work. Everyone will know you are pure evil."

I saw a new side of Daviana I loved but did not want people to see and misunderstand her. She was crying and shouting at the same time. Her words were not clear, nor did they make sense. I knew she was speaking from emotional pain. I worried if others would see it that way or would they too think she is mental?

Daviana shouted at her husband who was just standing there and said, "You have been giving me drinks that put me to sleep. You have been drugging me. I don't know how I came here, nor do I know where and how long I have been in and out. I don't have any lovers and if I did have one, he would not be anything like you. I will prove to this world I am not crazy, but you are. Like you, I too am a doctor aside from being a lawyer. I will prove to the world who and what you really are. Your downfall was marrying me. I am your downfall."

Daviana's husband laughed like a madman. He shook his head and rolled his eyes. His face showed no anger but just sadness.

He said very quietly so only Daviana and I could hear, "Did I hurt you, sweetheart? Also, I don't want you talking with your elderly boyfriends. I'm scared how you are hurting yourself. These acts need to stop. I can't be babysitting you all the time. Now, stop screaming and getting more attention than what we need. Why are you bleeding?"

I walked out from the church as I saw Daviana and her husband walk out after me. I stood outside looking at nothing but just wondered how my life went from worst to a disaster. A wild and angry storm hit my life. I was trying to stay calm, yet the relentless storm would not give up. It wanted to ravish my life.

I did not know what I heard or maybe I heard wrong, however he had placed his hand on top of her bruised hand. As a doctor, he should have known you don't press or touch bruises. It seemed he didn't care for her, but he acted to care. A group of doctors came this way and as they all came closer, Daviana's husband introduced himself to the group.

It was strange though as why did he introduce himself again to a group he supposedly came with?

He said, "Hey guys, I am Dr. Samar Kapoor. It's so nice to see new and old faces. I hope you all go and enjoy your dinners. My wife has been a little under the weather as she is from India and not used to this climate. I believe she also has some kind of emotional issues, which we need to deal with sooner rather than later. As a doctor, I believe in being an enduring and a supportive husband."

His colleagues seemed uninterested in his blabbering words. These days, no one wants to be involved in any kind of emotional issues or marital troubles. They all ignored him. Some did try to check Daviana, and then just totally ignored her. It was so obvious he was trying to either attract their attention, or maybe he was acting like a guilty person.

Samar then said, "I'll come and join all of you soon. I just need to take my wife to our room first as I want to let her rest. She is having some mental adjustment problems but is on medication and her doctors told us she will be fine. I just hope my in-laws and my mother didn't force a mental woman on me. I hope I can heal her."

It was like the very clever doctor was now twisting and preplanning his games early on. I knew there was a doctor's convention happening at MacNider Hospital and

David's Retreat, both of which my family owned. The group of doctors was now sniggering and making fun of my daughter Daviana. A person from the group laughed as she walked past us.

The woman said, "So, this is your wife? Why do you say she is from India and is having adjustment problems? I thought she studied in New York, not in India? Also, was she not the one who sponsored your visa too? I heard her family had put you through medical school. I guess some women are just shy. She will get over it soon if she is not mental because she has no shame in screaming publicly."

I could hear angry sounds coming out of Samar's nose. He was so angry and furious after the female doctor's comments. I probably could have seen smoke come out of his nose if I tried hard. It was then I saw a blonde-haired, blue-eyed nurse walk around the couple. She touched Samar's hands weirdly as she said something in his ears.

I followed the three and saw their room at David's Retreat was in the corner. Samar locked the door to Daviana's room from the outside and left a do-not-disturb sign on it. He walked to the connecting room next door with the nurse who looked a lot older in his arms. He gave me a look as I walked past them pretending to be in the room next to theirs. I saw them hold hands very weirdly and walk into the room next door.

I heard the nurse say, "When will you tell them everything? How long will you keep her drugged? The medication could be dangerous for her heart. It gives her uncontrollable temper tantrums. I don't want to be involved in anything harmful. You are too public and will ruin everything."

I saw the nurse shove his hands off her hands. She was emotionally disturbed and didn't like what was happening. Suddenly the thought came to my mind what if she was one of my hospital employees.

The nurse then said, "This was supposed to be your honeymoon. You were to make her fall in love with you, not make her hate you. I don't like how things are going. If you are telling me the truth that she knows about everything and doesn't care about open relationships and being tormented, and if she wants to be admitted into a mental hospital, then I will see if it's still okay with me or not. I need some time to adjust to all of this. I just don't like what is going on. She is your wife, and I am not to be in the picture. I don't want anyone to find out who I am, my age, or my relation to you."

Like the ravishing storm outside, I saw a weird relationship in front of my eyes. I could have questioned who she was or how she was related to him, but he could have easily refuted and said she is just a colleague. Their conversation, however, seemed mischievous.

When my son entered medical school instead of law school, I didn't get offended but had accepted his choice. My son David MacNider whom I call Dave was named after me. He had told me about a male Indian medical student who was charged for raping another student. The case went nowhere because no one could prove the rape. The predator in question was a very wealthy donor's son who had a brother who looked identical to him. No one could prove which brother was the one who raped. Both brothers were proven to be at different places. Like all rich donors, he too was proven innocent. We all let it pass and forgot all about it. Yet it still bothered me if one of the brothers was lying for the other one or protecting him.

Fate has a way of bringing everything back in circles. It matters not how much one wants to run away from the circle, we forget there is no place to go and hide in a circle. The rapist, the predator, who walked away free was the same man standing in front of me. I never forgot his face as I had promised myself if life ever gave me a chance, I would prove to this world he was a rapist who belonged behind bars, not in the society free to repeat his crimes.

It seemed he didn't remember me, nor did he link me to my son Dave. The very dangerous and arrogant rich man walked into the adjoining room together with his naïve elderly nurse girlfriend. I thought she looked like his grandmother but who am I to judge?

My son Dave arrived and held me from the back as he said, "Hey Dad, did you see Daviana was crying? Is she all right? I feel terrible for her. She married the same jerk no one could prove to be the rapist as he had an alibi. He was in class and even the professor testified. She married him because her family had forced her to do so. You know she is the same girl I had a huge crush on. I thought she was the love of my life. You had told me not to go close to her or hurt her, for she would never go against her family."

My son, the pride and joy of my life, was the only reason I survived and shall live only to make sure he has good health, a roof over his head, and a good soulmate to spend the rest of his life with.

Dave continued as he said, "Dad, listen. Like a man in love, I had watched her during school and college, yet she had said no to me as she would never go against her grandfather. Just like you had predicted. She told me you were her teacher, and I told her you didn't know how I felt about her. She knew I would never go against her family or society. Did you know the rape victim had committed suicide? Her family members didn't believe it was rape, but thought was consensual when they all found out she was pregnant. This guy swore he had no hand in it and had DNA to prove his innocence."

I tried to pay attention to his words but wondered why Viana and her family kept coming back into my life when I had just taught myself to live without her. I must now live with agony and the pain of her loss. After losing Viana, I tried to take my own life, but then I got a call. It was a call that saved my life, but the callers didn't live to see their newborn son.

Like it was yesterday, I still remember his last words as he had said, "David, I know you are very young, and I believe you will get over Viana as I have a gift for you. I know I don't have much time. I made a will and have transferred everything I have in your name. Never did I think of you as an adopted brother but my baby brother. Now you will be my newborn son's only living relative on this world. My wife gave birth to him, but didn't get to see him or hold him as she took her last breath. I guess the Lord wanted me to stay alive until I give you David, named after you."

My son became a successful doctor just like his father, Dr. Samuel MacNider. He somehow looks so much like me. People never question if I am his biological father. The Lord does miracles in strange ways. I lived to be the dad of the best son on this Earth.

My son opened the door to our hotel room a few rooms away from Daviana's one. When we get too tired to go home, we stay here in the owner's suite. I debated if we should go home or stay the night as all the attendees were staying there for the conference. We both decided to just stay there for the night as it was paid for.

No, I didn't know about the rape victim's suicide. I closed my eyes as this knowledge tore something inside my inner soul. I could still hear my own beloved's voice who had one day told me she would commit suicide. I made her promise me she would never take her own life as whatever happened, her life belonged to me and mine to her. So even from far away, I would love her and watch her be happy.

I realized how this story was becoming a circle, so I took a vow. I would not let this story end without getting justice for Daviana as she was an innocent woman. She was not only being tormented but was being brainwashed by a famous doctor to think she had killed someone. She screams and shouts in public which she forgets soon too. Was there really someone or some people who was or were murdered? Or was this a phony story made up to make Daviana think she is crazy? I prayed whoever was doing this would leave my daughter alone.

For some weird reason, I prayed for her husband to live because if he was evil, I wanted to catch him and not have my daughter sent to prison for his murder. I feared what was going on. Was it that my inner fatherly intuitions had kicked in and I knew my daughter was in some grave danger? I tried to breathe out all my negative thoughts and only think positive thoughts. I didn't fear she would be murdered as I would protect her with everything I had. From afar, I would protect her and maybe the love of my nephew whom I raised like my own son.

One day, I had told her mother, "True lovers don't always unite but even in separation, they remember and cherish their lost love. Promises made to one another will be kept in this life or another."

This world has come to a stage where one can very easily with power and money change the fate of an innocent. How could someone with no support or power fight back and prove to this world, not everything is what it looks like? What happens in a couple's bedroom only has the two witnesses. If there are three witnesses, then the vows of a marriage have been broken.

I am David MacNider, and this is my diary where I prove the innocence of Daviana Shaw, my biological daughter. She was the victim of forced marriage. She was not mental or crazy. Nor was she imagining anything as she was being administered drugs to make her look crazy in front of the society. For what reason was she being made to look crazy, I had no idea. Yet I knew something more was cooking up. I must prove she had entered a forced marriage which is a violation of human rights. Daviana was not the guilty, but she was the innocent victim.

THE INNOCENT VICTIM

A wild bird

Who flies around the

Amazing planet

With her open wings,

Flying liberally

Without hunting

Or hurting anyone,

Has been captured.

She has been placed

In a cage

Where she can't fly,

Nor can she talk,

Nor can she sing.

Her singing

Has turned into weeping.

She can't sit on the trees

As she watches

The weeping willows too are

Weeping for her.

Her sweet voice

Makes no sounds

For she is the prisoner

Of her captor who has

Shackled her freedom.

Her hands and feet

Are shackled.

Her eyes are blindfolded

Through the society's

Forced marriage vows.

She is the one

Who can't speak

Nor voice her worries.

She is a prisoner

In a cage that

Can be opened,

Can be unlocked,

Even from the inside.

Yet the weak and fragile

Bird is trained

To know she is a prisoner,

As she is a criminal.

She only

Needs to know

She can raise her hands,

Get on her own feet,

And open the door

Of the cage,

And sing the song

Of her life,

And let all

Know,

She

Is not

The guilty

But

She is

This society's

This culture's

THE INNOCENT VICTIM.

CHAPTER ONE:

Promises Kept

"Converting
Truth
Into false,
And false into reality
Through the power
Of deception
Only generates
Instability,
But that's
What
Deception
Is."

The rays of the morning sun peeked through the windows of my bedroom. Dawn broke open as my dream shattered like broken glass. The shattered glass turned into tears as they fell from my eyes and wet my pillows. I so much wanted to see her and find out her identity and why she kept calling me. The same scent my Viana had, I could smell on her even in my dreams. I wanted to hold her just once and ask her if she truly loved me or was everything just my imagination. I couldn't say anything as words didn't come out of my mouth.

It was like I had tape on my mouth. I worried what if she was a stranger and not my Viana, as my beloved was placed under the cold Earth. Then, I got scared for the stranger and wanted to forget all about my Viana. I hoped the woman who called me during the night was all right and everything was just a fragment of my imagination.

Again, I had a nightmare that tortured me throughout the night. Every time I saw the same dream, I lit a candle in hope that maybe, just maybe Viana was alive. She might be hidden in a tower far away somewhere; however, this nightmare was the same one on repeat. A woman was crying as she called me to come and rescue her. The woman was wearing all white. Her gown looked worn out. Her hair was long and unkept, hanging beyond her lower back. I didn't remember her hair color, the color of her eyes, or her face. All I remembered was how my heart ached for her. It was as if she was someone very close and dear to my inner soul.

I saw a woman chained to a brick wall trying to walk toward a door. There was a single bed, and a curtain which gave some privacy from the toilet in the room. A plate with some food was laying on the floor. The woman could somehow see me as she made direct eye contact with me. Shivers ran down my spine, and I felt like I had to rescue her right away. I saw there was a red thread tied from her head to mine. That was the strangest part of the dream. Even though she was suffering, I could feel the pain and the struggles through this red rope.

She said to me, "What about our vows? Have you forgotten them? Please know this, I have not forgotten nor betrayed you. As long as this body breathes, my vows too will live. If my body is no more, then know I never broke my given vows for they are eternal, yet death came in between. Please find me and know I will keep beating death. Even if Mr. Death comes to me, I will let him know I had given my mind, body, and soul to you. He must find and go through you to take me, just like he must go through me to take you. I love you for all of eternity."

It was then I heard screams of a woman in pain. There was not one but two people hurting her. One was scraping her back with a sharp claw-like object. Everything was fuzzy as if there was a fog in between her and me. Blood fell all over the ground. I stood in between her and the two attackers. I pushed the attackers back and saw they fell backward.

The helpless frail woman laughed and watched them run out of the room screaming, "Ghosts!"

She stood up and said, "You're here! I can feel your presence. Please, don't shed tears for me. That will prove to the world our love was weak and frail. I am strong and I have faith in my love as my prayers have reached the door of the Omnipotent. I know you have come!"

I saw she was excited and overjoyed with victory as she forgot her pain and her dripping blood.

She tried to glance toward the place where I stood as she then said, "Please know, I your beloved am still alive. How could I die if you are still breathing? My eyes open each dawn wishing once more to only see you before I do eventually die from this torture. Please pray for me that I live and can take this torture until I can see you one more time. I know you will see me as you must be a dreamer, like your grandmother."

My dream broke and again, I felt so tired and restless. My pillow covers were all wet from my tears. I only hoped my beloved who passed away wouldn't be jealous of this dream maiden who kept calling me. I wanted to know if these dreams were my imagination or if there was someone who was calling me from the beyond. I wondered though how she knew my paternal grandmother was a dreamer.

My grandmother, Grace MacNider, had traveled to places through her dreams and prophesized the future. She also had the ability to visit the past. The only person I had told this truth was to my beloved Viana. My adoptive parents, Dr. Daniel MacNider and Dr. Brianna MacNider, had a dream diary given to them by my grandmother, who at her deathbed wanted them to adopt me. With my adoption, they were given all my grandmother's properties and cash, as my grandmother was one of the richest women during her time. Everything was later transferred to me.

I stood in the shower for a while trying to wash away my tears that fell for this unknown woman; however, I cried for my beloved dead twin flame. Nothing or no one could convince me anyone else was made for me. I was made only for my beloved, who I saw was buried years ago.

Nonetheless, why was I still alive? How could my love not keep her alive? I walked away not because I didn't love her but because I loved her more than being with her if that was not her will. If my going away would keep her alive, I would do it all over again.

Like all other days, I placed a cloak over my emotions. With the pouring shower water, I wiped away all my emotional pain. I had to be there for the one and only person on Earth who needed me, that would be my son, my beloved son who gave me another lease on life.

I rushed to the doctor's office and because of my haste, I forgot my morning coffee. I would take the cup at the doctor's office, the same coffee which people swear could be poison. The doctor's office was busy with patients. I didn't have any appointment, so I had to wait.

The funny story was the doctor in question was my son. It was close to 8 AM and I knew this doctor always left around 5 PM. This day was different as he would leave early. I walked into my son's private clinic, thinking of only happy thoughts. For months, my son and I had planned a cross-country vacation in a recreational vehicle. I knew to beat the Long Island traffic and get off this island, we would need to leave in a few hours. I love driving my camper because we can park and stay wherever we want to as long as there are RV parks. Dave and I both loved our new RV even more as it's our own private hotel on wheels.

The smell of hospitals always made me a little nauseous. I had to remember to differentiate a hospital from a hotel. Even some hotels make me nauseous. I keep thinking, or you could say imagining, what had taken place in the same room, on the same bed before I entered the room. How many people were sick? How many people had died in the same hospital bed? My son told me to think how many people have been saved in the same hospital room. He also says to imagine how many children or adults had been overjoyed of being able to have a vacation in a hotel room. How could I tell everyone that I can somehow feel the past residents?

A long time ago, I had sat holding on to the hands of a newborn baby boy in my arms, I knew I had become a father in one horrible night. I lost my doctor brother Samuel and his beloved wife Riva. They were both killed by a drunk driver. They were brought back to life for a few minutes after the accident as they fought to see me with their newborn son. I would become the sole owner of the property my biological grandmother had left my adoptive parents to give to me after their passing.

My grandmother lost her only son and daughter-in-law, my biological parents John MacNider and Jenny MacNider, in a plane crash when I was two months old. She then gave me away to my adoptive parents when I was five months old after she was diagnosed with a terminal illness. They were both her doctors, the only people on Earth she was not related to yet trusted and loved. Miraculously, I didn't have to change my surname when my adoptive parents had legally adopted me. My biological grandmother's surname and my adoptive parents' last name were both MacNider. She left all her properties to me, saying her wish was to have a hospital built here when I was able to build it.

My grandmother's stone manor on the hill was where we all stayed and enjoyed our life together as a family as this was our family estate. The estate was a forty-acre lot with an ocean view stone manor. Little did my parents, or my brother, know we would all have a short time together. My brother's son survived. He is a doctor just like them and is my only son.

I know my grandmother to this day watches over all of us. Some say they see the old woman go for her morning walks by the lighthouse nearby. She is loved and called by the locals as the woman on the hill with long gray hair. She has a big smile and still roams around the property as a free, happy, and good-spirited ghost.

Medical science made it possible for me to become a father even after my sister-in-law's death. I still don't like visiting hospitals. The smell of death overshadows all the joys of new birth. I had to walk across the path of death and bury my brother and his wife while I rejoiced and celebrated the birth of my nephew. I did not legally adopt my nephew but am his guardian. I wanted my brother's name to be tied with his forever.

It took years but I was able to build a hospital on the same property after I became a successful lawyer. With my grown-up medical doctor son's help and my financial support as an attorney, the two of us had the financial support to build this luxurious high-rise hospital on our ancestral estate. The stone manor we call David's Retreat still stands as a retreat for the visiting doctors which is on a different parcel of the property where my grandmother's original stone manor was. I found it was better and healthier for me to live far away from the hospital with my son in our small cottage.

My inner heart was facing turmoil wondering how I could tell Dave if we could delay or maybe reschedule our vacation. Daviana's personal situation was none of my business, yet I am her father. It tore me apart thinking my child needed me, but I couldn't be there for her. In some weird way, it felt like I lost her again, or did I give up on her again?

My son walked over to me as he said, "Dad, are you all right? I know you hate hospitals. Why didn't you wait at home? It would have been better. Dad, let's cancel our trip with everything that's going on. On top of everything else, there is some kind of a mystery going on here in the hospital. We must figure it out and get to the bottom of it. Everyone is on high alert as the patients who reside on the 13th floor are going missing. Dead bodies are appearing at the morgue even though we don't have any patients who have died."

I had personally financed this hospital to completion in memory of my departed brother, his beloved wife, and my grandmother. It was built on my grandmother's land in a neighborhood with no other hospitals or care. My brother's last wish was for me to somehow fund and finish the hospital so it could become known as a healing center, a house for healing, not a scary place. My brother wanted to fulfill my grandmother's wishes, but financial troubles prevented everyone from completing this wish until I was able to do so.

I thought about what my son was saying. The 13th floor was the morgue. How could those patients walk in or out on their own? If I recall correctly, no one entered that floor intentionally nor could anyone walk out.

Announcements overhead paged Dr. David MacNider to go to the 13th floor. I realized our cross-country trip would have to wait. The only thing I dreaded more than a hospital, dead bodies, and illnesses was managing such a big hospital. There were no shareholders as this private hospital had always run solely on my family funds.

We did, however, create a board so that board members can decide what to do when and how. Basically, they run the hospital for a pay. Running a private hospital was only possible as we had guidance and help from a Dutch family who have private hospitals across the globe. My son's famous doctor friend, Dr. Jacobus Vrederic van Phillip, and his family members, had kindly donated their services for free, and helped us get this hospital going. I had made sure my son followed his father's footsteps and became a doctor to handle all of this.

Before leaving, I told Dave that I would go home and let him handle all the hospital business as this hospital now belonged to him. I stood up and walked ahead as a young nurse came flying and bumped into me. She came from nowhere and she was screaming something in German, which I understood nothing of.

The poor frightened woman was terrified. She was shivering and shaking and felt extremely cold. I somehow knew her blank frightened face told me the story, she just witnessed death. This for a nurse, I thought was normal, but looking at this woman I wondered what was going on. She couldn't have been witnessing her first death. A friend had told me people are more scared of their own death than anything else on Earth. I thought those people can't be parents nor had they fallen in love.

The sounds of curses got my attention as curses in all languages were curses. Now the woman was sweating, and her face was blank and traumatized. She was shaking and swirling her words. Dave came running from a room and grabbed the nurse in his arms as he steadied her calmly.

He then hugged her and calmly asked her, "In English please. What is wrong and why are you screaming in a hospital wing where we have serious patients fighting for their lives? Please get a grip on yourself at least for the patients. Also, why do you look so unfamiliar? I know all the nurses and doctors of this hospital. Are you a substitute? Jacobus, do you know Jacobus? Did he send you here?"

Sweet musical piano notes were playing harmoniously on the overhead speakers. Calming ocean waves mixed with reassuring sounds of the wind were playing in the background. It felt so relaxing that I could fall asleep through all the frightful events. Yet falling asleep here gave me the chills. The woman who was still shaking froze in space as she was giving everything around her a blank stare. I wondered was she okay or was she dead? She looked like a dead person walking.

I didn't know why, but I saw the husband of my biological daughter walk toward us with his so-called girlfriend assistant walking by his side. She looked so much younger today. Maybe she just had some blood for her morning coffee, as she sure looked like a vampire woman. I wondered if those two were glued to each other. Looking at the woman so close now, however, made me wonder was she young like him or much older than him?

He smiled at us and asked the nurse directly, "Why did you run out from surgery like you just saw a ghost? It's not the way we handle business here. If you can't do the job, then don't be a nurse. Never ever repeat what you just did because you could have risked my patient's life by running out in between a surgery. And who is he? No one is allowed in this part of the hospital. That is a specific rule of the founders. I've been called in to do a procedure."

My daughter's so-called husband was pointing his finger at me. He was making gestures to have me removed.

45

I watched the newcomers and smiled at them both. I wondered if he had a memory problem because he didn't recognize me, but he was obviously talking about me. We had only met recently, and he still watched me strangely. Was it a fashion statement these days to either ignore and pretend you don't remember your last encounters, or act like you're always on drugs or are drunk?

He was clenching his teeth as he talked and whispered his words. He also rolled his head back and forth in authoritative teasing manner. I screamed in my head and told him to just act normal. I ask so many young and old people these days to just be normal and not follow any trends but just be yourself. I train my clients to act normal in court or remember you have a big chance of losing your case.

My son broke the awkward situation and said, "This is the famous Attorney David MacNider, and my beloved and dear father, the owner of MacNider Hospital. I will not allow any visiting or permanent employees to insult my family. I believe you know this is a family business. This hospital was built completely with private family funds on my father's ancestral grounds."

Dave was angry as he touched his head, and he rubbed his nose when he was angry. As a child, he would stomp his feet along with rubbing his nose. My son was the best baby boy, and now as a grown man, he still was the best son a father could ever pray for.

Dave with a raised voice continued, "I thought you know who he is. You just met him, remember? You met when you were being abusive toward your newlywed wife. As the owner of this private hospital and your bread giver, I believe it's his right to be present at any place he so wants as long as no patient is placed at risk."

The weird guy said nothing but just smirked at us. I could swear I saw smoke coming out of his elderly girlfriend's nose. He looked at me, up and down, as he twitched his eyes and lifted his lips in a shocking way. I could say these looks did not work with the fashion statement he wanted to display about himself. I knew he was trying to judge me from my attire. The world judges through attire, not the person inside of the attire.

I was wearing my favorite old jeans with a blue sweater. My son and I were supposed to be on the road. True my sneakers were worn out, but I liked them that way. I adjusted my glasses and paid more attention to my onlookers. I wanted to observe people as observations usually tell their own story. I saw Samar and the elderly nurse who was glued onto him. They were both watching me so critically. I laughed and thought how scrubs always look so perfectly ironed.

This man, my daughter's strange husband, had long brown hair tied in a bun behind his head. His eyes were blue even though his skin was brown. I knew he was of Indian and European descent. I wondered what the original color of his hair was. Was it originally brown, black, or blond? It's hard to say. He reminded me of my daughter and how so many Indians do have colorful eyes as they too are bi-racial. The very uncomfortable woman who accompanied him was staring at me. She was trying to say something but did not.

The shoes, the watch, and the ring on her finger showed off money and class. The question that popped in my head was, why was she in scrubs and just got out of surgery but was allowed to keep these on? Even though the Indian doctor was married to my daughter, somehow, he and the woman were both always together, even in the hospital. I assumed doctors work with their teams and patients maybe as a group. I brushed away my awkward feelings and knew I had to concentrate on the mystery that was evolving in front of me, not on my suspicions or weird feelings.

At that time, suddenly the screaming panicked nurse stood up and went behind me as if the five-foot-tall petite woman wanted to hide herself behind me. She was scratching me with her fingers. Luckily, she had short nurses' nails. She tried to grab my hands and show me something. She pointed toward Samar but froze again. I followed her gaze and saw both Samar and his nurse were observing the frightened nurse.

She said with a lot of courage and trembling voice, "My name is Lucy. I always wanted to meet the people who created this hospital. I wanted to thank you from the bottom of my heart and just hug you. I will haunt all who tried to hurt my little girl or me, even if I don't make it. I was forced into a marriage. A man who looked like my husband raped me. When I lost the rapist's baby, he came back and tried to kill me with a knife. It was then the brother of the man who raped me, married me to honor my character, not because he loved me."

Lucy cried and I watched her stand like a woman who lost everything in life and even now was devastated because life gave her only miseries. I wanted to tell her I would be there for her like a father or a friend, but I knew it wasn't possible. I dropped tears for her and watched her slowly fade away as she touched and wiped my tears and smiled back at me.

Lucy said, "Unexpectedly, I fell madly in love with my husband even though I knew he married me out of guilt.

I was pregnant with my husband's child. He knew and still went ahead and remarried as if our wedding vows meant nothing to him. He said in his line of work, marriage wasn't on the plate. I ran away from him as Dr. Jacobus and his family helped me. It always felt like he married me to save me, yet from my end, it was complete love. I wish maybe one day, he will also say from his end it was also love. My husband, now another woman's husband, had searched for me."

I hugged the nurse. She was trembling and was having a hard time controlling herself. I heard her whisper in my ears as she held on to me as hard as she could. Her body and whispers were getting cold.

She whispered very quietly, "Help me, please. They will kill me. They are not who they pretend to be. In this hospital, people who come to be treated are all in danger. Some people are here to take life, not to treat and save lives."

If she was an employee, then why didn't Dave recognize her? I held on to her. She was shaking a little less and settled down.

I told all the hospital staff who were standing there ready to scrutinize, "Why don't you go back to your respective jobs? We can't have the hospital run on its own. Even though you personally don't know me, I'm positive your wallets do. As you know, private hospitals close more often than anyone realizes. I am blessed as the Kasteel Vrederic family from the Netherlands has supported this hospital by not only being here but keeping an eye on all our doctors, nurses, and support staff. Also, someone please find out when and how this nurse was employed. Did she come with the visiting doctor? Or was she hired by Dr. Jacobus as she implied?"

The odd couple silently without saying anything started to walk away. Neither did they try to introduce themselves nor did they try to make small talk or explain the inconstancies of the nurse's employment. They were, however, eyeing the young nurse from afar. It was as if they would hold her in a prison or make sure she never spoke. I wanted to ask her so many questions. Instead, I watched her faint within my arms. The poor woman couldn't take the evil stare the two had given her.

The thought irked me of how I never noticed this hospital had an employee whom I had no clue of or about. I needed to talk with my Dutch friends to make sure they had employed this one nurse, because I surely knew no one at the hospital had. There were so many strange faces all around as the hospital grew faster than I realized. I still didn't recognize the woman in my arms, nor the doctor who had an ID card with the name Dr. Samar Kapoor.

Even in this large hospital, we're usually able to keep our eyes on all employees, and all the small and big details, making sure our hospital provides the best possible care through medicine and technology. This family-oriented, very high-tech hospital was built with all the facilities that modern medicine could give us. My son had been running the hospital with his Dutch friends. Our Dutch team was led by the famous Dr. Jacobus, son of the famous Kasteel Vrederic of Naarden, the Netherlands. His mother, the famous author, takes care of all the living and education expenses of orphans around the globe. His father, the famous artist, has been one of our main financiers for years.

Over time, our hospital has grown healthily. Great news is the hospital is never short on doctors, nurses, or technicians. We always have a huge international group of visiting doctors training with our local doctors every day.

Dave took over as he said, "Lucy, what is the problem? Why are you here and not at the station? I realize you work at three different places, but I don't know why I can't place your name and face together. You said you are an orphan? And Jacobus and his family wanted you to be here?"

Dave took her hands and froze. I knew from his face that something was wrong. As he called for help, he pressed an emergency buzzer. Others rushed in and they all took the nurse into a private room. Everyone was screaming. In a short period of time, Lucy the nurse who was here to help and nurture so many sick people became a patient herself. I was sitting with one of Lucy's friends as she had no living family members. All her nurse friends were praying for Lucy to recover miraculously.

Out of nowhere and without any reason, Lucy's heart stopped. She was pronounced clinically dead. I had wanted to ask Lucy what staff members were whispering about. After investigating the situation, we found out staff members were witnessing ghosts walking out of the morgue for days. They began quitting as rumors started to spread within and outside the hospital walls that this hospital was haunted.

Dave then told me even though he didn't recognize Lucy initially, he recalled how Lucy was hired by Dr. Jacobus. She had actually assisted in a few surgeries that Dave and Dr. Jacobus did together. Lucy was one such nurse who was loved by the family members of Kasteel Vrederic. As Dr. Jacobus is my son's close friend and our hospital's biggest support, I knew any harm on Lucy would be a personal war between us the owners of this hospital and the perpetrator of these crimes.

My son also told me no one knew who employed the strange doctor husband of my daughter. So, I began an investigation into the fishy doctor and the nurse who accompanied him. There were no hiring files on them. They had arrived a few weeks ago and were using different operation theater rooms to perform different surgeries. According to the records, most of his patients had passed away. Strange, he was never investigated as he kept moving from hospital to hospital.

Before I left, I walked by the morgue with Dave. For some reason, I felt icky maybe because I knew it was a morgue. Then, I thought I saw a young woman walking inside of the morgue wearing all white. Her eyes were all black with huge circles around them. She was trying to show me something when I made a sound. Dave gave me his hand. I did manage to see she was bleeding. In that room, there was a huge crowd of people. They were all wearing white, and they were all watching me.

Dave held my hands and asked, "Dad, are you all right? You don't have to be here. I can handle these things. Maybe you should go home and just take the rest of the day off."

I ignored my son because I wanted to go and talk with the people wearing white. As I walked toward the others, however, they disappeared. For some reason, the woman in white kept pointing toward her chest. I stood there and thought my tired brain was imagining things. I didn't say anything to my son, nor did he say anything to me. The vision I could not forget, and I knew I must keep it safely within my chest until the time came for it to make sense.

The visit to the morgue did not end well as there were no dead bodies in the morgue. There were a lot of blood stains and some kind of rancid smell was all over the morgue rooms. Dave was furious because it was obvious something very suspicious was going on. The apparitions continued as did the moaning sounds. A cleaning crew walked in and ran out of the floor, screaming in fear. Dave and I said nothing as we both knew it's better to say nothing unless we knew what was going on.

I did say to my son, "I think I'll camp in your room tonight. You grew up too fast. I really miss my baby boy. So, Dad will join you and it will be like camping."

Dave laughed and held me tightly as he kissed my head and hugged me. He said nothing as I knew when we went home, we would both probably just camp in the family room, like we did most of the time anyway.

The walk to the coffee shop seemed longer than usual. The coffee tasted bitter and cold, as did the scones I ordered at the coffee shop a few blocks from MacNider Hospital. The hospital had my name, or I would say my son's name as he is also David from David and son, half owner of the hospital. We all call him Dave to differentiate him from me, as I am known as David.

For my son, in the medical field, Dr. Jacobus is the whole world. The whole world knew him, but I had never met the famous Dr. Jacobus. I knew him as a nice family man as his family always came first and that's why he was even more famous. I waited to meet him one day.

Dr. Jacobus was the world-renowned doctor who took upon his hands issues everyone would avoid and stay away from. Dave said if there was a burning building, everyone would run out of it, but Jacobus would run into it. He would never give up if there was anyone else to save. He would die trying to save that one person.

Dr. Jacobus had believed in Dave, his dear friend, when no one else wanted to help convert his dream into reality. The hospital my brother had started took years. With moral, financial, and technical support from Dr. Jacobus and his family, we were able to finally convert our dream into reality. We needed their help with whatever was going on at the hospital. When medical science and a lawyer's basic intuitions fail, the Kasteel Vrederic family members believe in their dreams. I must let them know and get some kind of guidance from them as to why I too see dreams. I wondered if I was dreamer like them.

The door opened and a beautiful woman with long black hair and beautiful blue eyes walked into the coffee shop. She walked and banged into my son who was trying to get his coffee and pastry. Dave had brown hair and brown eyes just like his father did. He was six feet tall, and I assumed the woman was five feet, five inches. For some strange reason, she jumped into his arms. She was shaking and looked terrified. She looked like she walked out of a movie representing victims of abuse.

My hands and feet froze. I made a fist trying to control my inner emotions. My biological daughter stood in front of me. This was the child I gave up to only keep her alive. For her, I did not fight with the love of my life, her mother. I knew I won the battle of love by giving them both up. In my mind, I told my Viana, love is eternal in union or in separation as my love for her never betrayed our love story.

I wanted to hold Daviana in my chest and ask her what was wrong? Why did she seem so lost and oblivious to everything around her? She was walking like she was sick and would fall and faint at any moment. Dave tried to steady her by holding on to her hands. She screamed in pain. I saw blood was dripping from her hands.

She said immediately, "I am so sorry for whatever I did now. I didn't mean it. I promise I will change and never do it again. Please don't hurt me. My bruises hurt a lot. I never called anyone, I promise. I won't call the police. Please don't let my family know. They won't be able to take the pain."

I stood up and started walking toward her, yet an invisible shackle grew and entwined around my feet. Yes, my feet stopped by the given promises that tied me up eternally. I just wanted to see what was going on. I gave up my daughter, not so that she would live a life in fear and pain. I gave her up so she would live happily with her mother, as that's what her mother wanted. Never did I ask for any fatherly rights. Yet why was my daughter shaking in fear, even in public?

Dave indicated to me to sit down and not get involved. How could I tell him I was involved even before she was born? She was living and breathing because I was involved in her birth. She was the only proof of my love. She was the only proof that I the evergreen bachelor too one day had loved someone so dearly. To this day, I live with those sweet memories.

The Earth shifted when I heard my beloved Viana try to hide in my chest. She was shy and so sweet when I carried her to our bedroom in the house we built together, yet to this day I sleep alone in the same room. We spent our honeymoon in our own home, planting flowers and creating a dream home until our dreams shattered. Like shattered glass, I too jolted back to reality. Dave was very gently helping Daviana sit at a small table for two, right next to my table.

He took her coat as she said, "No, I am cold. I will keep this on. I like having something on. I really don't have much time. I wanted to get some pastries as my father whom I call Bapu is coming. He likes Danish pastries. This is close to David's Retreat where I am staying. My husband and I will move into our apartment soon, so Bapu is coming to help us settle down. I love having Bapu around. That's when I can be free like a bird and don't have to watch all my footsteps. I don't get hurt and no one dares to hurt me. I only wish he could live with me forever."

I let out a breath of relief. At least the man who took my child away from me was taking care of her. Dave got up, holding her coat, as he watched her very carefully. She did not complain, nor did she say anything but just cried. In front of my eyes, sat a very sad and fragile woman. She was frightened and was trying to wake up from her sleep. Or was she trying to fall back to sleep? It was hard to comprehend. My whole being tore apart as I witnessed the only candle of hope left by Viana was shattered.

Daviana then said, "I asked you to meet me here so you can give me some medication for my bruises. I really don't want to bother Bapu. He will ask questions, and I don't want any argument. Samar is my grandfather's stepbrother's son. My grandfather lost his stepbrother a long time ago as he was murdered in their own home by intruders. We never saw Samar because his mother, a German woman, never kept in touch with us until recently. She is the same nurse who always travels with Samar. Never speaks to me as she hates my grandfather, my mother, and me."

My daughter got up and tried to see if anyone was coming. She felt better seeing no one was there. Daviana sat down and rearranged her thoughts. She was smiling and happy. Whoever she was thinking about gave her good memories or made her happy.

She smiled and took a deep breath as she said, "Bapu is kind, but Samar's mother somehow came back into the family, and she wants to take all our family properties in

India and internationally. My grandfather had transferred everything to my name. So, this woman hates me and wants me to give her all my properties as I am the sole heiress of my family. She lives all over the world and wants to have all the properties worldwide."

Dave gave her a cup of apple juice and took away her coffee. I didn't think she even realized since she was deeply absorbed by her thoughts. She took a sip of the juice and made a face. I took a mental note, not fond of apple juice like her biological father. I didn't like it either. It reminded me of the time I had to have my gallstones removed and was on a BRAT diet. My mother only gave me apple juice. Since then, I absolutely couldn't have it without the horrid memories.

Daviana then started to talk again. I realized she was in this manner just like her mother who spoke nonstop when she wanted to, but she wouldn't talk at all if she didn't feel like talking.

Daviana then said, "I never knew my mother. Everyone told me she died when I was a baby. My grandfather, Edward Kapoor, whom I call Nana is 96 years old and still going strong. He is coming with Bapu. Nana is very sad. I believe he been sad ever since my grandmother passed away and my mother was buried. He only lived for Bapu and me. Nana keeps saying he must go on until he can undo his mistakes. He is strict and still to this day, very kind toward Bapu and me. I don't know what everyone has against Bapu. He is a live-in prisoner who could leave but maybe for me he never did leave and has been a prisoner by choice."

I realized my past would come back to bite me if I got eye-to-eye with that man, Daviana's grandfather, ever again in my life. He knew Daviana was my daughter. He was the person who had broken us up and would do anything to break up my daughter and her chosen man to only honor family and tradition or maybe his own made-up rules.

Yet I did wonder why he allowed my Daviana to marry a biracial man if he so valued his cultural values. Maybe he had become elderly through the years and changed his way of thinking. I had to leave the coffee shop before everything got out of hand. I wanted what had happened to me and Viana to be left buried in the past. I didn't want to dig up anything unpleasant.

I wanted to leave the coffee shop where the last symbol of our love was. I just took a deep breath, however, and told myself to live with the memories of my beloved and not let my emotions ruin my child's life. I remembered the phrase that kept me going all these years.

I had told my Viana years ago, "For you my beloved, I shall live. For your love, I shall let you go. For your memories, I shall keep breathing. Never separated by time or place as we are always united through love."

I heard the screams of a prisoner break through even the daylight hours in the coffee shop. Dreams come and visit me in the darkest part of the night, yet now for me it seemed like they were arriving even when I was wide awake and not fast asleep. Somehow, I felt dizzy as I knew the screams belonged to a woman who came and visited me from dusk through dawn. She disappeared at the first sight of dawn like a vampire. Yet her screams I could hear even then. I wondered if everyone else had heard them or if I was the only one.

The warm, bright, and clear skies suddenly roared with thunder. I couldn't let my dizziness hold me back, so I jumped up. I had so much to achieve, but so little time. I needed to investigate what happened to the nurse Lucy. The roaring thunder then brought in the two men from my past, whom I dreaded the most in my life. One was walking with a cane, and the other one was helping him.

Both were very visible and were walking toward me. I wished there was a secret trap box under the coffee shop where I could jump in and hide. I didn't fear these two men, but they brought back to life my love story that never found its ending, never found its beginning or its middle. My love story was buried alive within my chest to keep the other half of the beholder alive. Yet that too had ended, and that had kept me neither alive nor dead. Somewhere in between life and death, I live.

All my life I wanted to ask this cruel man why he thought forced arranged marriages worked in his eyes. Why did he think love marriages, especially interracial marriages, did not work? Why could we not love, live, and learn from our own mistakes? Why must we live with your forced mistakes?

Daviana helped both her Bapu and Nana sit next to my son who spoke with them and said, "My medical assistant will call and set up the dates for the surgery. I will not do it as I have a Dutch team coming next month who will do it if they think it's necessary. Again, I don't like to do any surgeries if I don't have to at your age. The surgery could be a higher risk than not doing anything. My advice would be to just enjoy the rest of your life knowing we all did our best. That includes getting opinions from other doctors, especially from Dr. Jacobus."

The men saw me and stared at me directly. They smiled warmly toward me as I tried to avoid eye contact with them. I realized Dave saw the exchange and he will have a million questions when we will be alone. Yet now I saw a doctor worried for his patient talking.

He said, "We would want you to take a second opinion before anything else. We know heart transplant patients have a lot of qualifications they must go through. You can't just buy a heart, it's a dead person who donates a heart. Also, there is a long line ahead of you on the transplant waiting list who will get priority because of your age."

The two men came to my table and shook my hand. The elderly man said, "Miracles happen when you least expect them. Don't believe everything your eyes see as they don't tell you the whole story. I do understand life is not fair, yet I beg of you to keep an eye out for my granddaughter. Also promise me, if she ever needs help, you will help her."

I only nodded and assured him I would be there for her if she so needed me to be there for her. Both men had some water and then left abruptly. I knew they thought money could buy anything, yet not there. It was so strange to see life take a twist. The person who had taken everything away from me was in front of me, near my own hospital. Yet again, I remained quiet for the sake of my beloved daughter.

As her mother had taken my heart away, I stopped living by learning to keep my heartbeats quiet. My daughter had increased my pulse, and I only worried why my sacrifice seemed hollow. How many people around me were sacrificing their lives too? Why did everything seem so complicated?

The question remained if Daviana was loved by her grandfather and stepfather, then how was she so bruised and why had no one said anything? Her bruises were displaying a pallet of colors, all over. Under her eyes there were black and blue bruises. Her wrists had marks of cuts. Her fingers seemed cut and irritated. Clear signs of abuse were displayed all over her body. No one in public or in private said anything, nor did it seem anyone was even worried. These days, it's better that words were not uttered than uttering. Also worries are just left behind in the closets, and only belong to the person wearing the clothes.

A cold shivering breeze filled my heart. The drapes in the coffee shop were moving even though there was no wind outside or inside. I felt like a fog was filling the room. It was then I heard a very familiar voice whisper in the air.

I heard, "Help her. Help me as I wait for you to break me out, to break the lock and rescue a psychologically tormented and abused woman who waits to be rescued. I am the prisoner who waits for you to rescue me. I can help her as she too is on her way walking toward a prison, yet please help her as she is innocent."

I tried to see who was talking as the voice was so familiar and I had been hearing these words more and more recently. I knew it couldn't be her but just my mind playing tricks. Our daughter needed help to be rescued. Or could it be that a dead person was trying to get in touch with me? Maybe my beloved was there watching over both of us somehow. So, I must have been daydreaming. I thought I was the dreamer who saw dreams, but this was getting weird. I shivered away my worries.

The thought of a ghost trying to communicate with me completely drained out all the hope I had of my beloved walking out of her grave, standing in front of me, and saying, she was alive as she was buried alive. To this day I keep on imagining she would knock on my door and will say all of this was just a nightmare. I closed my eyes and tried hard to bring myself back to reality. I needed to hide all my selfish tears so I could be there for my son and my daughter.

That's when I heard Dave say, "Spill it! I walked away and let you be with your family. I let you have your way because I loved you and will always love only you. How could I sit in front of you and ignore your bruises? You're being tortured. I can see them and so can everyone else. Your father or grandfather do not see them."

Dave was furious. He gave me the look, and I knew I would get some of that anger displayed toward me tonight. I would wait for all of his queries as he deserved answers at least from me.

Dave said to Daviana, "Your mother passed away at your birth, right? So, she can't ever help or probably would have kept quiet as she too probably never had a voice or choice. Your family is mixed with interracial marriages, so why did you have a problem? Your father is still here, or is he not your father? He somehow looks different. I can't quite touch the truth but as a doctor, I know when something is amiss. Is your biological father dead? This man is biracial, just like you. Your eyes are so much like his but somehow look a lot like my father's."

It was that one sentence that got Daviana up as she stood up and screamed and started to cry, "Take it back! Please take it back now! Take it back! My father is alive and may he always be. I pray may my lifeline be given to him if he has less. I pray may my life be gifted to him because that's what my mother would have wanted."

I closed my eyes and prayed for her to live, laugh, and find love. Daviana walked closer to the windows. As she saw me, she ran and came and hugged me. I was crying, so she wiped my tears with her soft bruised hands. Her shaking hand took a bit of her eyeliner from the corner of her eyes as she made a dot with it on my forehead. I knew it was a nazar sign as Indian women do that, so no evil touches your loved ones. Viana used to do it to me.

Daviana watched me for a long time, as she again poured her tears without any words being uttered. She opened a locket that was on her neck. In front of me was a picture of myself and her mother in an embrace. It was our wedding picture. A very happy couple who had so many promises and dreams filled in their hearts. I stood up and watched her for a while. I wondered how long she knew.

She said, "My name is Daviana and it's Scottish. My mother was very bitter and angry all her life as she was a prisoner of her society. She had named me just before she passed away when I was a baby. She left a note privately with Bapu for me. My mother said she had fallen in love with David and as her name was Viana, I was named Daviana. David had told her that Daviana means beloved."

I saw a happy girl in front of me. I realized anything that relates her with her mother made her smile and be happy.

Daviana then said, "My mother and grandmother were both prisoners, not by choice but by force. My grandaunt, a European American international trafficker, had imprisoned my grandmother and mother as both had voiced their objection to this criminal's path. All my family members from that day have become victims. My mother gave up her life to save her mother's life. My grandfather had done everything to save his wife and daughter. So, he lived a loveless life, for the love of his wife and daughter."

Daviana sipped her apple juice and jumped up to see if anyone was there. She was relaxed when she realized no one was there.

She continued talking as if she was in a rush, "My grandmother eventually was supposedly murdered, and her ashes were scattered in the river Ganges. My grandmother died trying to protect her daughter. My grandfather who is the only one who loves me is petrified by my grandaunt. She has some kind of leash on him. My grandfather witnessed everything and still has no voice. Now, he is trying to protect his only child who was already dead to this society, yet for some reason I'm still alive. My grandaunt said she has her European crime family control all our investments as she is the jailer who takes anyone who objects her ways as prisoners."

I wondered how long she knew. Why did she never call me or let me know? I realized how could I have gone against a belief and a society which had no place for brokenhearted Romeos? The Earth beneath my feet was shaking but I had to make sure I could stand steady and walk. Everything was so strange as I thought it was family and society which held my wedding vows captive. Yet it seemed like money and greed won the battle as they take societies, countries, and all greedy people as their army.

Dave then said, "Why didn't you accept my love? You knew I always loved you. I would have protected you from all the societal harms. I'm not scared of any tyrant, trafficker, or drug lord."

Daviana said, "I couldn't be in love with my own brother or cousin, could I? Strange, I thought you knew too."

I watched both and realized it was too late, but I whispered out loud for all to hear, "I was adopted by my parents. I am not blood related to my brother whose son I have raised like my own. So, sweetheart, if only you could have told us before. No, Dave is not biologically my son or my nephew. I consider Dave to be the son and the child I never had. If only you had asked."

That's when I saw the infamous doctor walk in. He was six feet tall with shoulder length brown hair, blue eyes, and brown skin. I realized again, biracial. He could have been a star with a lot of fans behind him. He could belong to any ethnicity. Somehow, he had a very mean and cruel look on his face. I felt like he was born to be evil.

He went straight to his wife, my Daviana who had beautiful long raven black hair, olive-colored skin, and blue eyes. As he held her hand very tightly, I watched Daviana whimper silently in pain. I could have sworn he had his nails in her skin.

Daviana's husband, Samar said, "She has some mental issues. See all these bruises? She does them to herself. It's all self-inflicted. I'm the only one who can understand her day-to-day issues. She has gone through a lot of psychological traumas. I'm trying to help her by understanding the reason to why she is like this, before we can treat her. That's why I am trying to get miraculous treatments for her because I believe in love and healing together."

He held her hand even tighter as he made a hissing sound in her ears. Everyone could hear him yet said nothing.

Samar then said, "My mother is her grandaunt, and the relationship is all so weird, but in my family, everything is as my family so wishes. I am not by blood a Kapoor as my mother had me through an Indian sperm donor. My father

Dr. Doug Kapoor had adopted me. These are notorious secrets that can't be shared with anyone. We don't follow any religious or societal rules, but we do as we wish. We try to teach societies to make their own rules as we travel around the globe."

I called Samar by his first name, not last, because I didn't want to take my father-in-law's name out of both respect and disrespect. I saw he had blood on his hands as I watched Daviana's blood drip on the floor. I wanted to shout as my son pinched me. I saw there were guards wearing all black standing inside and outside of the small café.

Without being given any permission, I rebuked and said, "If you are breaking any international law or not, it is up to the courts to decide. By squeezing blood out of her hands, however, you have broken the state law under domestic abuse. It seems your intent is to do her bodily harm as you have pressed her hands causing her to bleed publicly. By humiliating her in public, you have just committed a federal crime. I can go after you anywhere. I can prosecute you in any US state. If I were you at this time, I would really be worried."

The strange doctor just laughed and hissed at the same time. It was the ugliest laugh I had ever heard come out of the mouth of the man who was wearing a wedding band in my daughter's name.

Samar said, "You see, you don't have any authority in India. Daviana is a weak Indian woman who knows not to argue with her husband. It's culture, not law. Also, I am the only one who is willing to treat this mentally ill woman, the daughter of another mentally ill person. That's why I must always keep her under my surveillance. Her family has said her mother and grandmother, were like this, mental. Their house should have been an asylum, not a home with all the crazy women. My mother saved their home, and she is dangerous, so don't come after me. I would not if I were you."

He pulled Daviana and walked out of the coffee shop. Daviana never uttered a word as she walked out silently without complaining about anything.

I shouted after him, "Maybe I will catch your mother in an international crime, so then I will come after both of you. Promises I make, I keep."

I only wondered how Daviana managed to bruise her back, where she couldn't possibly touch. We could all see the dark bruises of a belt whipping her back. Her hair blowing in the wind uncovered the bruises on her back. At such a young age, she was tackling a society that had accepted abusers and who knows what kind of criminals in their own families, who walk and roam around freely without having any consequences.

Dave patted my back and said nothing. I saw how he too was angry and furious but kept quiet as he had asked me to keep quiet. I had to get it out as it hurt me too much being a firsthand witness to domestic violence and intent to do harm. Neither I nor Dave said anything. As all left, I had the memories of my beloved daughter being in pain in my head that I could not get out. I felt lost as I saw my son Dave come and grab a napkin from my table.

He said, "She was scribbling on this paper. I saw her, but I don't know what she wrote. She dropped it on your table when she hugged you. Look! Dad! It has a note!"

I unfolded the napkin and saw a note:

I am not mentally unstable. I am the abused. Please help me. I am your biological daughter. I have nothing to prove I am your daughter but my tears, and my mother's necklace and note. My family members will disprove all my words by denying everything.

I need your help to prove my mother and grandmother were not crazy but prisoners of a society where love is not accepted, where abuse and beatings are all accepted as just normal, where tyrants rule the society. Being happy means smiling and just saying you are happy, even though tears wet the pillows.

I can't sleep because I am in so much pain. I can't even write this note without bleeding and dripping all over the napkin. My fingers hurt, Dad. I need you please. I want you to prove I am the innocent.

Also, a secret I shall only write to you is, I need your help in reawakening my mother. She is not dead, but we must all publicly pretend she is. Bapu told me she is not, and he has been trying to find out where she is being held as a prisoner.

Maybe you will know as Bapu said she is your twin flame. She was yours and shall always be yours. She never was his and never will be. He tried to keep your love intact to only have her reunite with you, but my grandaunt and her criminal family members found out and had removed her.

Please from the power of a twin flame, let half of your flame lead you to her. She is a prisoner held at an unknown place, I don't know where. Please help her even if you can't help me. My grandfather said he was wrong in separating you two but did it because his wife was being held a prisoner. Now he lost his wife and daughter. For years, he did as they said but now my life is in danger. I would want to only unite you with her even if that means it would be my last breath. Bapu said my mother kept uttering your name until she fainted from abuse.

She had uttered your name because that was her only strength. I am not crazy. They will all say I am crazy like my mother had been crazy for a white man who had made her pregnant and dumped her.

My grandaunt is a white woman herself. She is preaching division and racism. She uses these teachings to create division and harm. They will say everything is my imagination as how could a buried woman be alive? I say because she was buried alive, and Bapu rescued her. She was abducted and sent away to an unknown prison somewhere on this Earth.

My extended family members are having a woman dress up in white and pretend to be the dead ghost of my mother only to make me crazy. My husband married me for my family's money and his family members are all trying to have me committed to a mental hospital declaring me to be crazy.

Somehow, they have been involved in killing people and making them disappear. I heard Samar say they will have me arrested for murder. Please help me.

With love,

Your daughter

Daviana

Again, I heard screams and cries of a woman who kept asking me for help. I knew twin flames can call one another, yet how could Viana call me and be my twin flame when she was married to another man? Also, I had witnessed her burial. I had to find out what was happening, but I couldn't share my dreams with anyone. If I shared my dreams, they would say I am crazy and so my daughter too is mental. They probably would say it runs in the family.

I gave Dave the note to read. I also gave him my diary which I brought along to write about today's events.

I told Dave, "My son, read the diary and you will be caught up with my tragic love story. I will share my love story, a very short story which started and finished so quickly, so soon. The best part of this short story is it was enough to keep me going through my very long life."

Before we left the café, everyone saw a lady shackled with chains appear like a ghost and scream she was in pain. Everyone in the café jumped up and ran out saying the small café was haunted. Some people took cell phone pictures and videos, but nothing showed up on their phones. I knew who she was as she was coming for me. She was somehow getting stronger as she could travel even outside of dreams.

Trying to avoid any more attention, I walked out of the café in the middle of the screams and rush. The people said because it was a hospital café, the ghost probably was a dead person who wasn't able to pass on. People kept talking about the incident. As I left quietly, so did my son.

He said in a very calm and silent tone, "I have seen a lot of ghosts in hospitals, but this woman looked so real. She disappeared as quickly as she arrived. She was calling someone. I thought she was saying my name. I wonder if anyone else has passed away."

I wanted to tell him she did say David, not my son's name, but my name. I decided not to say anything. I went home and tried to sleep out my worries. Maybe some would say I quit or gave up on my beloved and our daughter. How could I tell everyone that I was a burned-out soul? I was like a candle who burned itself to wax. As I burned out, I spread an invisible carbon dioxide gas and water vapor all around me. I kept all my pain inside of myself, so I wouldn't harm anyone else.

I had nothing left inside of my soul. My wound had never healed and now a very old wound had been opened. How would I recover or heal those who have reopened my raw wounds? Who was this woman who only appeared in my dreams, who was now appearing in daylight hours in front of a crowd?

Dear Viana, I will keep my wounds hidden inside of my soul and be there for you as you call me. From far away, I will help you and will try to be there for you without allowing my open wounds to burden you or toxify you or our child. For you, I have lived my life and for you, I shall give up my life.

Who said love and lovers write their love stories in union? This love story will survive and be immortal even in separation. I know my daughter is the strongest woman on

Earth as I will prove for our love, our child Daviana is not crazy. Neither were you nor your mother as you were all psychologically tortured. So, my beloved, like our wedding vows, these are my promises kept.

PROMISES KEPT

Love stories are made through

Two beloveds

Falling in love.

In separation,

They are incomplete.

In union,

They become one.

Yet even

In separation,

True love

Never dies

For it becomes

Immortal

As the vows

Of the two beloveds

Remain eternal

Through love

And tears of the

Two beloveds.

This story is written

Not through a pen,

Yet through

Tears of

Eternal promises

Given

And

PROMISES KEPT.

CHAPTER TWO:

The Walking Dead

"Could the dead
Walk on
Their own?
The dead who have
Been sleeping,
Could they walk
On their own?
Or is it that
The living
Today are,
The walking
Dead?"

 aybreak arrived too soon and the horror-filled dreams never seemed to find any answers. I was breathless under the amazing stars, running away from a woman with long black hair. She was running toward me, yet in my dream I was running backward. No matter how much I tried to go toward her, my feet kept on going backward. I saw tears fall from her beautiful innocent eyes. She tried to come near me as she fought on her own.

She cried and was staring toward the same stars as she uttered, "Why don't you come to me? I have been waiting for years. I could just accept defeat and fall asleep. It would be easier, but then I know I would be separated from you even in death. Is it not enough punishment that I have been separated from you all my life? I just want to take my last breath telling you, my beloved, I too kept my vows. I want to sleep next to you, not far away from you. I'm always trying to find you in the dark, but I find you have evaporated at dawn."

Again, she had shackles on her feet. Her hands and feet were stained with blood. I asked her so many questions, yet she only repeated the same phrases.

She said, "Where are you? Why are you so late? When will you come? I'm scared and worried I won't make it. My earthly body can only take so much. I just want to see you at least once please before my death on Earth. I don't want to become an unrestful soul, so I want to die after I see you."

My sleep seemed sleepless as even after a long sleepful night, I woke up so tired. People love peace and quiet. As a single father, however, I had to keep my doors and my ears open during all times of the day and night. Dave was a very mischievous little boy. Peace and quiet meant Dave was up to something. Quietness always gave me more stress as it wrapped me up in a blanket of fears. I didn't know what happened as I knew I was awake, but I couldn't get up. I was trying to call Dave my son as I forgot Dave was a grown-up man. I had always woken up worrying for my child, my young mischievous boy.

My dream shifted. I saw a man dressed in all black was trying to suffocate a woman.

She was crying and said, "Please let me go. I never did anything wrong. Why are you lying? You are lying about me. What do you want? Do you want someone to die and blame it on me? But why? What have I done to you?"

The man wearing all black now had all white on as he jumped up and down in a clown costume. I wondered why he was in a clown costume. He was trying to hide his face.

Then, I saw an ambulance. The paramedics came out with a stretcher and left with a dead body. I tried to see who was dead. I cried for my daughter whom I never held, never fed dinner, and never gave a bottle of milk to. I was the unluckiest father who never got to see his own daughter grow up or walk her down the aisle in a wedding gown.

I heard Dave call me as he said something I couldn't hear. His words seemed so far away. My son was very slowly trying to wake me up. I somehow was screaming and crying. I repeated "Viana" nonstop. I sat up and had a cold glass of water. Dave had the glass in his hands for me. With time, my son Dave became the caretaker, and I became the one who kept asking him for help. It felt like I was sweating and had run for miles. My pulse was high, so I tried to calm myself and watched my son staring at me with a million questions in his eyes.

Dave teared up as he helped me up and said, "Dad, what is it? I did read your diary and am so sorry I could not help. If only we could time travel and go back in time, I would be there for you. I will try now, and we will together win this part of the battle. At least now I know who Viana is and why you always wake up crying for her."

Dave placed the glass of water on the bedside table. He then gave me slices of oranges and I took them as did he. We both enjoyed the cold slices of juicy oranges.

Dave then kissed my forehead and said, "I am a doctor but am your son first. You're the only family I have, so I don't plan to lose you anytime soon. No funny thoughts, and don't even think of anything weird. Please share your pain and let's investigate everything through the lens of my father and his famous prosecutor mind. We will win this case together. Remember we are together father and son, joint mystery solvers."

The doorbell rang as I wondered who could be ringing our doorbell at this hour. I told my son I would share everything with him soon as we saw a very familiar face staring directly at the cameras outside the gate.

Dave went to the speaker system and said, "Hello. May I help you?"

On the speaker, we heard a deep male voice. He was feeling awkward and looked in different directions. He ran to his car as if he wanted to leave. But then somehow with a lot of willpower and courage, he walked back to the camera.

He said, "Hi, this is Dr. Jay Shaw. I am Daviana's father. I got your address through a lot of hardship and would really like to talk with you without any eyes prying on us. In my life, I fear the walls too have eyes. I had to run away from the hospital as my father-in-law is in the hospital now. So is my son-in-law, who I fear is not there to save my father-in-law, but to harm him."

Dave opened the gate as we watched a compact rental car enter our driveway. We were in our very small, cute cottage I had with Viana where I didn't raise Daviana, but raised my son Dave. The four-bedroom cottage won best garden of the year for a few years in a row. Our garden was a flower lover's paradise. We had a wraparound porch with hanging plants, ceiling fans, and cottage style seating arrangements. The huge privacy gate was installed to keep my little boy inside and all the nosy busybodies outside. Our white picket fence which granted us good neighbors was covered with fragrant filler flowers. The heavenly scents from our yard go to all the people who pass us by.

After reading my diary, Dave sighed as he gave me a big bear hug and said, "I will never leave you Dad or this home. I feel like she was supposed to grow up here, maybe because I did, she will grow old here. If I ever decide to marry, she too will have to live in this home with you. We will raise our family here. You will be here with your grandchildren forever. If no woman agrees, then it's just father and son eternally. I will never ever let you go Dad."

We watched a very rich person enter our small cottage. He said nothing nor did he see anything around him as he was nervous and seemed like he might faint out of nervousness. I wondered what bothered him so much that neither did he stop to smell the flowers, nor did he see the porch swing which he bumped into even though it was not even near the front door. The funniest part was he almost knocked on Dave's nose as he was oblivious to the fact that the front door was open. Seeing Dave's face shocked him more than knocking on the door.

Dr. Shaw walked in as he very loudly said, "I'm not a medical doctor, but a PhD. Just wanted that out of the way. I really need to talk in complete privacy and whatever I say must never leave this room. I am an introvert, from birth. It feels like I was cursed, and I'm shackled with an invisible chain, so I can't say or ever share anything in my life."

I served some hot tea with fresh baked pastries, hot from the oven. My son loved making pastries and bread before I could even come downstairs. Dave would have done well as a baker, but he chose to save lives. He said he would retire as a baker and feed all the people he had helped live long healthy lives through proper healthy diets.

As Dave was serving and helping himself, he said, "It's all right. Just calm down, sip the tea, and speak your mind. I hope Daviana is all right. It can't escape anyone's eyes, she is being battered and abused. She is a victim of domestic abuse. I hope her family members see her bruises for as a doctor, I know they are not self-inflicted. I will have to file a report with the police as that's my job. They will find out she was also a victim of forced marriage. This will cause harm and shame to the family name Kapoor which the family wants to keep clean."

Dr. Shaw looked at me directly as he tried to see through me. I never felt uncomfortable, nor do I shift eye contact when someone gives me the looks. It's a habit I have trained myself to do as I had spent most of my life defending or prosecuting people in courtrooms. I observed the man sitting in front of me did not seem Indian. He had blue eyes, dark brown hair, and something about him was strange. Sadness surrounded him like a fog. He had bags under his eyes maybe from worrying or sleepless nights. Did he have European genes? Something about him made me think Dutch.

Dr. Shaw smiled as he knew I was observing him, and said, "I will be completely honest with you. Never was I jealous of you David, yes Viana's beloved David. When we lost Viana, I heard her repeat nonstop like a prayer, 'David's Viana and Viana's David.' I cried for her and for you. I knew it was a sin to separate true lovers. After you held Daviana and left her with me, I have done my best to be her loving father. Never did I see her as my stepdaughter or adopted daughter, but as my own. I don't believe in stepchildren, as all children are innocent, and the parents are blessed to have them through birth or adoption."

Dr. Shaw helped himself to a pastry and poured himself a cup of tea. I observed his hands were shaking. The man who I thought I would hate and kick out of my house, was sitting in my own living room. Oddly, I felt no anger or grudge against him. I thought three lives had been ruined.

Dr. Shaw looked at me directly and said, "I am half Dutch and half Indian. You see if you are even half Indian, then you don't get as scrutinized as you would if you are completely from another race. You look guilty, but don't ever feel guilty. You saved my life by giving me your daughter. Now she is through the oath of love, my daughter too."

He smiled and knew I had this question in my heart for as long as I could think back. I nodded and smiled at Dr. Shaw with acknowledgement. He smiled back. I felt lucky to have Dave. In the same way, I guess he had Daviana.

He then said, "I veiled her and protected her from the enemies within her own family. Her life is in danger, and I am helpless. I have a secret, for which life has been tormenting me from within my own body. I fear something big is going on, but I don't know what it is. If I could, then I would carry Daviana back to the past and hide her within my arms as I did when she was a baby."

Suddenly the air felt cold and chilly. The wind blew inside through the open windows. I stood up and wanted to just erase and forget everything. Selfish maybe, but I wanted to hide my feelings and myself from this nightmare that was taking place in the daylight hours. Maybe all of this was a dream, and I would wake up soon to know all of this was just a dream.

Yet nothing changed as I heard Dr. Shaw say, "Please call me Jay as that's what my Dutch mother used to call me. She was the only person who loved me for who I was. I was born as an intersex person. My genitals, my chromosomes, or any reproductive organs I might have don't fit the male or the female sex binary. Even though I dress and live like a man, I am not a male or female. I feel like I was born in a prison, yet Daviana made me her father. Through her, I found my identity."

The whole room fell silent. I stopped sipping my tea and my pastry froze in the middle of my mouth and my hand. If we were in a movie, this would be where everything pauses. As Dave pinched me, I remembered to take a bite and almost choked on my little piece of pastry. I was shocked I still didn't wake up from my dream as I realized it was not my dream but my reality. Still somehow, I was able to unfreeze myself.

I watched Dave say, "Intersex is a natural distinction, and within our world, 1.7% of humans are intersex. As a doctor, I have seen others who are also intersex. There is nothing wrong. It's just how you are. Will everyone know when they see you? I assume no. Intersexuality was one of my research projects and involves a lot of physical and psychological trauma. We must be happy with the bodies our Creator bestows upon us. If not happy, then there are doctors like me who can help."

Why would Viana's family force her to marry Jay if they all knew about his condition? Nothing made sense. Why would a father make his daughter go through this nightmare of separating her from me? Why did he separate me from my daughter to only have her married off to a person who never loved her?

Jay watched me and smiled as he said, "Viana's family used my condition to blackmail my family members to agree and marry a very pregnant woman. My Indian family members were ashamed of my condition, so they hid this truth from the world. In return we had agreed to everything Mr. Kapoor had asked us to do. We told everyone Daviana was mine. It was easy for them as I am half Dutch and half Indian."

Jay closed his eyes as I saw tears fall from them. It was then I realized how both of us were cheated by life. I asked myself why?

Jay then continued and said, "You see, my family's honor was at stake. My family had sworn to never let anyone know about my situation. My sisters, nieces, all the men, and women would have been discriminated and judged if my condition did not meet the society's expectation. So, I hid myself inside of myself. You see, it's not something I chose but was born with. Everyone shows sympathy and say they understand, yet a lot of people are actually scared to touch people like me."

I had so many questions but asked nothing. I had to let Jay talk. For the first time in his life, he was free and was letting go of the biggest burden of his life. I felt so bad for him. Yet suddenly it dawned on me, my Daviana must have known as a doctor on top of being a lawyer. She had said how much she loved her Bapu. I am so proud of my child and knew her Bapu was a great guy as he raised her like a great father.

I blurted out without thinking, "Daviana knows, I am guessing. So, she too is being blackmailed by the same people to be exposed and shamed if she doesn't cooperate. What else is she being blackmailed with? I would have just told everyone the truth and let everything play out in real time. She knows you love her. In my eyes, you're the best father Daviana could have asked for, obviously aside from me."

Jay laughed as he finished his pastry and sipped his tea. He walked to the window and tried to see something. I asked myself if he was scared that he was being followed by the same people who were blackmailing him.

Jay saw me and said, "Yes, she knew always, even before she became a doctor. My daughter and I have no secrets. I am completely honest with her. I need your help now. I have been protecting Daviana as she is my daughter, whom I could never have had but she was God's gift to me. You should know, I never married Viana, Daviana's mother. Viana tried to commit suicide when I tried to marry her. She said her mind, body, and soul belonged to only you. Viana said she would commit suicide if anyone else touched her. I couldn't have sex with her even if I had tried. I told her that her body would be safe from me ever touching her. She said it mattered not if our relationship was physical or not. She was married and would die before she let other men touch her or fake marry her. So, I kept her secret and lived in the same house like her brother, not husband. Yes, it was a small lie which kept her dignity and my family's honor. It also kept both of us safe from Daviana's grandaunt, who is German and Indian mix. She had a huge leash on the family as she at that time had one member of our family imprisoned."

Dave got up and refilled his tea while looking out the windows. He closed the curtains and walked back to the couch.

Dave then said, "Why is Daviana's life in danger? Why is she married to an abuser who is keeping her like a prisoner? If everything is out in the open, then I hope you know Daviana's husband Dr. Samar Kapoor is in my eyes, a suspicious character. Why aren't you worried for her? She is living in grave danger. If her so-called husband attacks her on the wrong place, Daviana won't have bruises. Rather, she won't live to tell the story. He is a visiting doctor and has never been employed by our hospital."

I felt numb thinking about how the last symbol of my love, my daughter might be in real danger. What should I do? Who do I call when I had nowhere to go or no one to call?

I asked Jay for the first time, "Why did you allow Daviana's grandaunt's son to marry her? Is he not her uncle somehow? He isn't related by blood, but something is weird. How could you let this happen?"

Jay laughed aloud and was shaking his head. He placed his hands on his head as he made a fist.

He got up, walked, and stood next to me as he said, "No, he is not related by blood, but in some horrific way is her uncle. This whole family needs to get a wake-up call. That's why I'm here. I protected her all these years somehow, some way. I was against this forced marriage. Yet I was held a prisoner through the wedding as I was in the hospital. My heart stopped and only Samar had the cure. The marriage was a forced marriage. My baby girl went through it to save my life. I told her to let go of me, but she said I was the only person she knew as her father and mother figure."

I heard him and felt a knife go through my gut. My daughter was forced to marry a demon because no one was able to save her. Just like right now, she is in his care. I remembered how he left last time I saw him. He bent his head and waved backward with a smirk on his face. Something was wrong.

My mind drifted back to the same question if that family accepted everything like marrying off their daughter to an uncle character, then why was my wedding to Viana not accepted? Was it religion, race, or money? Or were there secrets that were buried within the walls that couldn't be opened? Did they just leave the secrets buried within the past?

Again, I heard the screams of a woman shatter my small cottage. This time, however, Dave and Jay too heard the screams. They both jumped up and tried to see where the sound was coming from.

Jay got up and said, "We must find the evil woman. I don't know why Viana's aunt, and her evil group forced Daviana to marry her son. My whole family tried to help Daviana. Viana and I tried to run away with baby Daviana, but whenever others tried to help us run away, they killed them. They killed Viana because she tried to escape and come to you. I tried to help but then everything changed and Viana was being buried dead."

Jay was shaking in fear as he kept peeking through the curtains out the windows. I wondered what he thought would happen. Would someone just come flying in through the window? I didn't believe in any ghosts or vampires and wouldn't unless I see one with my own eyes. I did, however, believe there was some kind of horrific evil people in my daughter's family who needed to be caught and prosecuted. I only worried why Jay was so scared.

He continued, "I was there at Viana's funeral. I knew the nurse who helped give birth to Daviana tried to help. You saw the woman who let you hold Daviana as a newborn. After that one time, we never saw her again as if she had just vanished. I tried to search for her, but she didn't exist. Later, I have received a letter signed by an unknown person stating Viana is still alive. The woman buried was her nurse who tried to help her run away. Anyone who tried to help, met with the same fate."

Jay refilled his cup with more tea as he kept looking at his wristwatch. I realized he feared his father-in-law, but maybe even Edward feared someone else for him to let his family members fall and not help them or be there for them. I only wondered why Jay allowed others to force him to hide his identity. At least by revealing his identity, he could have been free.

Jay knew I was thinking about all these things. I took a vow if my Viana was alive and hidden somewhere, I would find her. I would not rest until I found my Viana.

Jay shook his head and bit his lip as he said, "My father-in-law is very rich. His family members are extremely dangerous. They have all kinds of illegal businesses and will not hesitate to murder or even be murdered to hide their identities or their businesses."

Jay got up as we again heard cries of a young woman. She was crying out of pain. We ignored the sounds as we knew something was going on which we could not explain. Jay, however, was scared and shaking as he kept standing up and sitting down again. He tried to find some comfortable space for himself.

He stood up and walked back and forth as he said, "My father-in-law made his money from drugs, prostitution, and selling human body parts. He walked out of his illegal business after his family members started going missing. Money robbed him from his basic moral values. Viana was the love of his life. Through her, he found hope for his reform, but it was too late as he was fighting with the assailants, he had created himself."

Jay watched the ceiling as he walked to the stone wall where I had framed wedding photos of Viana and myself. I also had Dave and his parents, Dave and myself, my adoptive parents, and my grandmother's photos on the same stone wall. The photos were the only bridge that tied me to all my beloved family members.

Dave had never asked me who the woman in the photos was as I had told him she passed away around the time of his birth. The subject was very raw. My way of dealing with it was never speaking about it, so we never spoke about it until now. Dave understood he was all the family I had and needed. Jay saw the photos and smiled as for a minute I thought he was happy.

He was busy thinking and only said after he gathered himself, "Samar was a nice boy in a way that he refused to marry Daviana but agreed when they all said it would be a fake marriage. It was so he could take all her properties, money, and investments in his name. Edward, Daviana's grandfather, had drawn up a prenuptial agreement for them. It says Samar can't have any of Daviana's properties as she can't have any of his unless one dies. This is why I believe my daughter's life is at risk. He is a doctor who took an oath to save lives, but I fear he will take any life that might threaten his way of living."

Jay's phone rang. As he got nervous, he jumped up and spilled his tea all over himself. He was shaking so much in fear that I had to grab his hands and calm him down. After that, we remained quiet as he answered the call.

A deep voice could be heard from the other side as the man said, "I don't know where you are, but remember your daughter will be hurt. Your wife remains my prisoner. Don't act smart or else I will have both killed. Just keep on playing your role and everything will be all right. I believe your daughter burned her hands, so she will be in pain and won't be able to eat her food by herself. Do tell the police you were there when she burned her beautiful fingers in anger and fury. If you don't say it, then she will have more injuries. Also, I hear your wife's fingers are being burned at this moment. Another thing, if someone does happen to die, then it's your daughter who did it. Don't act smart and run away like the chicken you are."

Jay was white like he just saw a ghost. He somehow stayed silent and gathered his strength from somewhere. I watched as he opened the locket on the gold chain around his neck to kiss the picture inside. Daviana as a child was on one side and Daviana the grown-up woman was on the other side.

Jay screeched in fear and anger, yet with confidence he said, "Don't even dream of harming my child! Then, you get nothing. I made sure if something happens to my child, you will get nothing. She had nothing to do with why God made me like this. Neither did she have any hand in her birth or her marriage. Please let her be free from your attacks. Take me and I will write all my properties, and everything I have, or she has, to your name. Just let my child go. She is innocent. I will say I did the crimes, just let her go! Also, I don't believe my wife is alive. If she is, then show me some proof. With proof, I will wire all my money to you."

There were a lot of sounds on the other side. Dave told us to not say anything but to let the guy talk, so we all remained quiet for a while. The few seconds seemed like a million years.

I heard the unknown voice say, "If you want your daughter to not suffer, then make sure there is a heart ready for me before it's too late. I don't care about your father-in-law. He can die. Make sure all the organs are fresh. Don't stop me from getting fresh organs. I don't want to lose any other body parts because your people can't perform the transplants in time. Also, I will make sure the organs arrive to my clinic in time. Don't stop my work and don't ever come in between to try to be a hero. You should always remember you are a big fat zero. Don't ever get in between our work. We can't have the bodies in the morgue sent to burials without removing the organs. I want more live victims to enter the morgue and dead bodies to disappear. Remember, Lucy's story can't be repeated. We don't want any more walking dead."

I realized weird things were happening in the hospital. We had more bodies in the morgue than we had patients for all our patients were in and out surgeries. How was the morgue so overcrowded? Suddenly, my life seemed like a gruesome horror movie set. I heard Dave say he was going to call in special investigating teams who I knew wouldn't help unless we had solid proof.

As soon as the phone disconnected, I ran to the bathroom to splash some cold water on my face. I could take physical pain, but emotional torture was another topic. People were being killed for their organs, and my hospital was being used for these gruesome crimes. My stomach grumbled as I felt nauseous knowing my hospital was a crime scene.

Dave got up and walked back and forth. I saw he had placed a call to someone. A calming and uplifting voice answered the phone. The voice said, "This is Dr. Jacobus Vrederic van Phillip. How may I help you?"

My son smiled like he was in a happy place. He looked like he finally found the solution to all of his troubles. I saw Dave smiling and look worried at the same time. Dave placed his hands on his head as he spoke on the speaker phone without using his hands.

He nervously said, "Jacobus, I need your help. I have an issue, and I will tell you all about it in person. We have a trafficker of some kind who has taken over our hospital. The morgue is being used to illegally harvest organs. Living people are being brought in and killed so their organs can be sold in the underworld market. Some people are walking into the morgue alive, and some dead are walking out after death. Everyone is calling this phenomenon the walking dead."

THE WALKING DEAD

The living people need

Healing.

They need care

And nurturing.

For them,

We create a safe

And secure haven,

Where we close the door to

The fearful

And frightening ends

All people

Avoid seeing,

Avoid hearing,

Or knowing

About.

We the healers keep

The doors closed

Between the

Living and

The Dead.

Yet how do we,

The healers,

The guardians,

The keepers

Of all who come to

Our place of healing,

Be safe?

When the door

In between

The living,

And the dead,

Opens,

We all witness

THE WALKING DEAD.

CHAPTER THREE:

Murder

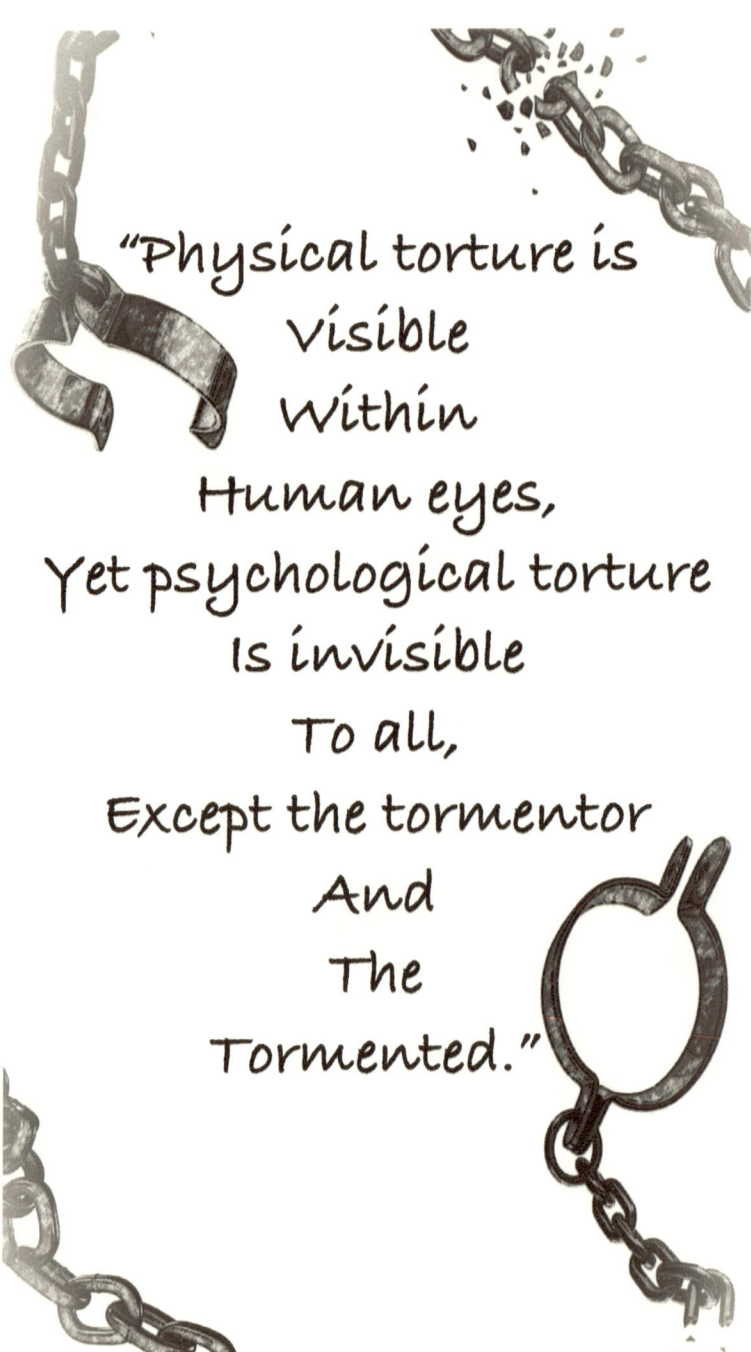

"Physical torture is
Visible
Within
Human eyes,
Yet psychological torture
Is invisible
To all,
Except the tormentor
And
The
Tormented."

T he very familiar voice of a fragile woman shattered through the quiet and peaceful night as Jay, Dave, and I walked through the corridors of David's Retreat, near MacNider Hospital. Situated in Montauk, New York, a famous beach town. Some call it a summer party town. When tourists enter this part, they often call it "The End" as it's located at the very end of the Long Island peninsula. We get a lot of tourists here. Because it's far away from any hospital emergency rooms, we built our hospital here on my grandmother's property as it was her final wish. I did comply with her wish with the help of my adoptive parents and my brother.

Montauk is where you can hear the Atlantic Ocean's waves if you just stand and try to listen. No, you don't need to place a seashell to your ear. You just need to be here and listen to the natural sounds of the Atlantic Ocean. The Montauk Point Lighthouse was built in 1796, after it was authorized by President George Washington. There are World War II bunkers here which sometimes just give me a strange eerie feeling.

When we moved to my grandmother's estate, I had asked my parents why this place was called the "end of the world." They told me it was because the world ends here. The land meets the Atlantic Ocean here.

David's Retreat was my home where I grew up. My parents built this stone manor with so much love, I had a very hard time making this decision. Yet after watching the doctors and families of some of the employees use it like a break away from their daily struggles, it was worth it. I let my son Dave decide what he wanted to do before everything was finalized. So, we had to wait years for him to be old enough to decide.

The warm home away from home for so many hardworking staff, was shattered with a woman's frightening shrieking cries. Her shrieks were so clear as if she was inside our private owner's wing crying. We jumped up and ran outside. The hallways were empty and the doors to everyone's rooms were closed.

A shadow of a woman running appeared by the bay windows near the elevators. There were two chairs and a small table by the bay windows. Every corridor of a long hallway had the bay windows and floor-to-ceiling glass walls in between the stone walls. The hospital standing a few acres away was visible. The well-lit hospital seemed like a very weary place as the screams shattered the peaceful night.

A chemical-like horrid smell covered the air. The tide was high tonight, so the waves could be heard from everywhere.

A woman wearing all white, was running from the hospital to the water fountain in the courtyard. She was being witnessed by all the visitors and patients of the hospital. She was screaming, crying, and shrieking in fear as we reached her. People were screaming and shrieking by her sight as they ran away in all different directions.

People were all screaming, "A ghost! A woman in white! A ghost dressed in a nurse's attires is haunting MacNider Hospital!"

We ran toward the ghost as everyone else ran away from the ghost. Like a shattering mirror, in front of us was nurse Lucy, standing with black eye bags and blood dripping from her mouth. Her white nurse's coat, white dress underneath, and her white stockings and hair piece were covered with dried red blood, not fresh drops that were visible now.

She kept saying, "Jacobus, help me please! Where are you? How can I go to the Netherlands if you can't come to me?"

The dead nurse who never had a funeral service as we waited for the Kasteel Vrederic family members to come, was standing in front of us. She gave all three of us a stare. She tried to see Jay more than she was trying to see us.

I watched her gaze and for whatever reason said to her, "Lucy, I have not given up or quit on your case. That's why I have Jay here. I'm trying to question all who were in contact with you. I know you were in contact with Dr. Samar Kapoor. I also called Dr. Jacobus Vrederic van Phillip as I know his family was like your family."

She was trying to watch us from beneath her black eyes and bloody mouth. She screamed and began to cry again as people were running away from her in fear as she was floating. Her hair was tied in a hairpiece that came off and floated in the air. She was twirling in a circle and crying. Onlookers were horrified at this sight, in the dead night's air. They ran screaming and crying. Lucy tried to see me directly.

She came closer and said in a shriek, "I will haunt them eternally as they did this to me in your hospital. Can you believe it? They took my life in the hospital where I tried each day to heal and save lives. How is it fair? We the living and healthy become the walking dead. These innocent dead people are now stuck here and will never leave your hospital. I will murder all who try to harm any more innocent people at the hospital. There are now seven under and they have five more coming."

The floating shrieking woman disappeared like she was never there. Her smell remained in the air, as if she was burning within some kind of chemical. People were saying she smelled like a dead vampire and a ghost nurse. It was terrifying to watch people trying to run and go as far away from the hospital as they could. The quiet and peaceful night was shattered by a dead ghost woman drenched in blood. People were now spreading rumors that MacNider Hospital was haunted by Lucy, the vampire nurse. Her name spread like hot cakes.

Black cats and huge water rats appeared from the woods behind the hospital. It was bizarre how they all walked to the droplets of fresh blood and started to drink it. The droplets of blood felt like a stream of blood that seemed to never end. A river of blood ran from the hospital to the Atlantic Ocean as the stray animals were busy drinking the horrible smelling chemical looking blood. The white dressed Lucy showed up and was just watching Dave. I realized she was somewhat scared. Then, I wondered why she was lingering on and haunting the hospital she herself said she tried to save lives within.

Dave touched and smelled the blood. I warned him not to.

He looked at me and said, "Dad, I treat patients here. We converted our ancestral home, so people can have a place to come and be treated. They don't have to worry about the money if they can't afford it. Now our hospital and our whole life's devotion is being tormented by some unnatural beings. I don't believe in ghosts."

Lucy the ghost nurse was observing Dave as she floated above trying to see what was happening.

She looked angry as she hissed and told Dave, "Well I am a ghost, so start believing in ghosts because your hospital did this to me."

Jay sat down by Dave and tried to smell the blood. He walked back and forth and collected samples of the blood. He heard Lucy but did not respond to her. I didn't know how this happened in our private hospital.

Jay said shockingly, "It smells sweet and not at all like blood but a chemical. It is sweet and looks and feels like blood. I'm not a medical doctor but a chemist who works with chemicals. I know this is a chemical that has been made to look and smell like blood. Somehow, I feel like people were using these chemicals to perform surgeries illegally without proper certificates."

A huge crowd was gathering by our hotel behind us. In the Atlantic Ocean behind the hospital, we saw fire was burning. People were shouting how sail boats and fishing boats were on fire. I wondered what was going on. Maybe the burning boats were a distraction, so either the police or the fire crews wouldn't be able to come here quick enough as they were busy with the fire on the Atlantic Ocean.

We were all busy trying to figure out why Lucy had become a vampire or ghost, and she was now terrorizing innocent passersby. Something was happening behind us. The bizarre night had much more bizarre and terrorizing thrillers stored for us.

The three of us ran toward our room. A guard came and told us someone had broken into our room to get some of our secret conversations.

Jay said, "Oh no! That's why I was peeking through the windows. I assumed they were recording, and they probably were recording our conversation in your house. Now again, they will blackmail me even more. This vampire drama must have been a diversion of some kind."

I said nothing as I realized people in this world are all the same. Always thinking of what will hurt or affect them the most. Jay was worried his actions to help us or tell us his side of the story would now come back and haunt him.

Something in the air made me shiver in fear. I prayed my daughter Daviana was safe. I saw Viana standing in the hallway like an apparition. She saw me and was pointing her finger toward Daviana's room. The door was ajar as people were running out of the building in fear.

It felt so strange but still I pondered if all were scared of my Viana's apparition or something more was going on. Never in my life had I prayed harder than during these few minutes it took me to go from the apparition of Lucy to the hallways of the retreat hotel room where Daviana was staying.

There inside of the two-bedroom family suite Samar had rented for himself and his wife, a body laid on the carpet. Dave rushed in as he checked the pulse and shook his head. The same nurse that clung on to Samar was screaming and crying while standing in the corner.

She saw me and said, "Daviana murdered him. I saw it with my own eyes. She was stabbing him with the fruit knife she had in her hands. I heard her screams and rushed in here and saw she had a knife and was covered in blood as she was screaming and blabbering something."

We all rushed in and tried to check Samar's vitals. He felt stiff but not dead or cold. He had a pulse but then again, he did not. He had no hair yet looked like Samar. I was somehow shocked to see him bald. Then, I thought maybe he was wearing a wig.

Daviana watched the nurse as she said, "I am also a medical doctor, and a lawyer. I did not do any such thing. I was sleeping in my own room when you tapped my shoulders and woke me up. You helped me walk into this room as you gave me the knife to hold. I saw Samar was laying there on his own bed. There was no blood but then suddenly blood appeared, and you threw something on me, so I too was covered in blood. You did this! I saw you! How is it my husband had full hair and now is bald and bleeding? I did nothing."

The room filled up with police, cameras, and coroners. All were investigating the situation. All I could see was everyone was talking about how Daviana was abused and had bruises all over her, yet Samar was a kind gentle man, who tried to take care of a wife who was mental. Like an apparition, my Viana was standing and watching the child she birthed be accused of murder. I stood next to the apparitional form of my Viana and watched my daughter be charged with murder of her husband.

I became the lawyer and told my daughter, "Don't say anything until we have a chance to investigate everything. I will help you and I promise I will get you out of this mess."

Daviana only nodded as I knew being an attorney herself, she knew what she could do and what she had to avoid doing. The old nurse who always stood near Samar was screaming and crying as if her life was lost. I wondered if she was close to him, more than we assumed. I had to investigate.

Jay held Daviana and said, "I don't know how and why, but I know this is all a setup. It's made to make you look like a murderer. Bapu will get you out of this mess however or whichever way I can. I will. Also, Daviana why and when did your husband become bald? He had hair when he went to bed. So, are they saying you shaved the hair off his head too?"

Daviana was taken into custody. I tried to inspect Samar's body with Dave.

Dave said, "The cuts look superficial. Not deep at all. So why was there so much blood? How did he die from scratches that did not go deep enough to bleed? I wonder if he really was dead or not. Dad, he looked different. He had scratches all over his face, but the blood smelled like the blood we saw outside. I couldn't inspect him as the police covered him and rushed him out. I know as a doctor, I swear he had pulse and wasn't dead."

Jay was walking around in a panic mode. He was talking in different languages. I knew even without knowing any of the languages, he repeated nonstop, "It's not possible. It can't be! The blood wasn't real. It's fake blood. The injuries were all fake."

Jay touched the blood and gave me a stare. Then, he stood up and looked at Dave directly. Dave nodded in acknowledgement without say anything. We all knew something was not adding up.

I watched as my child was taken away, accused of murder without any resistance from her. She saw both of her fathers, her biological and adoptive father, and just poured her tears. She said nothing. Jay closed his eyes and made a fist.

He told her very clearly, "This father promises, I will get to the bottom of this. I will prove to this world a father's love can and will protect his daughter at any cost. For remember my child, you have two fathers, your biological and I your adoptive father. I will make sure no one insults or says an adoptive father's love goes in vain. Even if I must take my last breath, I will awaken from death beneath to prove to this world, my daughter is the victim of abuse. She is not the murderer as she is the innocent."

We took a short drive back home. As Dave drove, I closed my eyes worried because Daviana had to spend the night in prison and no bail was allowed. Somehow, I knew a bigger force was behind all these happenings. I sat on my recliner in the living room as I tried to contact everyone I knew for guidance. The first thing I had to do was talk with Daviana. Then, I could take the necessary steps. I called for all the security camera footage to be delivered to us as I knew all the doors had cameras on them for the safety of the doctors and their families. These were cameras not openly placed, but they were secretly placed as written clearly in the rental disclosures.

Dave was talking out loud to Jay as he said, "The blood that splattered around Samar was fake. It was the same chemical that was outside by the fountain. There were no deep cuts on his body. I checked him myself to see if he was dead or if he had a pulse."

The doorbell rang as Dave walked over and opened the front door. I wondered who would come this late in the night. Maybe the police and investigators who were trying to build up their case.

The guest walked in with his walking cane. His presence set the whole house on alert mode. Daviana's grandfather walked in. He seemed panicked as he walked in and asked for a glass of water. Even to this day, I feared him as his presence warned of danger.

He sat down on the recliner next to mine, opposite the couch, with a loud and deep breath. A small coffee table, two small side tables, a computer desk, and a 75-inch television set decorated the room. It was a small room with a lot of love as my walls had aside from a few family photos, my boy Dave's photos all around the cottage. Maybe I thought his parents would one day come and want to see his pictures, even though I buried them myself.

Daviana's grandfather, Edward Kapoor, said directly to me, "I am here, so now let's figure out how you will prove my Daviana is innocent. At least you can do something to earn the name of being her father. I will pay for your fees. I made a mistake and felt pressured into allowing my Daviana to be married off into that family. No, I will not apologize as at that time I knew it was my only choice."

He was a big man with a lot of pride. I tried to see the man who was on the wrong path all his life. How did he change and why now? Does he not even cringe thinking his ways cost him his family?

Edward said, "I don't walk in the past. I have tried to walk out of the life I enjoyed. I thought it could enrich me financially, but instead it made me a poor man as it cost me my family. These people will stop at nothing to ruin my family. My stepbrother was married to a German woman who tried to take over all my businesses after he was killed. She is a notorious trafficker whom my stepbrother tried to divorce, yet she murdered him and staged his death to look like a home invasion. I somehow thought if Daviana and Samar were married, then all my family's troubles would be over. She promised she would let go of all her evil doings on my family if I handed her my business empire and my granddaughter. Yet her evil doings only increased."

I knew why he came, but I didn't know why all of this was being told to me as I believed he was the one who separated Viana from me. I tried to observe the old and fragile man sitting in my living room. If only I could have forgotten the evil man who did everything to take my beloved wife away from me. He had a thick layer of gray hair, and a clean-shaven face. He was tall and overweight, but he didn't look Indian. He had fair skin and blue eyes. At 95 years of age, he was in remarkable condition.

The smell of fresh baked vegan mince pies and scones filled the air. My Dave knows his food and is a great chef. Jay helped him and I realized it kept him mentally busy. Dave served everyone his Australian vegan mince pies with a hot pot of tea. Even Edward helped himself to a slice of the pie.

Edward laughed and said, "My heart has given up, so I eat everything and don't worry about anything. I was her victim. My wife Devi was taken as a prisoner for years. That's why I separated you and Viana. They blackmailed me into letting Viana marry one of their goons. After they found out she was pregnant, however, they rejected the marriage. Strange they arranged her marriage with Jay, who rejected them and their ways. He became my son not son-in-law as he never married Viana. To this day, my child is yours and only yours. Viana tied rakhi on Jay's wrist during Raksha Bandhan which made them brother and sister, not husband and wife. Jay did, however, adopt Daviana as his own."

The whole room fell silent as no one spoke after this new information. I wondered why no one ever told me anything about these things. I was familiar with what Raksha Bandhan is. That's when people celebrate the pure relationship between a brother and a sister. The phrase which is Sanskrit means "bond of protection." By tying a thread on a brother's wrist, the sister is providing her love and protection.

It was as if Edward read my mind and said, "You adopted your dead brother's son as your own. So, I decided not to place him or you in any danger by allowing international criminals to be related to you. I only prayed my Daviana would grow up and solve all the mysteries. I let her be in your school, so you could see her from afar and be with her. I know by now, my wife probably is dead, and my daughter might as well be dead. No dear Jay, I did not bury any nurse, nor have I in my entire life taken any life. I am a father and Viana is my only child. I would rather have buried myself than my daughter or anyone else. I only tried to arrange organs for people who needed them legally."

I finished my slice of warm pie and sipped my tea. I knew it was time I must reexamine everything and start a case against the earthly and the supernatural beings. I would somehow prove to this world my daughter was neither crazy nor was she sick. Something was going on, and I would prove it. Before I could do anything, I needed all the truth I could get from Edward Kapoor. Suddenly, Dave sighed in sadness and fear.

I saw tears in his eyes as he said, "Dad, we must go to the hospital now. The hospital security just called and said Daviana was brought there from the prison. She is not responsive. She was attacked in the prison in the few hours

128

she was there. Dad, Daviana isn't breathing! Oh my God, they must have killed her!"

Again, I saw standing in front of Edward and me was Viana who watched us and said in a whisper, "Why Papa? Why Papa? Why Papa? Why did you take away everything from me? And now my daughter has been charged with murder? Did I not mean anything to you? I had given up my life, my love, and now my child only for you."

Everyone in the room jumped up as this time, we all saw my Viana. I didn't know if it was her ghost or somehow her soul was traveling to her only child who needed her now the most.

Edward said, "Your love must be so pure that she can travel to you. I guess your love has been accepted by God Himself as you two can go to one another or call one another even in separation. Guiding each other like a bridge over all the troubles of life. Forgive me, David, if you ever can."

I said nothing as all I could hear was my daughter, the one I gave away to be safe, so no troubles of this Earth touched her. I had given her away so no tears would fall from her eyes, and she would smile all her troubles away. She, however, suffered under the hands of the people I gave her away to and for. My Daviana, an innocent victim of abuse, had been tortured to her death yet this society did not see her tears, her pain, or her sufferings as my child was charged for murder.

MURDER

Victim or the assailant

Is defined

By the witness

Who sees the crime

And the authorities who put

The Assailants away.

Yet I ask you,

The judge,

What if the assailant

You have deemed

As guilty

Is the innocent,

Locked behind

The mischievous ploys

Of the real assailant who

Now goes free,

As you have charged

The innocent

Blindly and unjustly

With

MURDER.

CHAPTER FOUR:

The Missing Body

"Nothing
Adds
To nothing.
If nothing exists,
Then how could
Anything even be?
As from nothing,
We get
Nothing."

I closed my eyes for a minute and saw Viana crying as she said to me, "Please don't let our love story end with the death of our child. For as long as she is alive, our love story lives on. If you and I are not in existence, then let our daughter carry on the torch of love. Please help her or they will kill her. The world hates true love stories. They hate love stories with happy endings as only the saddest tragic love stories make it into songs. It's always the saddest stories that become alive as they get sealed within the pages of a book. I know my love story has no place anywhere on this Earth or beyond, but only within your memories. Please wake up and help our daughter. She has no one but you."

I jumped up as I knew my daughter was in police custody, and the lifeless body of Samar was at the coroner's office. When we walked into the hospital, we saw my daughter on the bed, bruised and battered. Her whole body was covered in black and blue bruises from clear abuse. Blood was dripping from all over her body. It seemed like someone took a butcher knife and butchered my daughter. She was unconscious and her life was hanging in there like a miracle. Before I could arrange for her bail or do anything through my sources, as the police were transporting Daviana from David's Retreat to the police station, she was brutally beaten up. We also learned that the lifeless body of Samar went missing.

My tears rolled out without any veil in between them and the world. I watched my daughter's nearly lifeless body on the hospital bed still in shackles. She was losing blood, her vital signs were all messed up, her oxygen level was low, and her pulse was low. Dave started to give her immediate needed care as he called for help.

We walked out of the room when Dave said, "Dad I can't have anyone in here right now. Please let me save her life first. Something went very wrong in police custody. We watched them take in a person who was bruised but alive and healthy. They overnight gave us back a person who is fighting for her life. All her major organs are failing. I need to find out if there is any internal bleeding."

A huge police presence crowded the hospital. They were all talking about how my daughter injured herself to the point where she was dying because of her self-inflicted injuries.

I sat down in the waiting room trying to figure out what I had done so wrong that my God was punishing me. All I wanted was for Daviana to once call me Papa. I kept thinking how I never taught her to walk, talk, or drive. Life was making a mockery of my life story.

Jay helped Edward sit and gave him a glass of water. He brought coffee for himself and me. My hands were shaking so bad I was worried I would drop my cup of coffee.

A police officer came toward me as he said, "We are sorry for all this mess. I went to get some coffee, and we saw the dead husband stand up and beat her until she fell. Then, the morgue called saying Samar's dead body was missing. We tried to check everywhere, but we saw no sign of any dead bodies or any living bodies for that matter. Now the District Attorney's office will charge Ms. Daviana Shaw with murder and abducting the dead body."

My entire life had been defending innocent people against the unjust world. I howled yet the words froze in my throat.

Jay walked over to the police officer and said, "The dead body was in your coroner's custody. My daughter was unconscious in your custody, so it's obvious you all should be charged for the death of the missing body, and my daughter's condition. I am not a lawyer but as far as I understand, dead bodies don't get up and beat people to death in front of the police force, while being recorded on camera. My daughter can't be charged for murder when the dead person she was charged with walked and escaped in your custody. Also, I have hired David MacNider to represent her on this matter. So, you all must go through him for all communications with her or the family. We will sue you and all who are responsible for her situation."

The night was very long as the three of us waited in the cold and scary waiting room. Daviana was shifted to surgery and was there for hours. Edward was visibly upset as he called a lot of people and tried to see if he could use power, position, and money to save my innocent child. I must say I was strong and knew my heart was still beating even though I kept seeing the newborn child I held in my hands for a few minutes being taken away from me all over again.

I started to prepare my case against Samar even though he was supposedly dead. In my eyes, whether dead or alive, he was the only one responsible for his own staged death, my daughter's condition, and all the things that went wrong with my hospital. I called my staff at my law firm and had them prepare our case.

A shrieking scream of a woman's voice terrorized the hospital just before dawn broke. All the hospital employees including the doctors, nurses, patients, and visitors heard the scream. In front of everyone, appeared the woman in white.

She ran through the corridors and screamed, "I murdered him. I did. Dr. Samar Kapoor, where are you? I murdered that man who raped me. I know it was him. He was trying to rape Daviana, so I hit him with a knife. Now in this life, we will meet again as I will murder him if he is not yet dead in this realm."

The police officers who were all waiting with us heard the conversation and got up trying to see where the voice was coming from. I hoped they could all now agree my daughter was innocent.

Yet one officer who looked like maybe he was the detective as he was in plain clothes said, "This is all their doing. They are trying to fool us into believing there is a higher spiritual being doing all of this. I know their daughter is responsible. This proves they too should be charged with their daughter."

He couldn't finish his words as Lucy the dead vampire nurse, dressed in a white nurse's uniform, appeared in front of him. She was not see-through or dead looking. Rather she just stood there staring at the group of police officers.

With a hiss in her tone, she said to them, "Oh boy, you really think this hospital is being terrorized by the owners themselves? Or is it that weak bruised and battered woman doing all of this? I wonder if an innocent person dies and the police officers are involved in the wrongful death, then who will solve this murder mystery? The victim, the accuser, or the innocent? Or maybe the dead nurse from the beyond."

Suddenly like a cloud of fog, Lucy started to float as she tied all the police officers in a knot. Then, she made them float upside down and watched them scream and cry in fear. I tried to help the guys, but each time I tried to get close to help them, I fell backward like there was an invisible force holding me back.

The police officers, all eight of them including three female officers were throwing up. They were then released. As all of them fell to the ground, they looked up and realized I was trying to help them.

That's when a female officer said, "In one of the David's Retreat hallway videos, the door was ajar, and we could clearly see Ms. Daviana Shaw was asleep when a woman in white stabbed the very bald Samar multiple times. The police force was told by our higher-ups to delete the video. I know the hotel still has copies, so you could get one and prove the woman in white did it. Either she is a spirit or is pretending to be one, but she did all this. It seems like a ghost nurse did try to kill him. So, the police are trying to frame an innocent woman."

I smiled as I forgot I had all the videos in our backup computers for events like these. I knew with it, I could prove my daughter was innocent. Yet how could I do anything with the victim's body missing? There was no dead body, so the ghost probably hurt him or tried to save Daviana.

The hospital corridors were all covered with the same blood that was spread outside. I walked over the chemical looking blood to visit the operation theater to see if there was any news on Daviana. That's when I saw Jay was crying as he knelt on his knees in front of a statue of baby Jesus and the Virgin Mary.

He said out loud, "Please God, answer this father's prayers and let my child live. For if you don't, then I will know my God too only answers the prayers of biological parents, not the prayers of an adoptive father. Oh my God, please take my life and grant my daughter a healthy, and happy life away from Samar. With my condition, I will never have any twin flame, but let my daughter have a twin flame and have children of her own."

Dave came out looking depressed, tired, and somewhat upset. Even as a child, he would show temper tantrums by stomping his feet.

He stomped his feet in front of the police and told them, "Since you all lost the body of the deceased you are accusing Ms. Daviana Shaw to have murdered, I suggest you find the body first and then charge the ghost that did or did not murder him. Try charging Samar for abuse and the attempted murder of his wife. Charge him also for faking his own death and walking out on his own. I spoke with the coroner, and he said the stabbings on Samar's body did not match the knife that was found. Daviana's hands were broken, burned, and not useable from two days ago. She could not have lifted a pen, forget a knife and stabbing. You all knew, yet you still wanted to charge an innocent woman. Why?"

The police chief came and apologized as he said, "We are sorry for everything. Initially, the murder had pointed toward Daviana. We considered her the main suspect as that's why she has been in custody. Where did the ghost nurse everyone is talking about come from? Maybe she was set up by Daviana herself. Although she is free due to the lack of evidence, the detectives will continue our investigation."

I walked to the police chief who was five feet, five inches tall, chubby in the middle, and bald. I looked him directly in the eyes and told him, "You won't let anyone go free? She is the innocent, and you tried to frame her. No one was murdered as he pretended to be dead. My hotel has video recordings of Daviana never moving from her place. We just received the videos that another woman was there who did the stabbing and placed the knife in my daughter's hands. The ghost nurse tried to save my child by pushing the woman away. She also tried to push Samar away from my daughter. Or else today, my child would have been dead. I know you all witnessed this video before and still locked up an innocent. Why is the dead body missing? Where is the knife that stabbed Samar? Where is the woman who disappeared right after the stabbing? Why have you all knowingly arrested an innocent? In your custody, someone tried to murder her. The case is very strong against you. It's not based on hearsay. There is video evidence supporting my daughter's innocence."

I watched Edward stand up and come close to the police chief. Edward watched him for a while as he stared at him up and down. He suddenly seemed weaker and sickly. Through his willpower, he was pushing himself.

Edward asked the police chief, "I hear you did this because you are racist. You wanted to blame a woman who looked Indian? I will be suing you for defamation, and false accusation on a very serious issue, a murder charge. If my granddaughter dies or something happens, I will make sure you all are charged with murder. Also, please investigate why and when Samar became bald."

The police left as they had no case. The security footage showed Lucy tried to stop Samar from stabbing Daviana. It also showed the other woman, Samar's mother, who tried to kill him or just pretended, so Daviana would be charged. The problem, however, was how would a police force tell the public this murder was committed by a vampire ghost nurse or a person maybe pretending to be a ghost. They now had a huge burden in their hands as they would need to inform the public that something supernatural might be happening.

I saw Dave and didn't have the courage to ask him anything. I just thought no news is good news. My daughter will walk in here soon, smiling, yet my paternal instincts told me we had a bigger problem in our hands.

Dave saw me directly and said, "Daviana is fighting for her life. Someone was trying to harvest her heart for a heart transplant surgery. Samar had everything ready to do a heart transplant surgery in the back room of his hotel suite. Except in this case, the donor Daviana was alive and did not consent. She was saved by that ghost nurse who fought with Samar to save Daviana's life and tried to kill Samar. Yet somehow now the dead body is missing. Also missing is that old brutal nurse, or Samar's evil mother."

I immediately saw Edward and had so many questions thrown at him. Yet I voiced nothing for I knew as an attorney defending so many people all my life, Edward was innocent. Who was doing all of this? Why did they choose my daughter?

Jay walked back and forth, looked at Edward directly, and asked him, "Did you have anything to do with this? Please tell me the truth. If I find out you did, then I will personally be guilty of your murder. I promise, I will murder you with my two hands if I find out you were involved."

Dave closed his eyes as he tried to answer the phone. I knew it must have been the same friend in the Netherlands.

Dave had tears pouring from his eyes as he answered and said, "Jacobus, I would like to thank Erasmus for everything he has been doing. The police are now helping us instead of accusing us after your intervention. Yet Jacobus, we are worried not only about the bodies that are missing from our morgue, but how Samar's body is missing from the coroner's office which the police were in charge of. They are charging Daviana for a crime that happened in their own care within the coroner's office. They are calling it the mystery of the missing body."

THE MISSING BODY

A murder has been committed.

A person has been charged

Even though

The victim

And the assailant

Are both

Incapable of testifying

If a crime was

Committed

Or not.

Yet then,

I ask

Why is the dead

Not testifying

As within

All crimes,

The dead body

Testifies

Of the crime

Committed against

The victim.

Yet here,

How is it

In this crime,

A murder

Has been committed

Of

THE MISSING BODY?

CHAPTER FIVE:

The Dead Nurse

"Earthbound spirits
Roam
Around
To quench their thirst,
Not to frighten
The living,
But to
Find justice and
Justify their
Thirst."

T hirst dried my inner soul as I slept sitting restless in my own hospital owner's waiting lounge. Was I having sleep paralysis or was I dreaming? I could hear the waves of the Atlantic Ocean hit land and huge water rocks. The moon hit the dark water, and everything was glowing in the dark. I saw the moon disappear as the scorching hot sun appeared in the sky above.

Viana, the love of my life, was standing and watching over me. She tried to cover my face from the burning rays of the sun as she stood in between the sun and me. She used to do this when we were married for a very short period. I saw Viana cry as she realized she was see-through, and the rays of the sun poured through her onto my face. I tried to listen to her.

She murmured slowly into my ears, "My beloved, why did you fall in love with me? You gave your heart and lost your heartbeats for me. Your life has been trying to keep my memories alive, but I want you to live and make memories. Don't live in the past. Live in the present. Please help our daughter live and find love like we had and will have eternally. I love you my beloved and I always will. I promise I will break through all the barriers of life and death to be with you."

I touched Viana and was screaming not to let go. Somehow, I wanted to bring her out of my dreams into my reality. Maybe if I pulled a little harder, she would just come through the invisible barrier. Dave touched my hands and was trying to see what was wrong with me. I could hear him and everyone, but I couldn't move or tell them anything. It was hard to breathe, but I knew I must let go and let everything take its course. I felt good thinking maybe I was dying and soon would see my beloved Viana.

I got up and asked, "Am I dead?"

Dave laughed and hugged me. He had a glass of water in his hands. He sat next to me and leaned his head back. I saw how tired my son looked for the first time in days. He hadn't shaven but he looked freshly showered here at the hospital. His hair was wet, and he smelled good. I knew that meant he tried to shower away all his tiredness. Somehow, it worked for him.

Dave was observing my observations and said, "Dad, you're still with the living. If it's up to me, you will stay with me for a long time. Remember, we will both get old and have our steaming pot of tea on our front porch. Also, stop giving me those looks. I am fine. You know I'm used to not sleeping for days. It's all in a doctor's resume. Fresh brewed coffee and breakfast will arrive soon. Jay and Edward already had breakfast. They are both sitting in front of the glass room Daviana is in. They have made it their own bedroom."

A carafe of fresh brewed coffee, toast, scrambled eggs, fruit, and orange juice came with a note from the hospital chef saying, "Enjoy your meal."

It was always nice to wake up to a cup of coffee. There was a meal for two as Dave sat next to me and helped himself to breakfast. I knew it was time I had to ask Dave some uncomfortable questions, but I pondered how to do it.

So, I just blurted out, "I know you love Daviana, but is it uncomfortable because she is my biological daughter? I tried to keep her and her mother away from you not because I didn't want to share, but because I didn't want to be a burden for them. I assumed they were both happy and wanted to stay away from me. So, I kept them away from my son."

Dave enjoyed his breakfast slowly. He got up and refilled his coffee. I realized my son had grown up nicely. Even without any other help, I raised my boy my way. I wouldn't change anything as he is the best son in the world.

Dave said after sipping his coffee, "In a lot of countries, biological cousins are allowed to marry. In my case, however, Daviana and I would not be biologically related. It is nice to know I loved her from the bottom of my heart maybe because she is your biological daughter. She is just like you. If I could choose anyone on this Earth, I would choose someone you brought up or helped come to this Earth, or someone related to you."

I realized maybe God created her for him and him for her, yet somehow, they too were taken away from one another through obstacles of life. I took a vow and promised myself when my daughter opens her eyes, and all of this is behind her I would ask for her hand in marriage for my son.

Dave whispered, "Dad, Daviana might not make it through today. Someone tried to take her heart and was trying to perform a live surgery when Lucy intervened. A nurse who took a vow to save lives saved Daviana's life even after death. A doctor who took the oath to save lives tried to kill her and take her heart out in the most horrific way possible."

I wiped the thought of Daviana dying or not being on Earth from my mind. I replaced the thought with how I would unite the two for I would make sure the angel of death stayed far away from my child. I had to think positively for everything to be positive. The amazing powers of a father's love will make my dreams come true as Daviana has the blessings of her two fathers.

It was then the hospital's quiet environment broke with horrific screams of people. Fearful screams coming from women, men, and children ripped through the hospital. I placed our trays of breakfast down on the table as a pair of hands came in from nowhere. The nails were done and the hands looked very soft and taken care of. The hands made a prayer gesture. Then, as the hands turned to ashes, from a different wall, a familiar yet unfamiliar voice spoke.

The female voice said, "I have a big army now. Everyone wants answers. My army was of seven dead and now the army has grown to twelve. Why were our lives cut short? We only came here to get treated, not to become victims. I helped your daughter but remember I too am a daughter. I don't know who my parents or family are, but I am a mother, and my daughter will be tormented forever as she doesn't know where I am."

Suddenly, a nurse dressed in all white was standing in front of us. She shrieked like a phantom and then disappeared. More than her words or her ghostly apparitions, her screams scared the life out of me. I dropped my coffee cup as it shattered on the tile floors it landed upon.

Dave hurt his feet trying to get a grip of me as he said, "For Heaven's sake, don't scream like that Dad. The hospital employees will think you are a banshee screaming in fear."

I was confused as I looked at him in astonishment for a while. Then, I wondered did he not see her? Oh, so if he missed her acquaintance, at least he must have heard her shrieks.

His next words confirmed he neither saw her nor heard her as he said, "Dad, please no screaming. Everything is okay. We just need to figure out why everyone is screaming outside."

I ran after my son as we went through the hospital hallways and corridors. There was absolute chaos everywhere eyes could see.

I pulled Dave by his scrubs and said, "Dear son, I never screamed or said a word. Lucy was there as she spoke and then while trying to leave, she screamed. I wonder if she is in pain."

Dave gave me the look as he said nothing. I remember when he was a tiny lad, all the looks went from me to him. I said nothing but followed him to the Intensive Care Unit. The whole wing had blood dripping from the ceiling. The patients were being shifted to other wings as we had a disaster on our hands. I forgot all about Lucy and thought about what I could do to help.

In the ICU, Jay and Edward were both with their bodies blocking the glass door, trying to keep the glass that separated Daviana from other patients closed without any impact. The glass doors all around were cracking. Broken glass pieces were flying in all directions. Bolts of lightning were flickering everywhere. I tried to mentally call Viana to help us through this ordeal. Yet I knew if she was dead, then she couldn't help me. If she was in prison somewhere locked up, even then she couldn't help me. I wished she was here with me today. I knew some wishes are just that, wishes that never come true.

Edward fell backward just in time for Dave and me to catch him in our arms.

The first thing that came out of my mouth was, "Oh boy, you're so heavy!"

Dave pinched me as I shut up and knew my resentment toward him was coming out. I hated the man all my life as I blamed him for ruining my marriage and separating my wife from me. Little did I know he ruined my marriage to save his own. I would have given up my life to save both my wife Viana and her mother if he had only shared the truth.

The head of the ICU unit came to Dave and me as she said, "Dr. MacNider, please advise what we should do.

There is a woman dressed in a white nurse's uniform, walking in and out of all the rooms. There are some orderlies who are walking around dressed in blue orderly uniforms, covered in blood, trying to do maintenance. If approached or anyone tries to converse with them, they attack. We're having more patients bruised and battered by our dead employees floating around."

Panic broke through as everyone was fleeing. The patients, employees, security, and even visitors all fled. A very familiar deep male voice was laughing and giggling through the hospital sound system.

I could hear his joy as he said, "You can try to prove your daughter is innocent. I know you're the best lawyer she can have; however, I won't let you enjoy this victory. I will prove for you, your daughter is not innocent. Remember though Edward, you are a stupid fool. You were never my target, but Daviana is and was. So, you, the stupid big old fool Edward, do as you are told, or your precious granddaughter will go to jail. All this spooky drama will be tied to you, through your history. David, the lover boy, stop with the Lucy drama. Yes, I confess I killed her for her body parts were valuable to my mother. Why would a woman who I never knew or loved matter to me? She too is a fool and thought of me to be her stupid husband. I don't care about the child she thought was mine. Also, I don't believe in ghosts. So, your tactic is not working. You all don't even know me. Try to catch the person you believe me to be for that would give me so much pleasure as he too is my target."

The laughter of a crazy man continued. I wondered how a person gets so much joy by hurting others. It was frightening how dangerous the man might be. I felt a chill run through my bones. I didn't share my fears with anyone as I knew we had so much at risk. I needed to stay focused on the present, not on my wandering mind. I was not frightened by the hauntings of the dead but the voices of the living.

The police officers were all gathering in the hospital as chaos and bone-chilling fear spread all over the hospital. A town which was already rumored to have more than its share of ghostly sightings didn't need another one. The good news was everyone in our small town loved our hospital and they admired my grandmother. So, everyone was trying to keep all the rumors under the rug.

Yet through the lips of visiting patients, family members, and friends, rumors of a haunted hospital spread. Somehow, bad news travels faster than the wind. It felt like gossip stories of the haunting of MacNider Hospital were floating in the air like hotcakes everyone wanted but also dreaded.

Headlines in the news read, "The famous stone building, David's Retreat, is also haunted just like MacNider Hospital." Another headline was, "Famous MacNider Hospital by the ocean is being haunted by the earthbound soul of the murder victim, the dead nurse."

THE DEAD NURSE

Today her heart

Breathes no more.

Her sweet kisses and

Greeting smiles

Don't touch

Any kids.

Her soft loving hands

Don't hold on to

Your trembling hands.

Her tears

Don't fall on you

When she

Listens to your

Painful stories.

She does not laugh

When you share your

Funny stories.

Today,

Her heart beats

No more.

Her breath

Doesn't touch

Your cheek.

Her cold hands

Can't feel or hold

On to your hands.

Today,

Her tears froze,

And they stopped

Falling on you.

Her words of wisdom

Can't be heard

As today,

There is a wall

Between you

And her.

It's because today,

You are still

Amongst the living,

And she is

With the dead.

Yesterday,

She was there

As yesterday,

She treated you.

Today,

You are scared

Of her to even be

Around you.

Today

You call her,

Not your caring nurse,

But

THE DEAD NURSE.

CHAPTER SIX:

MacNider Hospital Charged

"Liabilities
Find a
Path to the
Liable,
Yet how does
The liable
Prove he is
Not the predator
But the prey?"

ecember brought cold icy weather to Montauk earlier than usual. A famous beach town and vacationer's paradise was dressed up in Christmas decorations since November. Hot cocoa and gingerbread cookies brought in customers looking to celebrate the holidays. This December, an unusual amount of ice was visible on the roads. We already had 15 inches of snow during our frightful night.

Some were saying this is due to coastal nor'easters. I knew this was because of our ghostly apparitions. We didn't have to wait for the nightfall for the ghostly appearances as we were badgered during the daylight hours. I only wondered what would happen at night. Every day, we saw a line of blood covering the path leading to the hospital. The lampposts lighting the path displayed the eerie blood every night. The number of people trying to leave the hospital grew faster than patients checking in.

I looked at the blood-lined path to the hospital. The path was Dave and my favorite part of the hospital's construction. Every lamppost had a message of hope, faith, and healing. I walked over and stood by my daughter's bed while holding on to her hands. Dave said she was doing better. I held her hands and prayed for her. As I sat down on a recliner next to her bed, I saw a dream. Viana was standing over Daviana's bed as she tried to cover our daughter from all the evil of this world. She was crying and made a fog with her tears. She then placed her long black hair like a mosquito net over Daviana.

Viana kissed our daughter as she said, "Through the hands of my twin flame, your father, I can touch you. I can kiss you and feel you, my baby girl. Don't give up on life even though you believe life gave up on you. Live to fall in love with your twin flame, even if it is just for a day. Be the bride, the lover, the twin flame, and live or die with one another not without. Wake up my beautiful girl for him, if not for anyone else. Love is wonderful and this mother of yours is blessed as I found the love of my life, and we had you."

As I woke up, Viana vanished into thin air. Dave was standing there as were Jay and Edward. They were all praying for Daviana as her vital signs did not look good. The hospital was running on private generators because of the storm brewing outside and the ghostly storm that was brewing inside the hospital. I was scared as nightfall approached so fast. I worried if the generators would run out and maybe leave some parts of the hospital in the dark. Our enemies, living or dead, probably didn't need light to see or haunt. We, however, needed light to find our ways out. The generators somehow kept all the ICU patients and surgeries going.

Police sirens flooded the eerie nightfall. I wondered what more they needed. We all hoped they found out where Samar was. For some strange reason, I knew he was behind all of this. The police, on the other hand, had other thoughts. They were after the innocent, not the real criminals.

A group of police detectives walked in with papers in their hands. They came in and when they saw Daviana, they froze and tried to check on her. They asked about her for a while. They seemed sympathetic and had shifted their faces.

A certain detective named Jane Matthews said to Dave, "You have been served. Your hospital is being sued for disruption, for spreading rumors, and selling bodies, dead and living. You also are trying to frame an innocent man through some ghostly rumors."

I walked and stood in between the detective and Dave as I said, "I am representing this hospital. I will do everything in my power to make sure you and your department pay for spreading rumors and ruining my hospital's reputation. My abusive son-in-law's body went missing in your custody. You had video evidence of my daughter being innocent at the time you locked her up and now she is fighting for her life. She was beaten up and made like this in your custody. You stand in front of me trying to prove my hospital is haunted. We have video and written statements from the police that you were in the wrong. Come, let's go to court and find out how the truth and video evidence will ruin you and all your groups. We are filing for wrongful arrest, negligence, and attempted involuntary manslaughter charges against you."

The detectives were looking at one another in a strange, weird way. Oh my God were the detectives corrupted, yet how could all of them be involved in this huge defamation plot against my hospital and me. I heard rumors there were people who did not want the hospital here. I saw Lucy standing in front of me. As she appeared, all of the spectators were watching her float in front of the huge nurse's station.

I ignored Lucy and pretended not to even see her. That was it. I would just tell them I didn't see anything, and they must prove there were ghosts. I wouldn't have to.

I told them again, "You do understand, there is always a scientific reason behind all paranormal activities. I don't need to prove what I can't see or touch. Also, if there are no scientific reasons behind it, then it's just a phenomenon we will never know, as Montauk has all sorts of rumors hidden within this magical city. If you even try to harm my hospital, you and your buddies will all be investigated for something much bigger. Get out of here as you should all worry about saving your own skin, not ruining my hospital. You can't investigate my hospital for dead bodies being misplaced from your care, not mine. Your charges clearly state Samar went missing from my care, for which my hospital is being sued. I urge you to correct the mistakes. Samar's dead body went missing from your care. So, like you say in this charge sheet, the charges should be against the people in whose care the body was and went missing from. That is you, the police force."

They reread the charges and were asking one another as one said, "How are we charging the hospital if Dr. Samar Kapoor's body was in our care? Also, Ms. Daviana Shaw was beaten up and left to die in our care. We have proof of all of this. Then, how is it we are charging the hospital for something we did? Are we not opening a trap for ourselves?"

Lucy walked out from behind a stone wall as she laughed out loud ripping through the cold atmosphere. She walked closer to the group of detectives as she blew out air. The whole crowd froze like ice. She was laughing so loud it was hard to pretend I didn't see her. Jay, Edward, and Dave caught on quick, so did all of our staff. They all pretended quite nicely that we did not hear or see any paranormal activities.

Lucy then said directly to the detectives, "Your group has been involved in my death. You and Dr. Kapoor have been working together. His dead body went missing? Or did you hide him? I will prove how you all killed me for my body parts. I want my heart back. You left no fingerprints, no proof above the Earth. Little did you know the proof you buried will come and haunt you down. If you don't confess, my heart will call me until it comes back to me. I was never on an organ donor list. Don't worry MacNiders for even if you don't have any witnesses on Earth, you have a lot of us beneath Earth."

Suddenly like a lightning bolt, we watched a lot of people walk out of the walls. They had different body parts missing as they all said in union, "We were not on any organ donor list. We did not donate our organs or ask to be murdered for our organs. We want justice. Why is it only the living can ask for justice? When we the dead question, or ask, we are called ghostly predators."

The police and detectives left as they spoke with their lawyers and took the court papers back with them. I realized we had a short victory but knew they would come back with something even worse. I would be ready for anything at this point because I knew we had open enemies. Dave would say it's better to know what and who we are fighting so we have a better chance at winning.

The screams continued from MacNider Hospital's inhouse ghosts. Now the screams became cries and whimpers. I did not fear them as I felt fearful for them. I felt terrible for all of them now that I knew these were caretakers and patients of our hospital. Instead of getting a chance at life, they lost the chance of life. I can't give their lives back, yet I would make sure they get justice.

Lucy sat next to Dave as she asked, "How are my pets? Who is taking care of them, Dave? Why is everyone saying I have a daughter? I sometimes remember things and then forget everything as the days start all over again. I am trying to get over the memories and think clearly. Maybe after being a ghost for a longer period of time, I will be able to conquer this ghostly realm."

I saw my son look at Lucy with a smile, as he loved looking after each and all our staff, as much as he could. Like a saint on a mission, my son Dave walks the hospital at night. He sits with the staff and talks with them individually. He then makes time to visit the employees at their homes when anyone has an accident, is sick, or is in financial difficulties. He provides for the children of a lot of our staff.

A warm comforting feeling tickled my inner core as I recalled my conversation with Dave who had said, "Dad, our retirement is preplanned as we will get old in our home together. You can take care of me when I am old Dad. So, you are not upset if I donate all my income to the less fortunate, right? I have you my famous father to take care of me. Let my income take care of the less fortunate as not all of them are lucky and blessed to have a parent like you."

I laughed out loud recalling the words of my son. Even when I'm sad or upset, he somehow heals my inner soul. He doesn't look at all like me, as he has his biological father's eyes, hair, and looks. Yet somehow people still say he looks like me and talks like me as I was and am his mom and dad packed in one. I love him so much if only I had words to describe what he means to me. It's like the whole world was wrapped up in a gift box in which I found my son Dave.

Dave asked, "Dad, are you okay?"

I saw him standing next to me panicking and taking deep breaths. The only problem with my son was he panics if something is ever wrong with me. As a five-year-old, he ran all the way home from school when a house in my neighborhood burned down to ashes during an arson fire.

I hugged my son and assured my son I was okay and still amongst the living. Strangely we can communicate with one another without talking and even moving.

Dave then looked at Lucy directly and said, "I went to your home Lucy. The mortgage on your home has been paid off. As you had no family members, I did call Dr. Jacobus Vrederic van Phillip to take care of your things. He advised me to wait for him before we do anything, as his mother considered you like her daughter. They told me your pets are safe. I know you were an orphan. The Kasteel Vrederic family had taken care of you and all from the same orphanage."

Lucy looked pale and was in shock. She just stared at our direction without speaking. An elderly woman came forward. She looked so familiar that I jumped up in shock. That was my favorite cafeteria lady. The woman who never got sick and never took a day off work. She never married and didn't have any close relatives. This hospital for the last few years had become her home. Before this, she worked at the local school. She was Dave's favorite cafeteria lady, Ms. Johnson.

Ms. Johnson said, "David, Lucy has no close relatives. The Kasteel Vrederic family gave her to me as a young child. Her parents died when she was a child and I became like her mother, even though I never adopted her. If Lucy ever said she had family, then she probably meant all her orphanage sisters and brothers and the family of Kasteel Vrederic. For a while, she was under some kind of hypnotism as most of us were hypnotized to trust Dr. Kapoor and walk with him to the morgue where he operated on all of us. Something is wrong with my memory. I wonder if Lucy had a young daughter."

I walked back and forth as did Dave. I knew we had to do something fast. Yet how would we deal with a huge criminal group that had existed for years around the globe?

Edward said loudly to us, "Stop this pacing back and forth. You two are making me dizzy. Whatever happens, he will eventually come out of hiding. I never thought Samar was this evil as he had taken an oath to save people. I knew Samar was involved in a lot of things but to go this low is even beyond me. If he is involved, then his mother is behind everything because Samar is greedy and evil, but he is too stupid to plan all of this by himself. We need to solve how he is involved, and that's how we will figure out how to stop and beat him at his own game."

Nurse Lucy came closer to me and said, "I don't know how I did anything for him but if I did, then I want to correct my wrong during the time I have as a ghost. There are twelve of us here who want to help you. It was never our intention to do anything against our beloved community, which is our hospital. All the patients who come here to be healed are our family. I would again give up my life to help this hospital and my only family on Earth, the Kasteel Vrederic family anywhere, anytime."

I saw all twelve ghosts standing with some kind of remorse or regret, I couldn't tell. Each one thought they should be held accountable for their actions even though they were all hypnotized without their consent or knowledge. They all trusted Samar. It felt so scary to see what was going on, but I knew a big international criminal was involved in all of this. I wished Samar was an international spy, not an international criminal who abuses women and makes them bleed.

I spoke out loud or whispered to myself, "How big is this group? How will we ever fight them? Is the mother or the son the head? One of them is trying to fool everyone."

An orderly came forward as he said, "Remember me? I helped repair and maintain all the technical equipment. I am Dev, an Indian student here on a student visa. My family lives in India and they don't even know I have passed away. I will help you in this fight. There are twelve of us. Your daughter was number thirteen. They had everything ready for her to be the next donor. We interrupted and saved her life. We will save all the others as much as possible with your help. From now on, our goal is to keep the number of ghosts in this hospital to twelve, and never let this number grow to thirteen."

I saw the light above Daviana's room was green. She was breathing on her own but still in critical condition. How would I take care of my daughter when I didn't even know how deep her wound was? Dave was our only hope.

Again, a call came from the Netherlands, and a familiar deep male voice said, "I spoke with the police, and they will not be bothering any one of you or the hospital anymore. I checked over Daviana's files, and you are a hundred percent correct and are doing a great job keeping her alive. I don't know if she needs a heart transplant or if her wounds might be from some kind of medical overdose. A medical overdose could imitate to stop the heartbeats but places one to sleep. If she needs to have a heart transplant or not, only time would tell. Keep her stable until I am there. I will be there to do the surgery. Please have everything ready. We just need a donor and must keep Daviana medically induced in a coma, until we can do the procedure. I will call you when in town. My family members will come with me, so maybe we will stay at the famous hospital retreat. Also, my mother wants to take care of Lucy's funeral as she was very special, like a sister to me and a daughter of my family."

Dave went into a corridor and spoke silently, not on the speaker phone, as he knew I didn't like to hear the medical conversations. I only wondered where we could get the heart for Daviana if she needed it. I watched all the friendly ghosts of MacNider Hospital cry and drop tears for a stranger fighting for her life.

Lucy said, "She is the innocent victim who was abused by her husband, forced into marriage by her family, and tormented to be portrayed by her predators to the world as crazy. Now, we the twelve ghosts will protect her, so she does not become the thirteenth victim. Today, we the twelve ghosts of MacNider Hospital take a vow to help and fight for our hospital that provided for us in life and even after death. We the twelve ghosts promise to avenge the false claims that said, MacNider Hospital Charged."

MACNIDER HOSPITAL CHARGED

A healing house stands tall,

With the Atlantic Ocean

As its backyard,

A seaside village

As its frame, and

Loving residents

As its clients.

All are frightened

As rumors

Of floating ghosts,

Dead bodies,

And missing victims

Create an unsolved

Murder mystery house.

I ask you,

How do you come

To the house which

Had healed you,

Gave you hope, and

Awakened your faith

In cures,

Caregivers, and

Second chances in life,

Where you had bathed

And awakened,

Pain free

And completely healed,

Today,

You are the healed,

The cured, and

The pain free,

Yet you give notice

And say,

MACNIDER HOSPITAL CHARGED.

CHAPTER SEVEN:

The Twelve Ghosts Of MacNider Hospital

"What life could
Not achieve
When the
Heart was beating,
Must be achieved
Even after
The heart stops beating
For the soul
To find
Eternal
Peace."

T he smell of blood filled the air. I saw twelve people were floating together. From far away, they looked like they were having fun on break in between their busy day of work. They seemed happy to be chatting amongst themselves. From afar, perceptions can be deceiving, as they were anything but happy or chatting. Their teeth were clattering in fear of death. All of them smelled like death. The tragedy of this portrait was these twelve could not help the dying patients whom each day they had treated and reassured not to be scared for they were there. The patients now feared the same people they once trusted with the care of their lives.

Lucy was crying as she said, "I walked in to check up on a woman I had treated all these days. She is seriously ill and just needed someone to talk. I went and sat next to her, but she screamed and ran out with her IV still attached. She refuses to be treated in a hospital that has ghosts, even though she is in critical condition and battling death herself. I helped with her cure and today because I am dead, she fears me."

I heard her thoughts and knew the feelings on both sides. We don't fear the living, but as soon as the breath is no more, we the living and the dead are separated by fear.

Suddenly, a child ran out from somewhere, crying in fear. She ran toward Lucy and touched her hands.

The young girl with big curls and dimples smiled and said, "Aunt Nurse Lucy, why haven't you come and visit me? I'm getting better, see? They said I can go home soon. I went for an X-ray and saw you. So, I ran away from him. I have to go back before I get in trouble."

The child hugged Lucy and left with another nurse who didn't see Lucy or any ghosts and was just happy she found the missing child. The child left, busy talking with the nurse. I saw Lucy and knew she was happy not everyone was scared.

Patients in our hospital were checking out not because they were healed, but because no one wanted to be in the hospital. They feared a basically healthy person seeking basic treatment could become a resident of the thirteenth floor and be transported from the world of living to the world of the dead. I realized we had to take a temporary loss and that's all right. I was going to solve this mystery for I knew there was a very real culprit behind all this. The hunters of this show were not paranormal as the paranormal figures were standing with me, not against me.

I sat on a rough uncomfortable hospital chair that hurt my back. As soon as I placed my head back, there within a smoke-filled room, a woman was trying to escape.

She was screaming and asking her captor, "Why have you done this to me? My mother passed away and I am a living dead person. So, why are you still hurting me? Kill me or let me go! What have I ever done to you? Please let me go!"

I clearly saw this time, it was Viana. My beloved Viana was shackled from her feet and had a long chain that allowed her to move a little. She was trying to communicate with me. She showed me, she was at a place that felt like the end of Earth, where I could see the land met the sea. This room felt like it was within a lighthouse looking structure. There was a tower room where the windows and doors were all open. The sea breeze chilled the entire room.

It was dark but the moon's glow brightened the room. It felt like a vampire would come flying in through an open window looking out at the sea. I could see a room with steel doors. The waves were crashing against the rocks at high tide, drowning out all the screams coming from the room. So, no sound could ever be heard from below.

I knew Viana was beaten and bruised. She only held on to the hands of love as her last and only survival string.

Years of abuse showed on her fragile body. Her beautiful long braided hair seemed longer than the fairytale character Rapunzel. She could not, however, stand by the window as her chains blocked her from going too close to any window. I wondered if she was cold and frigid. What if she got ill? She was covered in blood and her whole body was bruised purple and black. I convinced my mind to think this was only a dream and nothing but a dream.

I tried through my inner soul to send my beloved strength and all my love. Maybe I could build a portal for her through this dream. Maybe she would be able to jump out of her prison and jump into my room. Like a jolt from reality, my dream broke, and the twelve ghosts were watching me intensely. I had fallen asleep for maybe a few minutes. The inhouse ghosts who were rumored to be haunting my hospital watched me like they had a lot of questions for me.

Lucy gave me a look, and she raised and lowered her eyebrows a few times. Somehow, she was silently talking with me. I could hear her, ahh so mind-to-mind talking. I thought these types of talks were for dreams only. I guess spirits can talk to you this way too.

Lucy said, "I could see your dream girl through the fog around you. That's called the television of dreams. I thought you had said your beloved wife was dead. If that was your wife, then she isn't in the land of the dead but still within the land of the living. She looks very fragile, so find her quickly."

Lucy stopped talking and went missing. I wanted to ask her so many questions, but I refrained myself from asking. I didn't want to be influenced by anything if she was wrong.

Suddenly Lucy came back running and said, "Oh no, she is dying. Please go help her. Otherwise, she won't make it. Daviana needs your help, please go and do something."

Lucy walked into the ICU through the glass barrier. Jay and Edward tried to follow her and before Dave or I could say anything, they bounced back rubbing their foreheads. I wondered who the leader in this team of two was.

Jay then moaned and wiped his eyes as he said to Edward, "That hurt but not more than watching my daughter fight for her life. It's all your fault. If you hadn't forced her to marry that idiot, then my child would have been happily married to Dave. We wouldn't have had any troubles. You even knew Dave isn't David's biological son. I wish I had known, then I wouldn't have told her the whole story of her mother and David. It's my fault. Oh God, I will be the first father who threw his daughter to her death bed. Please God, take me, not her. Please my God, give a life for a life."

Edward raised his hands in prayers as he knelt on his knees and prayed in front of the glass room. I saw how shocked Jay was to see this and he too followed and knelt on his knees and joined the prayer. The twelve ghosts came and knelt by them and started to pray quietly, in their own ways.

I followed Dave as he threw everyone including myself out of the room. Lucy, however, stayed in there as she tried to place her hands on Daviana and pray. Lucy was speaking with Dave as Dave spoke to other doctors in the room. I couldn't hear their conversation but knew they were not happy.

Dave came out and he sat down with his hands on his head. I sat next to him and let silence talk. Lucy also came out. The hallway and sitting area had a lot of paranormal activities going on. Things were flying, and doors were opening and closing. Fear gripped us as thoughts of our ICU patients and their health overrode everything else.

Never did I raise my voice before, but I did then as I cried, "What's going on? Are you the twelve ghosts unhappy my daughter is dying and might just be the thirteenth? What are you doing?"

In front of me stood the twelve ghosts of MacNider Hospital. They were all bleeding from different parts of their bodies. No blood dropped on the floor yet in the hospital corridors, emergency room, and even in front of the operating rooms, there were blood droppings spread out like a murder scene. A pungent smell filed the hospital air.

Lucy observed me for a while, then she walked closer to Dave and said, "I should introduce you to all of us because whoever is committing the gruesome scenes around the hospital is not one of us from the world of the dead. This crime is being committed by someone from the world of the living. We suggest you all find out sooner than later. Otherwise, there will be many more of us than you wish to see or know. Maybe close off the morgue and the thirteenth floor to start with. Don't delay the investigation as the people who are doing these acts have been at it for a long time."

She stood in front of us and at times she looked so real like a living breathing human. Then when she moved, she became clear and glowed like a ghost. It saddened my interior to see a healthy young person had to die because of some gruesome crimes. All around her chest, there were dried blood stains. It bothered me thinking how much pain she was in. All of them had some kind of blood stains on their bodies. They all had such friendly faces yet had suffered so much. The guilt of all of this was burying me alive. I would close the hospital if I couldn't catch the predators. When I thought out everything, I decided I should keep the hospital open to make it a trap to catch the whole group. Lucy smiled and agreed as she nodded her head.

A male nurse who still had a badge on him said, "Don't blame yourself for something you had no hand in. My name is Ahmed. I came from Egypt and was trying to earn some money for my family. I went to sleep one night and woke up like this the next morning. As a Muslim, my family members wanted to arrange my funeral immediately, but my body is still missing. I feel like my body was cremated against my will."

I saw he too had similar blood stains, on his white scrubs. The young nurse was floating in a see-through form. My inner soul cried for his family members who would be destitute and in need of financial help. How could I even tell them their son had died without a body or proof? They had nobody to even say if he was dead or alive. I needed to do something quickly. Lucy watched me so intently I knew she could read minds.

She only smiled and said, "Real quickly, I will introduce you to the twelve ghosts, I am Lucy as you all know. Ahmed is also a nurse who worked in the operating room as did Nurse Levi. Ms. Johnson whom you all had met worked in food services. Dev is a biomedical technician who just came from overseas. Jack the seven-foot-tall ghost who always smiled at everyone he encountered and spread happiness all around is a lab technician. You probably never met Nathan the medical assistant. Nancy is the always pleasant patient service representative. You knew the executive manager, Mandy. The three housekeeping service crew members whom no one probably even noticed are missing as they were temporary staff are Wanda, Brandy, and Paul. You all can get to know them better, but please remember, they need your help. As in life, even in death, we are still devoted to do our share of whatever needs to be done to keep the hospital going."

A huge group of doctors suddenly left my daughter's room. One doctor came closer to Dave.

He tried to compose himself and said, "Dave, she is in very critical condition. Clinging to life through a miracle. Otherwise, we would have declared her medically dead. Now we wait for Dr. Jacobus Vrederic van Phillip, the only hope for her survival. He will know what she needs and how to treat her. It is said he himself is a miracle. When he walks in, half of the miracle starts; however, he can do miracles only if you have a donor heart. I hear he is nearby somewhere, so he will be arriving soon."

Dave was shaking and I knew this wasn't normal for my son, so I held him from the back and told him, "Miracles are our saving grace. There shall be a miracle. I will keep holding on to that thread of hope and so should you."

Then again, the hospital corridors were filled with screams. This time, there was a young child's voice. I watched the twelve ghosts disappeared as we followed Lucy and went to the morgue on the thirteenth floor.

Security went beforehand and there was a young girl around three years old with long golden hair wearing a hospital gown walking out of the morgue. The new security was hired by Erasmus van Phillip, father of Dr. Jacobus.

A group of security guards spread over the hospital grounds. On live security cameras, we all saw an elderly woman. A man was there who was tied up from the back. We could only see his hair was shaved and for some reason, he was being pulled by the elderly woman and her goons.

The man was screaming, "A mother is fighting to save her child she never met. A father is fighting for a child he did not give birth to. A birth mother is fighting to kill her own son. It is better to die and be reborn from any other woman than you. You are a beast who swallows her own children."

We tried to find the people we saw in the security footage, but we could not figure out or find any proof of them. It seemed weird how the elderly woman was pulling the young man. My inner warning wires went off to not trust everything the eyes see. The young girl was taken to the ICU for further evaluation. It seemed she was in foster care because her mother went missing. She was only three years old. Her foster parents sold her to a woman who paid a huge amount of money. I let Dave handle the situation with the police as it was now a police case.

The toddler told us her name was Lucy. Our nurse Lucy started to cry as she saw her own short life's reflection play over through this child. Everything froze in front of me as I saw a child Lucy staring at me with huge brown innocent eyes. She tried to see Lucy the nurse in front of her.

She then ran toward Lucy and said, "Mama, I'm tired. Can we go home now?"

The child tried to hold Lucy but was not able to. Jay jumped up and picked her up in his arms.

He kissed the child on her head and said, "Your Mama is my friend. She is here. You see her, right? She wants you to come with me. I'll be your friend until your Mama comes home. Let's go and get some ice cream."

Lucy nodded her head and smiled toward her daughter. The child waved her hand and blew a flying kiss toward her mother. Lucy did the same thing and hid her tears until Jay and the child were no longer visible. All the ghosts hugged Lucy and tried to comfort her.

Lucy said to me in a whisper, "Please give her to Anadhi Newhouse van Phillip, Dr. Jacobus's mother. She will know what to do with her. Maybe she will give her to someone we wouldn't even think of, but Anadhi will know what's best for her. Anadhi gave me everything I could have asked for in this world when she picked me up from foster care at the age of seventeen."

The hospital grounds smelled like blood all over again. I ran toward the kitchen and saw the crew were all screaming in horror. Jay came toward me all by himself as baby Lucy was not with him.

He whispered in my ears, "The local law enforcement came and picked up baby Lucy. I hope she is safe as I had to give her to them."

A cold shivering feeling crept through my inner self. I didn't know what was going on. Yet I hoped and prayed an innocent child stayed safe in police custody.

One of the food service managers ran toward the corridors screaming, "I can't work here anymore. The waters are contaminated as all the faucets are now pouring out blood."

I turned on the tap water and red pungent-smelling water came out. People would think it was blood.

Jay smelled the water with me and said, "Chemical, not blood. How do you convince your hospital staff something is going on, not paranormal but horrific intentional sabotage that is scientifically explainable? The question remains how they are doing it. We can't even get help from the police or the FBI as so many of the corrupt officers are working with them. We are left here to work on our own and we shall."

I saw the whole hospital in front of me was basically closing. It was a nightmare or torture that was not explainable. My family's dream was being shut down. I would fight to my last breath and wouldn't allow anyone to shut down my hospital, be they living or dead.

Dev, Ahmed, and Levi held their hands as Dev said, "Now it's war between the living ghosts and the dead ghosts. Strange, right guys? You would think the living people would want to stop the war and work together, to live in peace. Let's teach them evil is bad on Earth and beyond. If you can get rid of ghosts, then we the ghosts can get rid of you the living evils who torment the innocent. Healers who worked to heal people while breathing won't stop their job just because they don't breathe anymore."

Jay ran back to the ICU and hovered over the glass wall crying and praying on his knees as he watched the child he raised fighting for her life. The daughter whom I was forced to give up, whom he was forced to hold within his chest, was fighting death. Mind-to-mind, I reassured my daughter to fight and never give up as this father would never give up on her. I knew she would fight for me.

I got on my knees and joined Jay. Edward got up as his phone rang. He answered the phone and was visibly having a hard time breathing. I couldn't tell if he was excited or sad.

Edward said, "They found a heart for me. I told them to see if it matches my granddaughter, and they said it was a perfect match. They will have to do the surgery tomorrow. Don't anyone say anything as this will be my gift to my granddaughter. Don't tell her anything when she wakes up with her new heart."

He sat down and was crying in happiness or guilt, I couldn't tell. Nothing felt good as everything seemed wrong. How could a life gone to save another ever feel good? I listened to an elderly man who wanted to live and now was looking for a donor for his granddaughter, even at the expense of his own life. He seemed so happy as if a huge burden was lifted from his heart.

He said with a broken voice, "I verbally abused Daviana, threatening her with lies. I allowed her husband to manipulate and humiliate her in front of the world. I allowed her to be in isolation where she was physically and mentally tortured, yet I kept silent. Now let me die with remorse as I pray for forgiveness that I can never give myself."

He sat down on a chair near the coffee stand in the waiting room. He asked Jay with his hands to give him something. Jay knew exactly what he wanted and brought him ice water with fresh lemons. He took a sip and placed his head back.

Edward then said, "I was the silent abuser. All grandmothers, mothers, daughters, sons, and sons-in-law should be aware of people like me. Silently walking away from torture be it physical or emotional to save the honor of a family for the society is wrong. People like me are the silent killers of all marriages, all happily-ever-after stories. People like me only see when something touches our own skin. I assumed my way was the right way, but each person is different. Each situation is different. So, how could we have the same solution?"

I wondered where the heart was suddenly arriving from and who the donor was. The donor wanted to be secret. The patient would be coming from another hospital and would be alive, but dying in a day or so. The donor wanted to give the heart to the old man. As the donor was told about Daviana, however, the donor requested if the heart could be given to her. The request was accepted by all. How did the donor know Daviana needed a heart transplant surgery? This was a complete secret. This was beyond a miracle.

Dave came and whispered in my ears, "We still can't tell for sure if Daviana even needs a transplant surgery. I've been looking at all her charts and something isn't adding up."

The twelve ubiquitous ghosts were walking around the hospital. They visited all twelve floors and avoided entering the thirteenth floor as it was the morgue. I had security guards scrambling from floor to floor searching for the culprits doing these incidents.

Lucy came forward as she sat next to me and said, "Do you really want to find out who the donor is? At times, is it not better just not to know? If it was me in that bed, what if the donor is a drug lord or a murderer or a thief? Maybe you should just let it go and be happy you have a donor. I have a weird feeling you won't like the donor, even if there is one."

Lucy walked toward the glass door and just went inside. I walked into my daughter's room with Dave. She was sleeping so peacefully. I wondered what she looked like when she was a baby. When did she learn to walk? What was her first word? Will I ever know? I had never wanted to know because I assumed by doing so, I was protecting her.

Suddenly Lucy was whispering something into Daviana's ear. I got scared and wanted her to stop as I saw the eleven ghosts come and block me from doing anything. They stood like a wall. I was forced to get out of the room. Jay tried to help me, but again the ghosts blocked Jay and me from going near the glass wall, forget going inside.

Like a television screen, we all through fog there was a staircase leading from Daviana to the skies above. Daviana was trying to go up but was blocked off by Lucy. My daughter was trying to walk toward the light, but Lucy was blocking her.

Daviana said, "Please, let me go to the top so I can be free. I don't want to be beaten and abused. I don't want to fight or try to protect myself. No one cares for a woman like me. I was born to be abused and tortured, not to be loved and

197

honored. My biological parents let go of me. I have been physically tortured. No one ever loved me. I am both a doctor and a lawyer, but I can't protect myself. Please let me go."

Lucy placed her hands around Daviana and tried to block her like a wall.

Lucy said, "No one ever loved you. No one taught you how to walk, or talk, or ace your first exam. No one stayed awake with you when you had a fever. If so, then for him come back. He would want you to bury him, not the other way around. It's time you must take care of him, if there ever was such a person.

Daviana stopped and saw the staircase. Her feet couldn't move as I saw she had tears in her eyes.

She screamed, "Bapu! My father, please don't cry. I'm coming back. How could I have forgotten you? You don't have anyone on this Earth but me, your daughter."

Jay got up and ran to the room as he fainted at his daughter's feet. Blocked off and stopped by the ghosts, we saw the staircase going up to the clouds was made from clouds. It was like soft creamy milk one can walk over. A canoe appeared and I watched Lucy block the staircase. Then, Jay appeared in a white gown. He stood there as he watched his daughter.

He nodded his head and said, "Daviana, listen to me. Come back to Bapu. I love you more than my heartbeats. I am blessed as your biological father not by choice but by force gave you away, so I caught you. You are my breath, my will, and my hope in this life. I live only for you. We, your two fathers, both love you and wait for you. Who cares if your fake husband never loved you. Maybe he wasn't your twin flame. Come back and find him. Maybe you knew who he was, as someone is trying to save you with all his love, even though you kept him far away from you. Tell us, Daviana, who did this to you? Samar and who else?"

Suddenly, we all saw a bald Samar and an elderly woman were furious and were planning something big. I saw Lucy fall to the ground as she walked outside and stood in front of Dave. Dave tried to air hug Lucy. I picked up Jay and hugged him like a brother. He hugged me back and we saw our daughter was breathing properly again.

Lucy was crying as she said, "Forgive me. I tried to show you what is going on in the world between life and death. Daviana found the only one well-wisher she had all her life who truly matters. I only wish I had someone like him. I would have given up everything in the whole world to have him as a father. My only fear is Samar, and the elderly woman brewing up more miseries."

The woman Lucy was talking about seemed like the woman I saw in my dreams who imprisoned Viana. I recalled seeing an elderly nurse with Samar a few times. The same face I saw in my dreams. I felt like something was not right. How could a woman from my dreams be here?

Dave saw me shaking and asked, "Dad what's wrong? Have faith. Daviana will survive. She is a fighter. What is it, Dad? Why are you shaking?

I saw my son and sat down on the nearest chair that was available. The whole room was shaking as if the building was collapsing, or we were having an earthquake. I had to get my thoughts out before they got out of control.

So, I said, "Dave, I don't know what is happening but that elderly nurse who was with Samar and just now we saw through the miraculous vision is the same woman I have been seeing in my dreams. It's like every night I see Viana imprisoned in a tower room inside a lighthouse. She is in a room where even the doors are made of soundproof iron or steel. I saw she was shackled, battered, and bruised. The same woman was there. I ignored my dreams because I thought my personal feelings were making me see things that weren't real. Dave, then why did I see that woman?"

Jay walked closer to me and sat down. He was listening to every single word I had uttered. Caught in between both Daviana and Viana, I wondered what Jay was feeling.

He said, "First thing, she is like my sister. Remember I have honored Raksha Bandhan each year, even though she was missing. I know everyone said she was dead and only Edward probably knows the truth. But my leads told me she was taken by someone who had also taken Edward's wife. I too have had dreams about her. She keeps asking me to help her. Then, she asks about Daviana and tells me to keep her safe. I never shared this as I thought all this was my wishful dreams not reality."

The floors in the hospital rocked sideways. Everyone tried to get up as I saw our hospital crews begin evacuation procedures. In a few seconds, the shaking stopped. We never lost power nor had time to even move before everything went back to normal. An announcement came on to inform all that everything was back to normal, and nothing was wrong with the building.

Dave said, "Dad, everything is scientifically explainable. Dreams are there to guide us and I believe a door of communication from the dead to the living. Also, a way of miraculous communication between the living who can't get in touch. They are messages from the past, the future, and at times just our minds playing games. The lighthouse tower room you described does exist. It has been abandoned for years, so no one has lived there for years. No known activities have been recorded there. I know the building will be demolished soon as it deemed unsafe. Oh my God, we must check the building."

Something inside of my soul rocked everything I believed and questioned. All I could think was I saw papers and posters saying the small and damaged lighthouse looking structure would be demolished this weekend. I knew I had to get a stop order from court so this process could be delayed. I had to find out if anyone was being hidden inside. The nightmare would be to get past all the bureaucracies and time.

Edward came close to me. Even though he was having a hard time speaking, he didn't like showing his weakness.

He smiled and said, "I am still alive and breathing at this age. I'm surprised I can take so many tragedies and still breathe. I really must be a bad person. My last wish would be if my daughter Viana is still alive, I would want you to rescue her. Free her from her thousands of nights of imprisonment. I her father had no hand in doing this. Yet, I never checked nor identified the woman in the coffin, whom I buried as my daughter. I was given the coffin box and was told if opened, then both my wife and daughter would be dead. So, I hoped my daughter was still alive."

Edward sat on the chair I just unoccupied. He placed his head back on the shoulder rest as he tried to rest. Jay rushed and placed another chair in front of his feet. I realized through the years, Jay became like his son more than his son-in-law as he was Viana's brother.

Silently under his breath, grinding his teeth, Edward said, "I checked and rechecked. First, there was the identical face of my daughter. Then, I heard everyone try to say I buried a nurse who I had murdered. I just don't know why such a game was being played with my life. I never hurt anyone in my life. I believe it had nothing to do with my family but everything to do with my pursuit of illegal sales of body organs over the world. I tried to prevent the poor people from selling their body parts and tried to prevent all kidnappings that occurred for body parts."

Jay gave Edward water to sip and placed his feet up on top of the chair he had brought. Jay took Edward's wristwatch off and placed it in his pocket. I guess it was uncomfortable.

Edward said, "I was not in illegal activities. Viana knew everything. I worked in the police force and with the police force all my life. My granddaughter fighting for her life knew everything. Samar aside from being a doctor also worked with the Central Intelligence Agency and had a lot of contacts within the US. He promised to bring my wife and my daughter back to me by hook or crook. I guess I judged him wrong. He said he would catch his mother red-handed. I don't know where and when he went rogue. I wonder if he ever was good or is still trying to catch the international organ trafficking criminals. That was his passion as his mother was the queen of organ trafficking. Everything would have been all right if I had not forced Viana into a marriage and ruined three lives."

His words shocked even Jay as he watched Edward in shock and just sat on the floor next to the old man. I knew everything the old man tried to do was to justify his marriage to his Indian wife. He declined my marriage to Viana because he believed interracial marriages never worked. He did everything for his wife and daughter. Now he has given up on life all together for them.

The twelve ghosts of MacNider Hospital were watching all of us. There were no dry eyes left in the room. The ghosts and the living were all crying for the loss of the old man. He gave up his faith in life as all he did was try to save his wife, and watch his daughter and granddaughter be physically tortured, mentally abused, and psychologically tormented by a woman for being a woman. I only wondered why and how long this was going on.

Mandy, the hospital's executive manager in ghost form, said, "I will help figure out what's going on here. Lucy will help all of you heal through whatever is after you anywhere and everywhere, as she can travel outside of the hospital while we are all stuck inside. I promise even if you have no living souls to help you, we will help you solve the mystery. This is a promise from us, the twelve ghosts of MacNider Hospital."

THE TWELVE GHOSTS OF MACNIDER HOSPITAL

Within our sacred walls,

Worked Lucy,

The beaming nurse,

Ahmed,

The robust nurse,

Levi,

The all-charitable nurse

Who never asked

But always had given.

Here in my walls

Also was,

Ms. Johnson,

Who forgot to eat

But never let you go hungry,

Dev,

The technician who handled

Everything without being asked,

Jack,

Who handled the lab even though

You never knew him.

Nathan

Was there assisting

With procedures you needed.

Remember Nancy,

Who represented

You the patient.

Oh yes,

Don't you remember Mandy,

Who managed everything?

How could you forget,

Wanda,

Brandy,

And

Paul?

They did all

The housekeeping

For you to be welcomed

Back to our

Healing home.

Today,

We are all forgotten.

We are all

Frozen in time.

We are all

The eerie entities

As we

Are

THE TWELVE GHOSTS OF MACNIDER HOSPITAL.

CHAPTER EIGHT:

The Forgotten Prisoner Who Escaped

"A mother's love
Protects
A child
From even beyond death.
No prison on Earth
Or beyond
Can keep an
Innocent mother
From
Protecting
An
Innocent
Child."

L ucy guided Dave, Jay, and me to the abandoned lighthouse looking structure that has been here for years, on Winter Solstice. This day marked the end of fall and beginning of a brutal cold winter. The day had the shortest amount of daylight hours and the longest night of the year which gave us more time in the dark than we had wished for. The roads were crowded with people rejoicing. Early pagan traditions celebrated this day to honor the birth of the sun. A lot of people had candles lit and cider brewed along the path celebrating this sacred day.

Viana and I had celebrated Winter Solstice years ago as runaway newlyweds. She loved the small shops, the smell of food and drinks, and people celebrating the night. I had held her in my arms as I was madly in love with her. I saw nothing or heard nothing as I only wanted to see, smell, and feel my wife.

She had teased me saying, "David, come on! You are missing out on all the celebrations. Look at the decorations. You can see me all your life, but this occasion only lasts one night each year."

I walked behind Dave as my feet felt numb. I didn't ask Lucy or Dave why we were walking on a road that was unused and had huge unkept bushes and knee-high weeds.

Suddenly the busy crowd celebrating Winter Solstice could not be seen anymore, as everything became quiet. The dark night became even darker and suddenly felt creepier and colder. The never used path somehow felt like someone other than our group had used. I hoped by a friend, not an enemy as the path seemed recently traveled upon.

Jay and Dave both told Lucy together, "We should call the police and inform them about our suspicion."

Lucy gave both a weird look as if she didn't hear them and kept walking.

Jay then said, "Lucy, I don't want to die without telling my daughter I loved her all her life and will love her all my living life. If death comes today, I want it to come after I let her know how much I treasured her."

Again, Lucy saw Jay and shrugged her shoulders. She kept walking ahead of us. I wondered was it even safe to follow a ghost who didn't actually care about death as she was already dead? Then, I hated myself for thinking like that as Lucy would give up her life over and over again to save another life.

Lucy suddenly stopped and said, "I know it's somewhere here, but I wonder why I can't see the entrance to the lighthouse looking structure. I had come here once with a group of nurses and Dr. Kapoor. He told us he comes here often and loves to stay here all by himself. I realized which lighthouse David was talking about right away. I can see or read minds as a ghost, but something is blocking it."

I tried to listen to Lucy, but I heard soft murmuring cries, very familiar to my dreams. I took lead as there was a light coming from somewhere behind the overgrown bushes. The pouring light danced and guided us to a very old stone structure. The stone house was not the famous lighthouse but somehow this building resembled a lighthouse. As we walked closer, this lighthouse looking structure was all covered in vines. A huge yellow tape circled the structure which read:

CAUTION

DO NOT ENTER. STRUCTURE IS DEEMED UNSAFE AND MAY COLLAPSE. FINE WILL BE ISSUED TO ALL SQUATTERS.

We walked ahead before I placed my hands on the wall. The old, heavy, rusted door suddenly opened. A man with thick hair wearing a black cloak came outside, carrying brown burlap. We hid behind a bush as he spoke to the person hidden in the burlap.

He said, "I must go back and get the other elderly person. Don't move or say anything if she comes. Just stay hidden behind this bush. I promise you, I will save both of you, even if that's the last thing I do. Also don't say anything about me when all of this is exposed. Otherwise, you two will be my last victories."

I saw the small person hidden in the burlap stayed quiet. I realized the person trusted the man. Lucy signaled us to stay hidden in our place and not to move. I could not tell Lucy why I felt like my whole being just froze like icicles. So many thoughts crowded my mind which was going to shatter if I did nothing. Then again, it would shatter if I did something wrong. The man then returned with another burlap.

He said, "She is breathing, but her pulse is very weak. I need to take her to a hospital or give her immediate medical care. I must somehow take both of you to a hospital, but I'm worried she will come back and look for both of you. I need miraculous help from somewhere. I've been trying to get you two alone without being exposed to her. Also, please remember when you are safe, even then don't tell anyone about my help or anything about me. There are a lot more people I must rescue worldwide, but I must stay hidden amongst them to be able to do this."

I stepped out from hiding as did Dave. We tried to see the man standing in front of us. He stood straight as he tried to see Lucy.

He saw her and whimpered as he said, "So, they did kill you too. I wonder how much you remember, or if you remember anything. Lucy, where is Lucy? They had her and told me they will murder her and sell her organs. Maybe I married you because you were pregnant, not for love. Sorry Lucy, but I do love my child Lucy, and I won't let anyone harm her. I won't lie. People like me only make love and never do fall in love. I almost fell in love with Daviana, but then I realized I love to rescue people from being thrown into slaughterhouses more, so I never touched her and honored our wedding vows."

Lucy sat down and cried as she woke up the night skies. I realized she was a ghost, and no one could hear her, but it still scared my inner soul. It was strange how this man saw her clearly.

I heard Lucy say, "I couldn't remember anything but how I was an orphan who was saved by the Kasteel Vrederic family. I forgot how we fell in love and had a daughter. You never acknowledged our child but went and married a woman from your own country. I thought you were half Indian and half German. Why were you against our marriage? What did I do wrong that you and your goons murdered me?"

Samar had tears rolling from his eyes as he tried to carry the two people he saved and placed them both on a wagon. He was doing something as he gave both injections hidden within in his cloak.

He told Lucy, "I am a doctor first and my oath is to save lives. I do not take lives and never will unless a life is in danger. As a CIA officer, however, I have been working undercover for them for a long time. I am working against my own mother, not for her. I made an oath to Daviana that I would never touch her or harm her. I had to as my mother would beat her up just to satisfy her mind. My mother's evil mind found peace by abusing another woman. She is this world's biggest body trafficker. She sells organs of the living people. She believes Edward dumped her and threw her love away for an Indian girl from his own village. So, she became the devil for all married, unmarried, men, and women. She hates the existence of happy people."

The CIA sent a few cars in collaboration with the Federal Bureau of Investigation and local agencies. They helped the two victims into an ambulance. Samar spoke with them for a while as they left and told us they would meet us at the hospital with the two recovered victims. I wanted to ask them if one of them was my Viana. Samar placed his fingers on his lips as he signaled me to remain quiet.

In my mind, my wishful thoughts were, was the person Viana? Oh no then he would have told us. Yet maybe they wanted this to be kept secret, so no one showed us the faces of the two victims who were still breathing. I only hoped the prisoners we were rescuing, or Samar rescued were our people, and one of them maybe was my Viana.

We had a ride to the hospital as we met Samar with his new looks. Blue eyes and a full head of long blackish brown hair in a ponytail. I wondered how he had grown his hair so fast. Coloring his hair with different shades was one thing but it takes time to grow one's hair back. It must be fake hair, yet it looked so real. I didn't know why it bothered me.

He waited in a private room with the recovered victims. The two victims were in the room next to Daviana. The separation was made through a glass wall barrier. Samar walked into Daviana's room as he sat there and just watched the victim he had abused and beaten up. Maybe for work or whatever, yet her bruises were all real. She was verbally humiliated, manipulated through control tactics, and isolated from the world through blackmail. I wondered why someone would do this even for work. Samar came and sat next to all of us as he tried to make direct eye contact with Edward.

He sat in silence and said, "So, how many women need to be humiliated, manipulated, gaslighted, and kept in isolation before you tell them why? Why did you use me as your pawn? I never touched Daviana, so who touched her? Who beat your wife, and why? Also, my biological mother, who is she to you and what is her contact with you? Why did you involve the CIA with this? Answer my questions or I am out. I have given up my life and had clenched my teeth as I tried to protect an abused and innocent woman. I need answers. When the CIA recruited me, they told me it was your wish I continue. You wanted me because I am her son. I joined because I want her, and all people like her to be stopped."

Edward tried to get up but was very weak. He tried to have direct eye contact with me but for some reason either failed or was too weak.

He somehow found the will and said, "My mother was a victim of abuse as was my grandmother. Victims of forced marriage. I thought it was normal and through time the victims too take these beatings and abuses as the normal ways of life. My sister was a victim as she died at the hands of her husband. I became a police officer to fight these crimes, yet I stumbled upon a bigger crime being committed in continents of Asia, Africa, Europe, North America, South

America, and Australia. Human organs were being sold worldwide. Women, men, girls, and boys, age made no difference. I joined to prevent these crimes and had lost my own family because of this. I continued as I have basic moral values."

Edward tried to rest his head as he looked very tired and I felt bad for him, but still didn't care as I kept seeing him separate me from my Viana. He chose his path and separated my daughter and me from our beloved twin flames for reasons only he knew.

Edward then said, "There is no justification for my actions. When I walked into a hospital morgue where bodies of abused and bruised victims laid dead with missing organs, my inner gut froze. A school bus filled with elementary school children were kidnapped and we were told to spread rumors. Women being abused by their spouses was the reason for a sudden rise in unjust deaths. To save unknown children, I gave up my wife, my daughter, and my granddaughter. All of this because I had told the organ traffickers that the children we saved would be sent to their parents and would not be returned to the traffickers. So, they became my biggest enemy. Sacrifice I made for them I did not think was a sacrifice, but a husband, a father, a grandfather's love."

Edward wiped his tears as he tried to see the glass room which had his granddaughter back on a ventilator. We all knew anything could happen if we did not get the heart that was promised. I still didn't know why he never tried to save his own daughter or wife.

Edward watched me and somehow knew what I was thinking as he said, "Judge me for that's your choice and freedom. I saved thirty buses filled with people from the age of two to fifty. Each time I saved one more bus of victims, I got a notice to let them go, so I could see my wife and daughter again. I asked myself should I save two in return for seventy people in each bus? No, I could not justify it."

Jay watched Samar directly as he had his head bowed down, looking at the floor.

Edward then said, "So, I shut myself up and let go of my beloveds to save the others. Daviana knew everything as she too helped the CIA for Samar. They were partners, and that's why he has lacked on his job and almost got fired as he risked his job and his identity by being exposed to save Daviana, and everyone else."

Tears fell from my eyes, yet I blinked and let them dry in the air. Like always, I only let my tears fall on my pillows. Dave saw me and I realized my son learned this character trait of mine as he too hid his feelings behind an empty and blank face. The emergency room had a lot of accident victims coming in. Dave and I wondered if there was a bus accident or if something was going on. We returned to Daviana's corner as we knew in a crowd, anyone could come and hurt my child.

Samar was listening to everyone as he said, "I was approached by my mother, a predator of these abuse victims. She is the one who kept Viana as her prisoner to blackmail Daviana. So, I let my work know and we planned this out. I spoke with Edward and married Daviana as Daviana was her next victim. My mother was forced to leave Daviana alone. I gave up on my beloved and pretended to be in a pretend abusive marriage. I still need to ask Daviana who did this to her. I did pretend but never did I touch her or abuse her. Yet I know someone has. I only wish I knew where my biological daughter is for it's hard for me to see Lucy is gone. Who will save my daughter? Dr. Jacobus Vrederic van Phillip knows of my identity as I am working with his family on another paranormal situation."

I stood up and tried to recall everything as it was too much for me. I wanted to ask Viana so many questions but realized she too had no answers. I knew she pretended to be to be Jay's wife so they could give Daviana honor in a society where everything is judged, and nothing is forgiven or understood.

I asked Edward, "How hard was it to give up your wife and daughter to be imprisoned for a lifetime to protect all others and not have a family, a wife or a child to come home to?"

No one said anything as I watched Lucy wipe her tears. She had said nothing about her relationship with Samar. I only wished things were different as I would give anything to save their child.

Edward looked at me directly as he said, "It was easy David. When I saw how many Vianas were being saved and how many Devis, like my wife Devi, were being saved, it was easy. My wife and daughter would never forgive me if I had exchanged their lives for another's, or in this case hundreds. Also, I was tied and wanted my son-in-law, you, to be safe and left far away from my bad luck. The society accepts abuse and psychological torture, yet they don't accept biracial marriages. I am not the instigator but the crusader against all physical or psychological torture. I can't end racial and interracial differences."

The lights were all flickering in the hospital. We saw the lights were flickering in the new room with the rescued patients. We heard gunfire erupted somewhere outside of the hospital.

Samar got up and he took out his gun as he called some people. We saw outside in the open courtyard stood the nurse we assumed Samar was having an affair with.

He said to all of us, "Forget everything you all know about me. Hate me and let that hate guide you."

He showed us a woman and said, "That's my mother who abuses women and men, who preys on the innocent and places financial burdens on others. She taught me to show strength by being abusive and never apologizing yet letting others know they are wrong not me. I changed and saw the light when I found Lucy. I had vowed to make our family complete through love, yet my family remains incomplete eternally. I thought I didn't love her. When I realized I was wrong, it was too late. Also, Dave, Daviana was yours, is yours, and shall be yours, if only life gives you a chance."

The gunfire stopped as a police officer came and said, "There were no gunfire, but we all lied."

The police chief came rushing in behind the officer as he said, "Everything is under control and Charlotte Amanda Kapoor, the woman everyone had been seeking for years, has escaped."

The police chief also arrested the police officer who was corrupt and obviously had helped Charlotte Amanda Kapoor, Samar's mother.

Before I said anything, a woman's voice was heard on the overhead speakers.

She spoke without any mercy or kindness in her voice, "My enmity is with Edward Kapoor. Look how young I still am at eighty-five years old. Edward rejected me, so I married his stepbrother only to take my revenge. Your father wanted a typical Indian wedding. He wanted his children to be of the same race. He is the racist, not I. Shame on him. The world now will forever call his family abusers, who psychologically and physically abuse women."

She was now laughing like a mad woman as the police force went all over the hospital to find out where the voice was coming from. I held my temper as I watched Dave hold his temper in control.

She said again, "Look how I ruined everything. His family's name has shattered like the broken mirrors. He couldn't even have his beloved wife all his life. Poor Edward, how was it to sleep all alone? You rejected me, so you sleep alone. How was it to not be able to make love to your precious wife? You wanted a virgin wife, not me who had many lovers. Or was it because I told you honestly? I will not be finished until I murder you."

She then broke out into a fit of laughter. She was talking with others as her group of people started to laugh with her. I wanted to kick her out of my building yet could not do anything as the police officers were handling the situation. I would make sure I would have my way and day at court.

She then screamed and said, "Edward has no lineage to continue after his death! I murdered your daughter! I murdered your granddaughter and your precious stupid loser stepbrother! I already have started to murder Samar too, ask him. Soon you will die, and my business of abusing and terrorizing families emotionally and physically will flourish as I rip out body parts of the so-called innocent people. Actually, the innocent people should rename themselves as the stupid."

No one replied to her or told her love was not about how long you have someone by your side. Love flourishes in unions and even in separations too. We all tried to go different ways hoping we would capture her, yet even the twelve ghosts couldn't find her.

Samar suddenly screamed as he said, "Everyone get back here and stay close to the two rooms. She is trying to get in there somehow while distracting us with her message. I know she will be dying to somehow get Daviana or those two at any cost. Don't get distracted even if I'm not here. Please remember, don't leave Daviana at any cost. She will try to fool you as Daviana and the two are the only ones who can identify her real face aside from me, even through all of her plastic surgeries."

Our twelve ghosts appeared in front of us as they showed us the light above Daviana's room was blinking red. The light above the room next door was blinking green. I knew that meant Daviana was dying, and the newcomers were waking up.

Samar ran to Daviana's room as he screamed and said, "Come on partner, you must pull through. I'm sorry I listened to your plans. I should never have left you when I knew your life might be at risk. I assumed our plan to make you look tortured was just pretense. Why didn't you tell me she was doing it to you physically? Just wait, you will have a new heart very soon."

I saw Dave was checking her vitals as Samar stood there watching everything. I still didn't know if he was good or bad as I learned to trust no one.

Samar shook Daviana and said, "Please, promise you will live a long healthy life. Jacobus promised me he would do the surgery himself. I spoke with him and Erasmus this morning. You remember right, Jacobus my buddy from the Netherlands. Dave can't identify me as I have had so many surgeries, but Jacobus will know me as he himself helped me get this face."

He was crying when he was forced out by Dave. I was lost as to what was going on. The lights were all blinking as I waited in the sitting area waiting for the miraculous heart to arrive soon. That's when I saw a woman walked out from the room adjacent to Daviana's room.

She had a long black coat on. Her head was covered with the hood of the cloak, and I could barely see her face as she had her head bent. She walked directly to Samar and kissed his head as he bent his head for her. She hugged him and asked something very softly which I couldn't hear. Samar said something as he then walked to the next room.

A light appeared from somewhere and I could feel the wind blow all over. The winter's cold shivering breeze became warm and sweet. Somehow, I knew I was in the presence of my dream woman. Yet I didn't dare to even imagine who the very small petite woman was. Maybe she was a friend of Samar, and my dream woman was hidden somewhere in a faraway prison, if not six feet underground.

I wanted to see what was going on with my child as I only wanted her to live through all these ordeals. Yet I knew even as the father, I had no right over her. I knew Jay was given that right and he too was helpless as we both just stood and watched our daughter fight for her life.

The frail woman walked into Daviana's room. She kissed her head and touched her heart. I walked in without anyone trying to force me to go in or force me out. I stood at the doorway as the frail woman stood near the bed with her back toward me.

Somehow, I felt like the breeze in the room changed. The Earth beneath my feet was moving forward. The air smelled like flowers were being spread out as if my beloved was there. The air conditioner was blowing silently to keep the room cool. The petite woman turned her head and stood facing me directly.

She said with a frail and shaking voice, "I took her away from you to save her and you both. Now I come back to you with hope of giving her back to you, if only she lives."

There in front of my eyes stood my beloved Viana. I said nothing as words failed me. My eyes betrayed me as tears fell and spoke what I could not say. Viana didn't try to hide her feelings as she let her tears fall over her battered and bruised cheeks. Her frail body was covered by a cloak, yet I could still see the colorful bruises and sufferings of being a prisoner for years.

I almost fell and as my knees started to buckle, Jay caught me. He steadied me up as I tried to walk forward closer to my Viana. I tried to capture the moment in my soul. Fear gripped my inner soul thinking what if all of this was a dream. I wanted to see her one more time before she faded away in the smoke.

Viana came closer to me. She was always the outspoken one and never did she keep anything inside. I called her my tough one who could take all the stones thrown her way to protect all she loved.

Her bruised and battered fingers touched my cheeks as she said in a frail voice, "My beloved, before the dream fades away and you leave me like the first morning dew, I love you and have always loved you and shall always love you. It matters not how much they beat me or even if they kill me, I will come to you through your dreams, like fog or smoke forever and ever."

I held her frail hands in my hands as I didn't want to let her go. We washed our hands through our combined teardrops. Was she real? Was she standing in front of me? After thousands of nights of prayers, was she in front of me in this life?

ANN MARIE RUBY

I told her softly, "Dear beloved, I was yours and only yours. I am yours and shall eternally only be yours. I will wait a thousand lifetimes if I must, only to be yours."

Jay walked into the room. She looked at both of us and we almost separated quickly, yet Jay held both of us and prevented us from separating.

Jay said, "My dear sister, I always am and shall always be your brother. I know you escaped the prison with the help of Samar. But who is the elderly woman who escaped with you? Also, as you both gave me Daviana, I must ask both of you to walk outside and let the doctors take care of my adopted daughter, both of your birth daughter. Dr. Jacobus is coming in the morning as he said the heart too will be here by then."

We walked outside and saw there was an elderly woman standing in the doorway. She walked outside with us as she watched Edward Kapoor from far away.

The old woman stood in front of him and said, "You know I am tough. I told you I would be back. Nothing can kill me or keep me apart from you, not even the beastly woman you almost married. You see, your beastly woman may be a beast, but she gave birth to a son who is a saint. This blessed saint saved me which even my own daughter thought was not possible. Within captivity, I raised her son as she was never there. I fed him from the food he stole and brought for me. I read nighttime stories to him from the books he would bring to me. Just a few years ago, he told me his mother had another prisoner, and he would rescue both of us when he grows up and becomes a cop and puts her the robber behind bars. Holding on to the hands of a saint, I am Devi, the forgotten prisoner who escaped."

THE FORGOTTEN PRISONER WHO ESCAPED

Forgotten by the world,

Left alone to die,

Bruised,

Battered,

And punished.

Chained to a wall for years

As thought to be dead

By the world,

But not you,

As your love,

Your given vows

Tied to

My given vows,

Made a sacred

Door through dreams,

Through immortal love,

Through a bridge

Created by

Twin flames

Who call out

One another,

Where there are no phones,

No messages,

No mail deliveries,

Yet there is

Faith.

There is love.

There is belief.

How could one die

If the other one still

Breathes?

The heartbeats of two

Become one as

Twin flames call

One another

As one says,

I am

THE FORGOTTEN PRISONER WHO ESCAPED.

CHAPTER NINE:

The Kasteel Vrederic Family Has Arrived

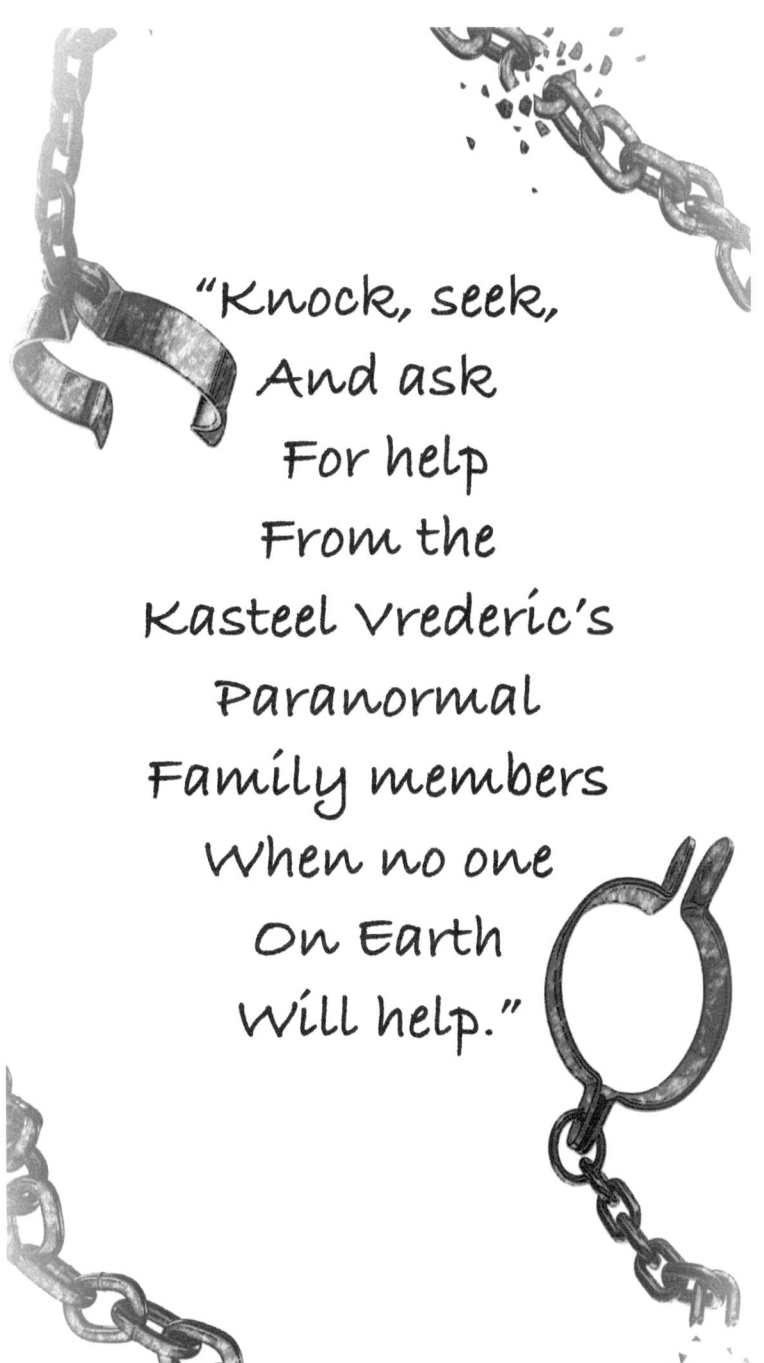

"Knock, seek,
And ask
For help
From the
Kasteel Vrederic's
Paranormal
Family members
When no one
On Earth
Will help."

The horrific screams continued throughout the hospital all night. Dawn broke open with two frail and bruised prisoners resting side by side. If only Daviana could have awakened and seen these two women, all her sacrifices and sufferings would have found some justice. My daughter woke up for the first time in days last night when her mother touched her chest.

She screamed and her words still came out as whispers as she said, "No Samar, please stop her. I will tell everyone I bruised myself and cut myself up. Just tell her to not hurt my mother. Please Samar, help. She can kill me, rip my heart out, take my organs. Just let my mother live. Samar, I think I'm crazy. I believe I must be. Samar, you are my partner, please help. I didn't sign up to be beaten and bruised. Please keep your promises. I'm scared you might break your vows as she is your mother."

My child sat down and saw everyone but somehow didn't see anyone as she just went back into a coma again. I realized she had seen too many women being beaten up as they were all forced into forced marriages. Abuse, manipulation, and intimidation were normal tactics of life. You either live within or die from it. Daviana gave up and became a victim. Her mother Viana never gave up and fought against it. Her grandmother Devi, fought against it.

They became prisoners of a woman who used factions within a society to harm other women.

Edward looked so much better, smiling obliviously to himself thinking about something as he said, "Hmm, David, did you know my family members, men and women, all used intimidation and forced people into marriages? They abused others tricking them through intimidation tactics. I assumed it was normal until Devi, my wife, objected. We too had a marriage of convenience. It wasn't a romantic love story. I was infatuated with Charlotte Amanda Kapoor, a German woman who became the biggest threat to my family."

I realized Samar's mother was Charlotte Amanda Kapoor the nurse, and his girlfriend. I wondered how she looked so young, but then I knew all blood eating vampires look young in novels. In real life, how did she look that young?

Edward held his wife's hand as he said, "I emotionally tortured Devi, for just being my wife. I blamed her for being there and ruining any chance of me being married to Charlotte Amanda, even though Devi was an innocent sacrifice sent to my home. She never complained and with time, I fell in love with my wife, as arranged marriage in my case worked for me."

Screaming sounds of fearful women and men filled our hospital. Everyone including our inhouse ghosts pretended not to hear the sounds.

Edward was in his own world as if he heard nothing, and he continued speaking from where he had stopped, "Charlotte Amanda, however, didn't give up and insisted I betrayed her. She married my stepbrother Doug to ruin my family. She never got over the simple issue of how a man could ever reject her, the great evil Charlotte Amanda. Her evilness became furious, and she took a vow of revenge. Yes, simple anger can ruin a person's entire life."

The sounds of screaming again ripped the walls of MacNider Hospital. I jumped up as I saw a huge group of police officers were coming toward me. They stopped in front of a room as they tried to hear and see where the screams were coming from.

A new face I had not seen yet came and introduced herself as she said, "I am Detective Delilah Sommers, and I was asked to look into the paranormal sightings and the missing patients' reports."

Then I heard a deep irritated voice speak in a foreign language with some people. I heard the sounds but saw no one near us.

The voice said in clear English, "If you can hear me, then know there are no evil ghosts or unexplainable activities going on in this hospital. I have not been to any hospital that did not have ghosts or dead bodies. The disgrace is on those who were asked and hired to catch the perpetrators, not spread rumors on and around the hospital. Now I will ask David MacNider to prepare the biggest lawsuit against these people for defaming MacNider Hospital and personal names."

I realized the voice had to belong to Dr. Jacobus, but when did he arrive? We were never told when he and his family had arrived or where they were staying.

From behind the fogs of unnatural happenings, four men walked toward us as they stepped out of the elevator. All of them at once and at the same time moved their heads toward the right and then toward the left. Then they so eloquently walked toward us. They were all tall Dutchmen. All looked similar in age, yet I must say they were all very handsome and elegantly dressed men.

The one with blue eyes had a very elegant warm hand-woven sweater with three buttons on the front. The rest had similar looking hand-woven warm sweaters on. All of them had black pants on that had no wrinkles and looked like they never saw a wrinkle in their life. They were somehow all related as two of them looked like twins and the other two also looked similar.

One of the men came and stood in front of me as he gave me his hand and said, "Erasmus van Phillip, from the Netherlands, and these three boys are my three sons, Jacobus, Antonius, and Andries. My family members are here and have decided to stay in our private yacht, instead of crowded hotels. That way, we can investigate on our own terms and be gone when our job here is done. Also, my wife will spend one day collecting shells with our grandchildren from this amazing beachside town."

Erasmus looked like he was in his mid-thirties, the same age as his three sons. I couldn't believe my eyes but knew the paranormal family members of the famous Kasteel Vrederic were compared to vampires, witches, psychics, and time travelers. Yet they were very well-respected throughout the world. If you meet them once, it is said you fall in love with this paranormal family.

I told myself not to think as maybe they could read minds too. One son I assumed and was confirmed later as Jacobus laughed and told me, "No we can't read minds. That would be intrusion of one's private space. Yet we could all hear your thoughts when you speak out loud. Maybe no one has told you, but you do think out loud."

I closed my eyes as I realized I spoke out loud. A very bad habit I've had for years. Somehow the four men laughed and made the whole firsthand embarrassment lighter. The three boys and the father seemed very close to one another. They all seemed to love and respect one another.

Dave went and hugged the man in the middle of the three sons. I realized I was correct as he was Jacobus. He tried to see something behind us as he kept on looking at the glass door separating Daviana from us.

Jacobus saw someone walking behind me as he sighed and said, "Samar, how are you buddy? I assumed you wouldn't be walking in public. That can't be safe for you. When did you last go into hiding? I can't help you if you don't stay hidden. Also, illegal organ trafficking has increased worldwide. We believe your mother and brother are at their highest points. I do hope your brother comes out of hiding as he was last seen in Africa going toward Asia."

Samar winked his eye and squeezed Jacobus's hand. Edward and Jay interrupted their private conversation as they walked over to Samar. They touched his shoulders and pulled his hair to see if it was real. They both tried to inspect him by touching and freaking him out.

Samar shook himself, shrieked and said, "Stop it. You two, no touching please. I do have a brother whom I had put in prison, but he has escaped. I asked Jacobus to help look for him as he and his organ trafficking will stay under the radar. As he escaped, I found out about how Devi and Viana were both in the same tower separated from one another. Devi and Viana were continuously shifted from one prison to another. My brother, however, was the top security for my mother and they were never inseparable. Our mother kept us separated from birth. I studied to become a doctor, and he became an organ trafficker. It's a multibillion-dollar underworld market. Yes, I joined the CIA as he joined the illegal organ and sex traffickers."

Samar looked pale and sat down on the nearest chair. Edward and Jay both came closer and tried to check him. Dave said nothing as he talked with Jacobus through with his eyes. Somehow, I missed a lot of things as I felt left out in the dark. So now, Samar has a brother. I did see him hold my daughter's hand and hurt her. I couldn't and wouldn't believe anything he said until I had proof standing in front of me that he was good. After all, as a lawyer, I could argue and say he was lying and making up stories as he went.

I had so many questions but knew now was not the time. Samar was rolled out in a hospital bed, as Jacobus took him holding his hand. Dave went with them, as he only winked at me to say it's all right, not to worry. Jacobus was looking at his father for a while. As Erasmus nodded, Jacobus left with Dave.

Then again, some kind of fear gripped my whole body. Suddenly it felt chilly as I worried about my daughter and Edward. Who was stealing bodies from our morgue? Why were we getting so many dead bodies when our patients were not dying? Why was our hospital even involved with organ trafficking in the underworld market? How did this even start?

Erasmus held my shoulders and said, "At times, the answers to our unanswered questions are in front of us, yet we don't see them. Just open your eyes and everything will be clear. I am told the answers are given through time, which allows us to adjust to the shocking answers."

Erasmus sat down next to me while his twin boys walked around the hospital talking with patients and giving them gifts. I knew one of the twin boys was the famous formerly blind painter, Antonius van Phillip, and the other one was the famous pianist, Andries van Phillip, for whom people wait in line for days to attend his concerts. All three of his boys were down to Earth men who didn't show off money or wealth. Erasmus was himself a famous painter and businessman who was known as one of the wealthiest people on Earth. They were all chatting with patients and employees as they inspected the hospital and searched for someone. The way they chatted with patients and staff, it felt like I had our hospital back even if it was for a few minutes.

Detective Sommers was walking around, taking pictures of our hospital as she came and stood in front of Erasmus. It was so strange I witnessed a detective flirt in the midst of the paranormal tragedies and enjoyed the drama taking place in front of me.

Detective Sommers laughed and giggled as she said, "I am a huge fan of your paintings. I have most of them in my house. Could I take you for a drink maybe?"

Erasmus didn't get up but just watched her for a while. He took out his phone and dialed a number. A woman's voice answered on the other side as Erasmus had his phone on speaker.

Erasmus said, "Anadhi, sweetheart, are you and the children all right? Why have you all not come yet? Did the driver go and pick you all up or is he late? Oh, I forgot to say, I love you and miss you already. Also, a detective here said she has most of my paintings."

I could not hear what was being said on the other side but whatever it was Erasmus laughed out loud. He almost choked as his twin boys ran to him and were standing by him like a tower.

They took turns as they said, "Big Mama, a woman is trying to flirt with Big Papa. You probably knew, right? That's why he called. How did she buy Big Papa's paintings? They are rare! How did she get them on a detective's income? Anyway, each painting was one-of-a-kind, so it's not possible for her to have one. Not fair Big Mama! Even we don't have one. She shamelessly lied."

Erasmus had the phone on speaker as I heard a soft woman's voice laughing.

She was not even worried as she said, "Big Mama will buy them for you if you two want sweethearts. Your Big Papa can be left on an island with all the women in the world, I won't worry, even then. I left him in one life as I crossed the ocean of death, but even death lost as your Big Papa managed to come find and rescue me even in this life. I will be there soon everyone."

Anadhi was still on the phone, but she was talking to children in the background. I enjoyed how nice and at home this family felt. I love how they always traveled together as they enjoyed business and pleasure together. I could hear children laughing and saying something I didn't understand as they spoke in Dutch.

Anadhi then said, "Hey Antonius, do tell Jacobus that Theunis said Samar's brother is hiding in the hospital. He is trying to ruin everything Samar had done. He will seem friendly if you get to see him. Don't trust him. She couldn't have done it on her own. Don't worry about a donor for Daviana. Jacobus has the answers. Also, Samar will be hurt if he is not careful as his brother has one job on his hands, to kill Samar, Daviana, Viana, and the elderly woman. Theunis is coming with us. He will explain."

I heard everything and wondered what was going on. Samar was at risk from a brother he mentioned yet avoided sharing details with us. Why was he risking his life when he could be here with everyone?

Viana came and stood in front of us, still fragile from all the years of confinement, and said, "Samar was there in the prison occasionally. He was extremely nice. I did see another man who abused and battered other prisoners before he took them away."

Her voice made my knees go weak as I really was in her presence after years of only praying for death to unite us.

Viana sat down near me, but not next to me. She watched yet said nothing. She also tried to avoid her father's eyes, and I wondered why. It was as if she was somehow scared of him. Or I would think upset at him yet wouldn't voice her feelings or thoughts. She was the kind of person who would burn herself to ashes for the lives of others.

She then quietly with a lot of hardship said, "Samar, however, did help with our escape. I always wondered if both men were the same, as he at times would say things only the other person knew. My mother was kept somewhere else until the day we escaped. Samar never spoke of her and his brother would joke about hurting her. I wondered how Samar helped with both of our escapes without his brother even noticing. Each time Samar and his brother Nimar came, they had different clothes, different hair colors, and different styles. Never did they wear the same clothes even once. Samar feared his mother and brother and tried to act mean if he thought they were watching. He closed his eyes and looked in the other direction when I got beaten up. His brother enjoyed beating me up. I could smell the vomit on Samar, when I was getting beaten up. I believe he threw up as he couldn't take it but said nothing. I always thought everything was in my dreams as I only saw David in my dreams, never in reality. He always left me at dawn."

Viana gazed at me with her bruised and tearful eyes, and I knew my love for her didn't fail as her love for me was there in her tears. I was told I would understand as twin flames are never separated. Even in tears, they are united.

Anadhi, a beautiful woman with long black hair and olive-colored skin, walked in with a halo of grace and elegance circling her. Her glow announced the most compassionate woman on Earth had just arrived. She had with her three charismatic women who held the hands of four children. Then, I saw two more children who were in a stroller. At first sight, I knew they were not twins but sisters.

Erasmus walked up to his wife and kissed her on the lips, a long kiss as if he missed her and hadn't seen her for a while. Antonius and Andries both went and kissed their mother, and I assumed their respective wives. They kissed and hugged Jacobus's wife. The family was so close knit, it warmed my cold heart. The rumor I heard was, wherever this family went, they warmed everyone's life for the better.

I assumed Jacobus's wife came and asked, "Where is Jacobus? I need to find the child Lucy. I am a pediatric surgeon, and I really need to operate on her or else she won't make it if we delay her surgery. She is the daughter of Lucy the nurse I had sent here. I hope the child is all right. She is Samar and Lucy's daughter. Lucy passed away, but I thought she had hidden baby Lucy from everyone. The child was my patient in the Netherlands but came here with her mother, to find her father."

The twelve ghosts of MacNider Hospital revealed themselves. I was worried what would our main supporters of the hospital say by seeing these ghosts? I only hoped they too didn't pull out and leave us alone. I knew the ghosts could be seen by people whom they wish to be seen by.

Lucy was crying as she tried to control herself. She covered her mouth so no sounds would come and the Kasteel Vrederic family wouldn't see her. I knew Anadhi was close to Lucy as was Dr. Margriete, Jacobus's wife. Anadhi walked to Lucy as she touched her face. Lucy was not see-through to her like she was to us.

Anadhi smiled and said, "There is so much more to my family. Our history is written in our diaries. Maybe you can all read them and get to know us better. Where is your daughter Lucy? How could you forget her when you tried to live just for her? Would Samar knowingly try to sell his own daughter's organs? I don't think so. Don't hate him so much as he isn't that bad. He was only born from the house of evil. He isn't evil himself."

The ghost of Lucy just stood there and tried to remember but it was as if she had forgotten the only reason she tried to live for. She forgot her own child somehow as days progressed. For some reason, she woke up and didn't leave the hospital. I worried if all twelve had something that was keeping them there.

I asked Anadhi, "Do you think it's coping mechanism? She intentionally forgot so she could pass on?"

It seemed Anadhi was not satisfied with my thoughts as she shook her head no, but she said nothing.

Jacobus came back with Dave, kissed his mother, and said, "Love you, Mama! You make the upside-down world better any day, anytime."

As Jacobus hugged her, his two brothers, the twins, ran and hugged and kissed her too. I wanted to ask though why he called his mother Mama, and the twins called her Big Mama. I did not, however, as I tried to find out what was going on with Samar. Why was he rushed out of here and was he good or bad?

Jacobus sat next to his father and said, "Papa, I don't believe Samar was intentionally pretending to be sick. I can't say anything but would advise everyone to not trust everything your eyes see or don't see. Samar is a doctor and won't do anything to harm people. I don't believe he will harm anyone intentionally. I don't know without checking if Daviana's heart has anything wrong or not. Why her heart isn't working properly, I will find out first. I will check Edward, Daviana, and Samar if needed, before making any medical conclusion, as Dave and I have discussed. We also have found Lucy's heart as they were going to give it to a buyer. Everything needs to be done soon."

Jacobus looked so fresh and alert even though he traveled from so far away. He had performed a lot of surgeries and still looked like he was on his feet ready to do so much more. I loved people with that kind of positive mindset and energy. I wish I had that.

Jacobus smiled at me and said, "Before we can do any surgeries, we must catch Charlotte Amanda and her team members. They have gone under and are hiding within different hospitals. Rather than trying to save lives, they are intentionally taking lives during surgeries. We must stop that at any cost. You will take this case to court as soon as we have all the proof. The evil raiders of this hospital will have a security breach somewhere, somehow."

Margriete went and knelt by a boy who looked a little different than the whole Kasteel Vrederic family. He grimaced at me and hugged Margriete. I heard her call him Theunis as she placed her ears near his mouth. I assumed then Margriete gave him permission to speak out loud.

He said out loud, "Margriete, there is a very bad person in this hospital. He hides and sleeps with the dead in the morgue. He is worse than the woman as he feeds off dead people. He travels to different hospitals, steals body parts from living people, and sells the parts. She is just a face as he is different. He is hiding in her team, that woman's, she knows him. They have hidden Lucy the child under a dead body in the morgue. That bad guy will kill her for her heart. Samar has been trying to find her and has damaged his own body through these physical fights. He is a doctor and is trying to save lives in their own group who are trying to take life."

Everyone turned and saw Detective Sommers. The woman was just sitting in the waiting room listening to everyone. She had told everyone the police had Lucy safely kept, but no one could find her. Detective Sommers didn't argue or question why a mere child was pointing fingers at her. Instead like a guilty person, she tried to flee. She had her guns pointing at everyone as she tried to run.

The twelve ghosts of the hospital made a circle around her as they held her in their ring. She couldn't see them or feel them. Yet she couldn't get out of the circle.

I said directly to Detective Sommers in front of everyone, "I called the police chief, and he is coming himself. This situation has gone too far. You will cooperate and tell us where the young child is now. Or maybe you too will find a place for yourself in the morgue with the people you are sending there."

The twelve ghosts had a lot of fun with Detective Sommers. They were trying to whisper scary words in her ears. They even blew wind on her clothes and hair.

She didn't flinch or seem scared, but sat there arrogantly as she said, "Fear is nothing if the person you are trying to frighten doesn't believe in it. I don't believe in ghosts, nor am I scared of any assailant."

She was making a scary laugh, and I saw Anadhi give her the looks, yet she said nothing. Theunis, however, was watching her and smiled to himself silently. He knew so much more as I wondered how a child was so brave and smart. He kept looking at the boy who sat quietly next to him.

He then said, "Alexander, let's go get Lucy the child and place this woman over there. Since she isn't scared of anything, she won't care about some dead bodies."

Alexander, the young child, stood up as we heard more gunshots fired somewhere. The screams of frightened voices flooded the hospital. Dave and Jacobus ran to a specific room as I ran with Edward and Jay to Daviana's room. My daughter was breathing and was trying to open her eyes. None of us were doctors as all the doctors were rushing from room to room.

Margriete walked in and said, "Please step outside and let me check her. I promise she will be fine. I will call Jacobus if there seems to be an emergency. Right now, Jacobus and Dave are both trying to see what is going on with Samar. Also, Lucy would you please come and help me. I can see you, and I know you can see me."

It was then I tried to walk out as I heard Daviana speak like a whisper into Margriete's ear. She tried to get up and it seemed like she was in pain. It looked like she was having sleep paralysis or something, where she could hear us but was having a hard time getting up.

Margriete said to her, "Calm down. You are in good hands. Don't fight the sleep. You will wake up slowly, just breathe. I am here and I won't leave you alone."

Jacobus rushed in and touched his wife and kissed her head. He walked over to the other side of Daviana and just stood there as Margriete was giving her an injection, while the ghost nurse Lucy was redoing her IV bag. It was surreal to witness a doctor working with a ghost like it was her daily work condition.

Jacobus said, "It seems like our Daviana is completely out of danger. She was given an injection which made it seem like her heart was giving up. I assume the same way they have been bringing in dead bodies. All were living people who walked into the morgue in a sleeping condition and died there after their organs were stolen. Everyone assumed their organs failed."

Daviana opened her eyes as she watched Jacobus and Margriete and in a shock screamed. Jacobus worried and made a face asking his wife something through their own eye language.

Daviana quietly with all of her willpower said, "I graduated as a doctor before I became a lawyer. You are Dr. Jacobus and Dr. Margriete from Kasteel Vrederic! I read about both of you and all the diaries of Kasteel Vrederic. Oh my God, I have the world's most famous doctors treating me. Did I die and go to Heaven to have you by my side? I could do it all over again to only have you by my side."

Jacobus laughed and made the whole atmosphere light and airy. He hugged Daviana as did Margriete.

Jacobus said, "Welcome back! I'm glad you have now entered the land of the living. You will still be a little drowsy, but take your time and try to adjust by waking up slowly."

Daviana saw the three of us, Jay, Edward, and me as she did a heart sign to the three of us. Then, she saw Dave and screamed again.

She said, "Dave! What are you doing here? I don't have any makeup on. You knew I was on my death bed. Go outside and someone get some makeup and a change of clothes for me. Also, where is my buddy, Samar?"

Everyone broke out laughing as I knew then something was going on between them. Why was she only concerned about what Dave thought of her looks? I was worried why she called Samar her buddy.

Dave smiled and said, "I have seen you bruised, battered, and know you are beautiful inside and outside. I like what I am seeing, in all the looks. Don't worry, just be healed."

Lost lovers lost in time were waking up. I prayed for my daughter Daviana. She had tears in her eye as I assumed she just walked down memory lane.

She closed her eyes and told everyone, "Samar is a secret agent. He has been trying to catch all sex and organ traffickers. Samar himself is a survivor from a kidney donor, who gave him his kidney in medical school. His brother and mother are manipulators. I was forced to marry him as his mother had my mother and grandmother hidden somewhere.

He promised if I do as he says and never open my mouth, he will help free them. Yet I could never tell anyone he was working for the CIA."

Daviana had a sip of drink from Margriete as she placed her head down on the pillow, and said, "I joined the CIA to help him with his cases as at first, I didn't know. Yet I realized how he never abused me but someone else did. We saved a lot of prisoners but could not find my mother and grandmother. I don't know how he found my family members as he kept it from me to keep me safe."

Dave tried to talk but then became quiet as he wanted Daviana to get everything off her chest. I worried if all these emotions were safe to let go at this time. I tried to see Dave and Jacobus, but both were just observing Daviana.

Margriete held my hand and squeezed it, as she told me without words it was all right. I remembered Daviana, my daughter, was in the care of the world's best doctors.

Margriete observed Lucy for a while. We all witnessed our ghost nurse was crying. She became very visible as she tried to be a good nurse and take care of her patient and the woman who was supposedly married to her husband.

I blurted out without thinking, "It's called bigamy. Samar was married to Lucy. Daviana's marriage to Samar would be void and automatically annulled. Daviana, you were married in New York, so Samar would be charged in a federal crime and could face imprisonment for this."

Daviana stared at everyone, "I knew about Lucy and baby girl Lucy. It was Lucy who brought the divorce papers to Samar because she suspected him of cheating as he was missing all the time. Samar didn't sign the divorce papers. The divorce papers were never filed. Our marriage was like Bapu and Mama, we did Raksha Bandhan. Brother and sister. He never touched me. I pretended to be a wife, yet I kept telling everyone he never touched me. That's what the CIA wanted us to do. Someone was beating me nonstop, so I was worried who was doing it. Every time Samar went somewhere, I woke up with bruises and there I saw Samar or someone who looked like him was watching me and had beaten me."

I wondered what kind of drug these people used that they could make people sleep for days. I knew Dave and Jacobus would get to the end of this. I saw them whispering to one another as they spoke quietly for their ears only.

Jacobus comforted everyone and said, "All is well. Daviana is a free woman and can marry the love of her life who still waits for her to make up her own mind. It's time we let the real ghosts haunt the pretend ghosts, as I can hear them becoming wild. Dave, I think Daviana is ready to be your patient. You can update her on all the things she had missed. I need to go and recheck all the dead bodies, if there is any hope for discovering even one living person."

We left the love birds alone. I felt like a burden had lifted from my chest. I know calculatedly we had hidden the facts of Daviana's mother and grandmother. We let Dave handle the details. I watched two very frail woman enter Daviana's new room. For security concerns, she was brought into a bigger and better private room for the owners.

I walked out and saw Detective Sommers was trying to escape; however, the twelve ghosts kept her in a circle.

She was screaming repeatedly, "I'm not scared of fake ghosts. I know how Samar and Charlotte Amanda are doing everything. I am a part of the group and so are many others across the world. I'm not scared."

Jacobus laughed at her and was just watching her with his father and brothers. I saw Theunis laugh and talk with Alexander. I assumed both were part of the Kasteel Vrederic family. It was then I saw a hand appeared from nowhere and went into the body of Detective Sommers. She screamed in pain as the hand tried to rip out her heart.

The hand asked, "Who is behind all of this? Tell me now or I will rip out your heart and donate it to a needy person. You have no heart, so why do you want to keep one that beats?"

She said, "Charlotte Amanda has bought out a lot of the police force. Call the FBI and let them know. They have agents who know much more. I only did it as they sent money to my account every time I gave them a body. They put the person to sleep as it fools even the doctors and usually the coroner declares them dead. That's when they send the bodies to different hospitals to sell the organs quietly, and we the police help them. Please stop! It hurts a lot! We all suspected Dr. Kapoor was betraying his own mother."

I heard her and everything really seemed impossible in my eyes. Doctors and law enforcement officers who had taken oaths to protect were involved in silently taking lives. I did, however, wonder who was doing this trickery and whose hand that was. The twelve ghosts were all watching in horror as the CIA, FBI, and local law enforcement officers came and took away Detective Sommers. They began to search the whole hospital for any and all bodies that were registered and not registered.

Lucy then said, "We are scared. Who is doing that? Whose hand was that? Because it wasn't ours. I wonder if the hospital is really haunted."

Erasmus walked up to the ghosts and looked them up and down. He was somehow amused as his three boys followed his gaze and laughed with him.

He said, "Please excuse my manners. You are scared of ghosts, but as far as I understand, you are all ghosts. This is a hospital. People either get healed and go home, or some die and pass on through the light. The others become ghosts and join their ghost friends. What is there to fear?"

Theunis stood up and started to walk. Margriete and her sisters-in-law followed the boy as did the other children. We all tried to keep up as we walked through the stairway, not the elevators. We ended up on the thirteenth floor. I felt a little nauseous as Dave wasn't with me. I left him with Daviana, her mother, and her grandmother. I kept wondering whose hand we saw.

The lights started to flicker on the thirteenth floor, and we smelled blood. The smell was so bad that everyone started to cringe, but we all were told silently through sign language by a child not to move or make sounds. I watched Anadhi and Erasmus hold Theunis as they signaled Jacobus to come near them.

Jacobus walked near the hands and said, "Beware, whomever these hands belong to. If you are good and here to protect the hospital, we will leave you alone. If you or anyone else is here and have died, try to find the light. Find peace. If you can't and you want to haunt the hospital, remember your lifeline has ended. Today is your doomsday as the Kasteel Vrederic family has arrived."

THE KASTEEL VREDERIC FAMILY HAS ARRIVED

When and where there is no help,

They arrive.

When a life is in danger,

They arrive

To spread love,

To give hope,

To strengthen faith.

They arrive

Never fearing the dead,

Or death.

Not giving up

On the living,

Or to communicate,

With the dead,

They arrive.

If anyone needs them

And gives them

A call to help,

And be there

For you,

And work with you,

Never leaving you

Stranded in danger,

Alone,

Or lonely,

They arrive.

Today

For all the

Inhabitants and employees of

MacNider Hospital,

THE KASTEEL VREDERIC FAMILY HAS ARRIVED.

CHAPTER TEN:

Manipulation And Intimidation

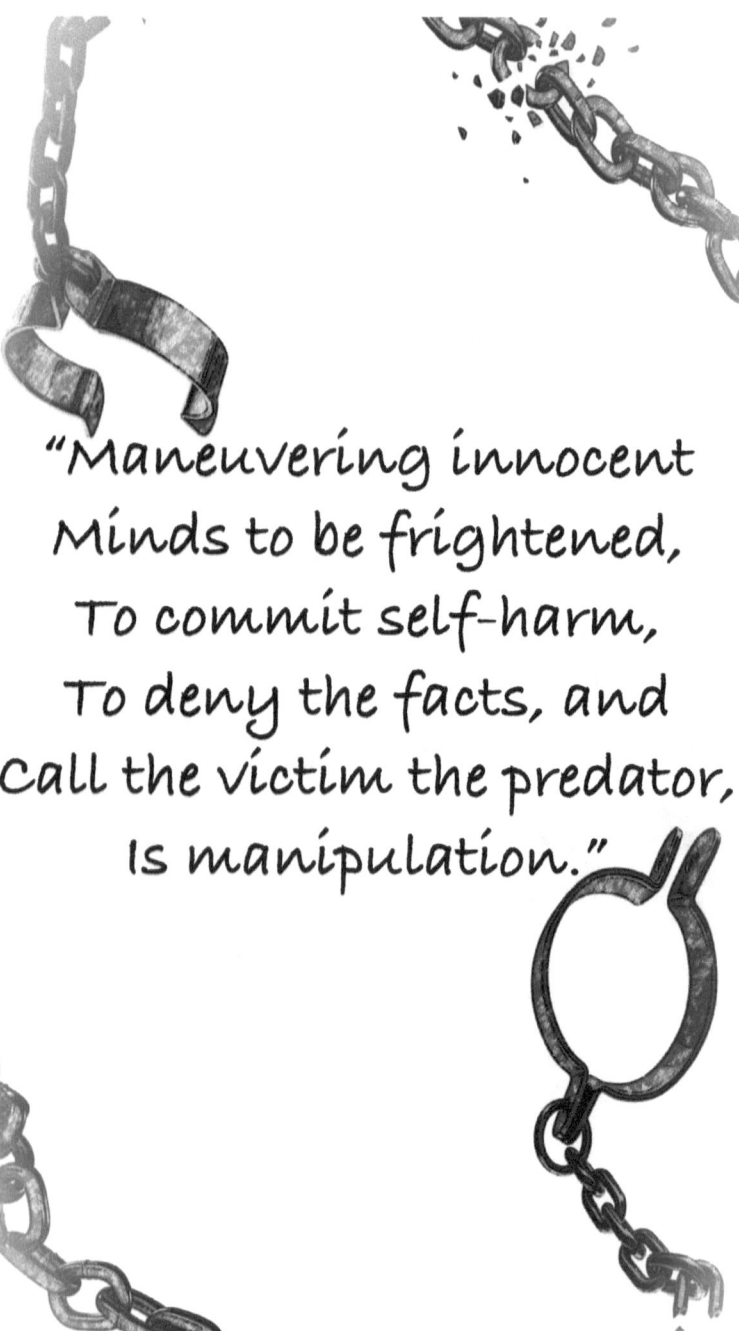

"Maneuvering innocent
Minds to be frightened,
To commit self-harm,
To deny the facts, and
Call the victim the predator,
Is manipulation."

F ire and smoke filled the thirteenth floor of MacNider Hospital. Alarms went off all over as announcements were playing asking all to evacuate the building and start the procedures of evacuating patients. Theunis the child in front of my eyes became a grown-up man. He had long blond hair, with blue eyes and a daredevil look. I was somewhat not even shocked there in front of me stood a person who looked like a superhero.

The rumors around the Kasteel Vrederic family had reached my ears but I learned to not pay any heed to rumors. My son Dave warned me beforehand to not question, remember, or repeat anything my eyes might witness regarding the family members of the famous Kasteel Vrederic.

Dave had also said, "Dad, if they just disappear in thin air and come back, act normal and know they are the only family aside from you whom I trust with my life."

Jacobus walked with so much confidence and elegance. I knew they must have faced all the obstacles life could give them and they persevered.

Jacobus winked at Theunis and said, "Welcome back Buddy. This place is like a picture from a horrid horror movie. Blood, dead bodies, living people dead, and the dead are walking all over the hospital."

Theunis, Jacobus, and his brothers were all talking in a low voice to one another I realized this family had a lot of secrets which the world didn't know, but they were really close to one another. People from all over the world always found these family members on their side if anyone ever needed them. They always found time to arrive. Theunis moved forward gracefully. Somehow, it seemed like he could walk on air or through fire and under water. He had a small crown on his head that glowed and was made of fire. Everyone followed him.

Theunis then stopped and said, "Jacobus, we need to rush and get the girl as this was all a distraction for them to again take Daviana, her family, and a girl named Lucy. Also, they will try to kill off Samar as he has been exposed."

I felt like a knife just stabbed through my gut, and thought it's just my feelings for Viana, Daviana, and Devi. I just wished that Viana and I would get a chance in love this time around. I prayed Viana always stays healthy and safe.

Dave walked in by himself as he rushed to my side. He held my stomach and pressed it hard. Somehow, the pain inside of my lower stomach became intense. I kept my feelings to myself as I saw everything around me became dark. Theunis was holding me as I heard him say something I didn't understand.

Dave was now panicking and all I heard him say was, "Someone, call a doctor please!"

Jacobus looked at him and placed his hands in the air and said, "Really? What are you?"

It was a strange pain that slowly got better. I felt much better in a few minutes.

I heard Jacobus say, "This is an illusion, nothing here is real but your blood and pain are. Someone here in the illusion stabbed you. Luckily Theunis was with us as he got the woman. She is being held in an illusion herself. She is a nurse who was hypnotized to kill. I must find out how Samar kept hurting himself. Dave and I dealt with him as soon as I had landed. I only hope he doesn't ignore the pain like he always does."

My stomach felt much better, and we all moved into a room in the morgue where aside from the morgue freezer drawers, there was a coffin. Theunis told us to move back and not get too close to the coffin as it's all an illusion. He opened the coffin and then he pressed a button. We saw the floor opened underneath us. It was a trap for people who might be opening this without knowing.

About thirty different bodies were hidden in there. All were dressed in their own clothing. They seemed to be just sleeping, not like how a dead body normally looks like. They looked like people who went to bed and never woke up. All of them had different drawings on different parts of their bodies where they would be operated on.

I watched Dave, Jacobus, and Margriete give them some kind of shots. They all slowly woke up trying to talk but only gasped as no words came out. Somehow, they all knew Dave and me. I felt terrible because I didn't even know if these thirty were patients or our staff as our hospital has around 4,800 staff members. I had no justification as all staff members must be treated as my family, and I shall. This will change.

Jacobus placed a finger on his lips and told all of them to be quiet. He helped all thirty people stand up and get on their feet. He and Margriete were both working together like they were made for one another as they knew exactly what to do next. Anadhi and Erasmus held one after another in a line as they were at the beginning of the line. Dave walked out with them one by one as he took them to safety.

Like a trained group of army officers, I saw Antonius and his wife Katelijne stand in the middle. Andries and his wife Tara Bella stood at the end. The children all were in between and walked on their own. Only the two young ones were being pushed in strollers by their parents.

Theunis signaled them all to go downstairs as he, Dave, and I remained with Jacobus. We opened drawer after drawer but found no child. It was then Theunis shrugged his shoulders and went to the computer room. In the computer room, I saw an old woman on a twin bed, deep in her sleep. She was getting blood transfusions through intravenous lines. She looked like a Dracula woman who was clinging on to life through illegal procedures.

Jacobus walked in and stopped the transfusions. He saw her sleeping like she was medically put to sleep during these procedures. She, however, opened her eyes and tried to muffle a sound. I hid away from her as did Dave. We knew if she saw us, she would try to escape.

Jacobus said, "Charlotte Amanda, don't fear. I am a doctor. I save lives. I don't take them. If you keep relying on these procedures, however, you will end your own life. You won't gain more days to live. Right now, the blood has gone bad and should have been stopped by the doctor who obviously has poor knowledge in handling these procedures."

There were a lot of machines in this room which were probably saving this woman's life or maybe she was trying to become a Dracula woman. I felt so irritated as to how we missed all of this.

Jacobus gave her a shot and said, "This should keep her sedated for a while, or until the FBI comes and takes her away for the remainder of her life. It's so strange as some people want to die with dignity and honor, while others will take a life to live. We need to find the person she is getting the blood from. I really don't know if these are medical experiments or some kind of cult who believe by doing this, they will become immortal. They want to get blood and sell body parts and blood they don't need."

Theunis touched a table that had the huge wall-to-wall computer screen. He pushed something and a drawer opened. In the drawer, was a young child about three years old. She was bruised and battered just like Daviana. The veins on her arms were bruised purple and black. She was sleeping, but she seemed so scared even in her sleep. I was shocked as this was the granddaughter of this Dracula woman, yet she was murdering the child ruthlessly.

The rest of the Kasteel Vrederic family came back upstairs. Erasmus carried the child and gave her to Anadhi. I watched Anadhi place her hands on the child. Margriete and Jacobus knelt by the child as they were both worried.

Jacobus nodded his head as Margriete held her and Dave started to give her CPR.

Lucy the ghost watched us as I saw she had tears in her eyes and tried to control her feelings. All the other ghosts held her in a circle as they all seemed helpless.

Jacobus jumped up and went to the computer as he carried the child to the bed the old woman was in. Somehow in that split second, I saw Antonius and Andries shift the old woman to the floor. Jacobus placed the child Lucy on the bed. It was then Daviana and Samar walked in and placed their hands on Jacobus.

Dave said, "Come on Buddy, you got this."

Somehow like a miracle, Margriete pushed everyone out of the room as Jacobus, Margriete, Dave, Samar, and Daviana started to do their medical procedures we could never understand. I was a proud father who for the first time watched Daviana become the doctor she was trained to be, aside from practicing law. Samar for the first time was crying to save his daughter.

Dave said, "Go and wait outside. It's for the best."

Samar walked back and forth and said, "No, I will watch. Let the world know how a grandmother kills her own granddaughter for organs. If I do survive, I will dedicate the journey of my life to fighting all organ and sex traffickers.

Today, I will learn from the best doctor in the world, who had believed in me even when the world did not."

Dave told all to be quiet as we watched from outside of the glass room. I prayed for the toddler fighting for her life.

In a few minutes, we heard a scream as everyone in the room shouted, "Yes! A complete success!"

Daviana came out first as she said, "I watched my favorite doctor in the world perform a miracle. He did what no one could have done and saved Lucy the toddler. She will be all right. She will be transported to the children's ward under heavy security because her uncle, Samar's brother, will try to harm her."

Theunis walked toward Erasmus as they walked outside. The FBI came and crowded the hospital as they took Charlotte Amanda Kapoor, who was wanted for sex trafficking, black-market organ trafficking, forcing women in poverty-stricken places into forced marriages to produce children for organ transplanting and sex trafficking. She was on all different wanted lists but was never arrested as she kept changing her looks through plastic surgery. It was shocking how she didn't yet become a plastic zombie.

As we entered the floor where Daviana had to return for some rest, we heard weird sounds. Someone was trying to hypnotize her over the sound system.

He was whispering, "Walk to the window Daviana. Open the windows. Remember, you will remain married to Samar or otherwise you will be blamed for ruining the reputation of your culture. This is not a forced marriage but an arranged one. Remember to always harm yourself. Beat yourself until you have fainted. Then do jump outside the window. Going against arranged marriage is a disgrace to your family."

I was horrified hearing the words from the sound system. I didn't know how much these people could do as I knew the hospital was crowded with agents from the FBI, CIA, and local law enforcement.

Erasmus came and placed his hand on my shoulder. With reassuring comfort, he said, "Listen, don't bother yourself with all of this. Now for them, it's a losing war. They can fight until the end. More than our reputation, for us it is about saving lives, not letting another innocent life be lost through these heinous crimes. The ghost stories, however, will linger on and become a part of the hospital's history."

I watched Daviana place her hands on her ears. I ran and held her in my chest. She hugged me back. Samar came and walked into her room.

He said, "Why are you allowing this nuisance to bother you? Even if the world doesn't know, you know I respect and love you like a brother. It was a hard played drama we had to endure, but we did it. Now I promise you, I will not rest until this world rids itself of all organ trafficking, sex trafficking, and forced marriage criminals."

Samar walked outside as he said he has unfinished business he must take care of.

I told Daviana, "I gave you up so you would be safe, away from my chest. Yet my child, I will break all my given promises so I can keep you safe in my arms. Never shall I let you go. You are brave. Fight him, fight them, and fight for your right. No one will force my child into any forced marriages. You are a free individual. Even if you want to stay a maiden all your life, this father will never, ever force you into doing anything against your own will."

I watched a very ill Edward watch me from the waiting room chair. He didn't say anything, but his eyes said it all.

As I approached him this time, I told him, "You forced my wife to marry a man whom you knew was intersex. He did not even know who he was. You thought I was not good enough for your daughter because I am white and am a Christian. You were wrong to push your grown-up daughter into a forced marriage as you were wrong to do it again to your granddaughter. I will stand up for their rights now even though I stayed away then."

Devi came and stood next to me. She was four feet, six inches tall. She had gray hair that landed at her knees but was now in a bun. Her hospital gown was gone and now she had a blue wool dress on that ended at her knees. By God, she was beautiful and so elegant, she didn't look like she was imprisoned by Charlotte Amanda for so many years.

Devi said, "Edward, he is correct. You were wrong. Our arranged marriage worked out as we were twin flames. There is a difference between arranged marriages and forcing someone to marry against their will. What if your infatuations and your fatal attraction to Charlotte Amanda would have broken our chance? That too is wrong. You also wronged Jay and his family by forcing him to pretend to be Viana's husband. So let people love, live, and learn from their own mistakes. It's better to make a mistake and learn from it than to be forced into something that might be good or bad for you as you would never know because you live with only the knowledge that you were forced into it."

I was so amused by the elderly woman's wisdom that it brought tears to my eyes. I remembered about Jay and now felt guilty for him. He was sitting in the corner, busy in conversation with Jacobus.

Anadhi came and said, "David, I would like to hug you. It renews my faith and belief every time I see another dream psychic who keeps his love and the love of his life alive through his belief in the power of dreams. I know you see dreams and are confused why you see dreams. Just remember, they are to guide you when you need them. Differentiate between different types of dreams and don't follow them blindly. You should fight for your love, not just let her go because you love her, but hold on to her because you love her."

Viana wore her hair in a French braided bun like she had always done years ago. Whenever she was in a rush, she opted for a quick elegant look. She wore a soft yellow dress. It was my favorite color as I told her a long time ago. Yellow on her always made me happy as it reminded me the sun does come back up after a dark and frightful night.

Edward looked at Jay and said, "I am sorry Jay for what I made you go through. If you can, please do forgive me. I thought I was doing the right thing as I assumed love marriages don't work. I thought people are blind and these are infatuations. I now know the differences between forced, love, and arranged marriages. In all of them, abuse and manipulation should never be accepted, and men like me must stand up to abusers."

I saw the twelve ghosts were all watching everyone and somehow were upset. I wanted them to be happy and enjoy their stay at MacNider Hospital. I wrote a letter to all of them as I gave them free lodging in the owner's quarter of the hospital and the retreat, until they could walk up the staircase.

Lucy came and sat in front of me, as she said, "What do I do about my daughter Lucy? She has no one in her life. the only living relations she had were Charlotte Amanda and Samar. I know Samar won't be able to care for her. I hear luckily Charlotte Amanda is now going to prison. I want her to stay far away from her uncle or any of the paternal family members. I know Anadhi will take care of her as she took care of me and made sure I became a nurse. I just hope Samar won't object."

I know a mother's love never dies. I watched Lucy and knew it's true. Samar didn't object to Lucy's decision and had agreed in writing to it. He left all the paperwork with Anadhi.

I told Lucy, "Please don't worry for your daughter Lucy. She is our responsibility. We will take care of her. If it is your wish Anadhi takes care of her, then I will let Anadhi decide. Otherwise, we will make sure she is taken care of."

Viana got up and slowly walked to Daviana. Erasmus was talking with his wife and both watched Viana sit back and look at Daviana. She was observing her daughter like a mother who missed her all these years.

Then, she went and touched Daviana's bruises as she said, "Who did this? How could you allow this Jay and Papa? I took her away from her father to keep her safe. What went wrong that you forced her to marry Samar? To save my life? But why? This world is mean and it's like we the abused and battered women are invisible. Why?"

Viana cried for a long time. The lights in the hospital were flickering again as we all became alert again. I watched Erasmus leave with some FBI agents as his three sons went with him. He gestured me to stay with everyone else.

Viana kissed Daviana's forehead, and said, "Get up Daviana and make sure nothing like this happens to Lucy the child. If everyone agrees, I would like to Jay to raise Lucy as he raised my daughter Daviana. Even to this day, he is sacrificing his own life to be the dad that everyone will one day remember. You don't have to be biologically related to be a dad. I know we will all be involved and make sure she has a safe, happy, and joyful life. I hope baby Lucy's mother Lucy agrees and gives us her blessing. Yes, I too can see all of you, as I see dreams and I see the dead. I thought it was a curse but now realized it is a blessing."

Nurse Lucy watched me as she came closer and hugged me. Somehow, she was even more like a ghost and less like a human.

She was crying and said, "If Anadhi and Erasmus agree, I would love that."

Jay walked outside to the balcony as he placed his hands on his head. I knew he was in another world thinking about something.

I asked him, "Is something bothering you?"

He did not answer my question but just took a deep breath. Then, he hugged me, and I just let him hug me.

He then said, "I am finally free. I had stayed with Daviana, so she could have a father and a mother. An intersex man was lucky to have a child. Yet I failed her as I failed to protect her from Samar. Even though he was good, his family ruined my family's life, only because I had no voice anywhere. Like the underprivileged women, I too had no voice, no choice in my life. Family name was more important than my existence. So not to cause shame, dishonor, or ruin the name of my family members, I had to hide my identity. I don't know if I am a man or a woman as I have no male or female body parts."

It was strange hearing from a person firsthand who had gone through this situation. It's like he became invisible as a human. I realized our world really is unjust and this too is a forced situation people are placed within. Jay was forced to marry and be with Viana even though it was not his choice, nor could he consummate the marriage.

Jay smiled and said, "I have a job offer from Jacobus to work in their science lab. Maybe, I can find help for some people who live in the closet as they can't identify as a man or a woman. Also, remember Viana is yours as we never married. Daviana is Dave's as her marriage to Samar was not even valid for he was married to Lucy."

Screams broke out in the hospital as our twelve ghosts tried to find out what was happening. A man walked out from behind a painting and screamed as he said, "I am a victim of this hospital, and I am not going to allow the organ traffickers to get away with my murder. I never signed up to be an organ donor but was waiting to receive an organ. They tricked me as I was never sick. Now, I want revenge. They too must become ghosts just like me."

Theunis who was sitting like a young boy, closed his eyes, and said nothing. He then walked up and in front of us was a grown-up man who looked at the ghost and said, "Unjust death can never be justified. I know we will get to the bottom of this and try to give you and everyone justice. Yet you can find justice through forgiveness as forgiveness doesn't free the criminal but sets your soul free to walk up to your Creator and find peace."

I saw the Kasteel Vrederic family rush back and witness the dead man's curses. Jacobus asked his mother, "Mama, what now? I assumed Samar had gone back to his CIA job, Charlotte Amanda is in custody, and now we only search for Samar's brother who I thought was in hiding so he wouldn't be coming out anytime soon. I thought we could now return, and everything would go back to normal."

We saw then an FBI agent walk in and say, "We have bad news. Dr. Kapoor's mother escaped from a maximum security prison. Last we heard is she crossed the border near Canada and boarded a plane for somewhere in Europe. We will let you know about the details."

Everyone was upset but knew we would all be ready for Charlotte Amanda and Nimar when and if they reappear. I saw the twelve ghosts of MacNider Hospital all line up and shake their heads.

They said in unison, "We will all be ready for when they do return. Until then, we would like your blessing to live here until we see the light and are ready to travel to the other side. We will make sure no one ever haunts our hospital for as long as we are here."

Theunis walked to the window with Alexander and showed us on the huge outdoor TV there he was, Samar. He waved his hands toward us as he knew we were all watching. He bent his head slightly toward the left as he does this gesture always. Maybe it's his signature move. He hit his head as he saw his mother who looked much younger walk into a car with a corrupt FBI agent, who I believed helped her escape again.

Theunis laughed and said, "There are two of them, remember, Samar and Nimar. Don't worry about Samar as he is the good one who always bends his head and waves as he smiles. Nimar looks just like him but is not his twin and he never smiles. He had a head injury which prevents his real hair from growing back. He is bald when not wearing a wig. The injury prevents him from smiling or bending his head, and one of Nimar's hands, the right hand is robotic. It is not real, so he can't wave either."

Theunis winked and leaned closer to Jacobus as they spoke quietly. They stood silently for a while as if they were trying to inspect the situation before sharing with others.

Jacobus very calmly said, "What a loser. You will have to live as an underworld criminal as we will haunt you from above the ground. You will be caught sooner or later. We know your secrets, so it will be easy to catch you."

It's strange how these underworld criminals work. They line up people everywhere, so they always have an escape route if they so need one. Seeing the extent of the work that the criminals had done, it seemed they were working behind the walls of our hospital for months if not years, or maybe ever since we built the hospital. From what we heard, these criminals target their victims and move slowly.

Nimar left a recorded video for all of us and especially for Samar with a hospital staff member. The staff member assumed it was Samar who had given him the video. Samar and his brother Nimar could fool anyone into believing they were the same person with slight makeup.

The long video played in front of us. Nimar was sitting in the office of an FBI agent, with his feet on top of the desk like he owned the FBI. He was completely bald and had no scars on him at all. We were all watching the video from our hospital computer lab lounge where we had huge screens and sofas in a room for doctors to meet and go over reports with visiting scholars.

He said to us, "I have to say, you are good. I really don't want to fight with the Kasteel Vrederic family as I know you have some kind of unnatural help. I can't put my finger on it, but I will, and I promise your secrets will be exposed by me. Yet Daviana, I wish you a happy married life. I only wish I could have raped you like I raped Lucy. I also think Viana had enough sufferings and know my mommy, the woman your grandfather dumped, has now moved on with younger and able men. David MacNider, remember, I will keep ruining the lives of men, women, and children, whoever we can fool, get, and grab. We will place them into forced marriages, let them become sex slaves, and we will sell their body parts as it's not our fault but the people who allow us to do so."

The man who resembled Samar stood there now sipping very expensive wine. He nibbled cheese for a while. He was showing off how he could have all the luxuries of life anywhere.

He then continued talking as he looked directly at the screen and said, "Why don't you all stop sex trafficking? Organ trafficking? Or stop forcing your men and women to be a situation they can't handle? The next woman I abuse won't be lucky like Daviana, Viana, or Devi, as this time I will make sure she does not live to talk. Maybe like how I raped and murdered Lucy. Yes, Samar if you are listening, I murdered your real wife. I did rape her before you married and had a child with her. I touched and ruined her first, before you could even marry her for honor I am assuming, not love. Now I am not stupid, so I will not come back to your town, but that doesn't mean I won't haunt other cities, towns, or countries. Maybe I will pay you all a visit. Bye for now everyone. It was fun. I like my kind of games where I eventually have to go back into hiding and you all must find me, don't you? Hey, in my kind of games, I always win. Also, my robotic hand is really a weapon against all my victims. Thanks Bro for giving it to me. I'll return the favor when I see you."

The video had gone on and on forever. I wondered how and when did this guy do all these tapings? He had preplanned for a while. After a lot of calls and pulling a lot of strings, I got a date for court where I would represent victims of forced marriage, sex trafficking, and organ trafficking including Daviana, four other women, and a young child who was only three years old. Without her parents' consent, her body parts were being sold as her biological mother had passed away. They all were going to testify against Charlotte Amanda Kapoor, Nimar Kapoor, and some more powerful names which had not been released.

The case was going to be very simple as we had enough evidence, yet it was very complicated. Some of the victims here had voluntarily participated. Others had some kind of paperwork that proved they knew they were being sold off as sex slaves. Some had marriage certificates but were clearly victims of forced marriages. All of the above were about money. Little did these victims know that their lives were going to be forever changed, and they would never have a life which they could live in freedom.

The whole story unbraided quickly as we recovered the thirty people who were put to sleep through an injection. That is still a mystery as this injection fooled everyone. The victims medically all seemed dead. We were lucky to have Jacobus, who had a hunch and tried his newly discovered injection and reversed the situation. All the victims woke up like they had just gone to sleep. They couldn't believe where they were and how much time had passed.

All the victims had medical evidence showing they wouldn't live long as they had some kind of illness, so they wanted to donate organs at the time of death. After receiving their accurate lab results, I was able to get statements from medical experts for the investigation. They confirmed the medical records were falsified for the purpose of selling human organs in the underworld market. The victims gave consent under deception as they were being treated for conditions they did not have. Victory would be easy as I had proof on my side. I got an arrest warrant issued for all of them, even to extradite the international criminals who had committed crimes in the United States, in a US hospital against US citizens.

The twelve ghosts of MacNider Hospital were watching everything unfold. A sudden sadness overshadowed my thoughts of victory as I realized it didn't matter how much I succeeded in the court or how many criminals we brought into custody, the twelve ghosts of MacNider Hospital would be just that, victims and now ghosts. As a lawyer, I knew I could bring justice to their cases, however, neither Dave, Jacobus, Samar, nor I could give life back to these innocent victims.

Anadhi the famous dream psychic stood and glanced at the rest of the group as she said, "Lucy and all the twelve ghosts of MacNider Hospital should know you can all walk toward the light when you are ready. It's not scary but really comforting, when and if you believe your job as a ghost or a spirit has been completed. I want peace, laughter, and joy to replace the fear and fury that spread within you and the walls of this hospital. Please be happy in whatever form you are as that's what will give you peace and be comforting to your soul."

Suddenly we all heard sounds of hurtful cries and howling, not from our twelve ghosts but somewhere else. No one wanted to say anything, but I knew everyone heard the noises. The lights flickered again in the hospital as the sounds of fear and anger overrode all the feeling of victory.

We saw people walking through the hospital who were dead but did not know who they were. They walked around the hospital freely. I wondered if our hospital would ever be free from the ghosts who roamed around without knowing they were dead. I realized a lot of the dead people were brought in from different parts of the world. The predators needed hospitals to do their dealings in the underworld market.

A woman was staring at me. She was crying and walked toward me. She spoke with me directly, "Hello, are you a doctor here? My son needs a bone marrow transplant. I became a donor, but my son walked up the staircase into the light. I saw him. Why didn't they take anything from me? Why didn't they start his treatments? How is it we are both dead? I wasn't even sick. My husband beat me up and my son tried to save my life. He got seriously injured in the one-sided beating. That's when we realized he was seriously ill or that's what they told us, even though he never had symptoms. Please help us. Don't let my death go in vain."

Jacobus stood next to me and closed his eyes. We all walked outside into the open courtyard. The bright sun was pouring its rays upon the hospital. I watched a newborn baby go home with his parents. Then, there was a breast cancer survivor going home with her husband as she hugged her doctors and nurses.

These actions gave me the strength to keep fighting for MacNider Hospital which stood at the end of Long Island next to the prestigious Montauk Point Lighthouse. Today, the lighthouse is a famous museum, so I am proud we have a view of this amazing structure.

The lighthouse that has been standing here for hundreds of years was the background for my childhood ghost stories made up maybe by my parents so I could go to bed without making a fuss, otherwise, the old lady would come. One could still see the lighthouse from far away and retell ghost stories. Now our hospital too became a hot spot for ghost hunters and ghost stories.

As a child was saying to her friends, "Did you know this hospital is haunted by Lucy the nurse? It is said her cries and yearning for her daughter could be heard all the way from the old lighthouse. Some say they see blood all over the grounds."

Daviana listened to the child talking and froze in spot. She was shaking in fear and had dropped her handbag on the ground.

The children talking about the ghosts said, "So funny! Look at that woman so scared and shaking by hearing a story!"

The young children left in their car. As the car became invisible in the fog, I saw Daviana was shaking in fear.

Daviana sat down on the grounds outside in the courtyard as she screamed and cried, "Please Nimar, don't touch me. It hurts and I can't take it anymore. It hurts! Oh my God, it hurts Bapu! It hurts David! Please save me. I am your child. Grandfather, please help me! No Samar, don't let Nimar touch me."

I ran and held my daughter in my arms tightly. I kept her in my chest for as long as I could. Jay came and held her from the other side. As we held her tightly within our embrace, we heard the laughter of Nimar flowing in through all the indoor and outdoor sound systems.

Jacobus said, "He is trying to manipulate your mind, Daviana. He knows since he can't physically be here to manipulate you, he will try to torture you through different sources. Remember, he can never win if you don't allow him. My mother says evil can enter your dreams if only you give him permission to enter. He got knocked out and now will hide in the criminal underworld. If he comes out from hiding, he will be caught. I know we will need to go to the criminal underworld to catch him."

Daviana stood up and took a deep breath. She hugged Jacobus and Margriete. She went and hugged Erasmus and Anadhi. She watched Theunis for a while and then went and gave him a big hug.

She said, "Since I can't be in the Kasteel Vrederic family, I am blessed I have the best two fathers a girl could hope for. The father who gave me up to protect me like the King Soloman story. Also, the father who picked me up and raised me within his embrace and never let me go."

Viana watched her own daughter and said nothing. I realized it was probably hard having a grown-up daughter when she left a newborn child. I nodded my head as she knew what I just thought.

Jay asked Jacobus, "What about Edward and his heart condition? Do we need to do anything, or should we wait?"

Jacobus was busy talking with the police and FBI agents. I assumed Jay's words went unheard as Jacobus didn't respond. After a while, Jacobus, however, came back and sat down.

He said, "No, Edward doesn't need to have any surgeries done. At his age, we will keep an eye out for all the needed procedures. I am shocked how everyone kept saying he needed surgery when he did not. He probably was drugged to make him look sick. We will keep an eye out for the drug interactions if there are any."

Edward laughed out loud as he was amazed at everything that was happening. His white hair and completely white beard made him look more like Santa Claus than anyone else.

He hugged Daviana and said, "Enough worries about me. Let's now concentrate on getting rid of all the ghosts, and Samar's family members."

We all said at once, "Not the twelve ghosts of MacNider Hospital."

They come with the hospital. We would keep them for as long as they would like to stay. The twelve ghosts were working alongside the living employees. No one questioned or asked questions about our twelve ghosts.

Daviana walked outside to the balcony of MacNider Hospital as she said, "David, I want to help you bring down Nimar and his group. I want everyone to say no to forced marriages. Say no to being a sex slave. Say no to illegally selling body parts as a part of victimization. I'm not afraid as I only agreed to be the victim to save my mother. Today, I will become the voice and the attorney who ends these crimes that are being committed by a criminal. I the innocent will fight for all the innocent victims. I am trained to recognize all the manipulative characteristics of an abuser as I have been abused by the master of abuse. So now, I will stand up and teach all victims how to protect themselves and not allow fear to enter the mind, the body, and the soul, as fear is the control system of manipulation and intimidation."

MANIPULATION AND INTIMIDATION

Forced to do

As they wish,

Or they would do it for

You.

Forced to walk

As they teach,

Or they would complete

Your walk.

Forced to marry

As they chose,

Or they would

Send you away.

Forced to be

A sex slave,

Or they would

Sell you off.

Forced to sell

Your organs,

Or they would

Sell them for you.

Now let's,

All the forced,

The manipulated,

The intimidated,

Victims in union,

Say,

No to

MANIPULATION AND INTIMIDATION.

CHAPTER ELEVEN:

The Haunting Of MacNider Hospital

"Dead bodies
Found at
A place
Is often engraved
As eerie or haunted.
I, however, say it's
Where the mystery
Had begun and
So therefore,
Was
Solved."

The survivors of abuse have brought to us the guiding stars of the darkest nights. The brave warriors have come forward as they shared their open wounds to heal not themselves but the others on the same path. The message they leave out there like a glowing star is that no pain or wounds should be buried, as the only thing buried upon Earth are dead bodies not the living.

The wounded need to be healed, not be hidden. Healing is an example of a current wound that has been treated. The injury that had caused the impairment no longer is in control of our body. For example, now the survivor realizes she is not the dead casualty but the surviving innocent.

As everyone walked out from the hospital to the retreat, we all stood in the courtyard. There was a huge water fountain which was called the wishing well. Dave and I had placed this fountain there with prayers written on stones like plaques. You can see prayers from all different faiths there. I believe prayers are answered here as all the different prayers from all different faiths made this wishing well a sacred ground. Underneath the ground where the fountain was installed, the original stone well still functions and is the main water source of the wishing well.

Daviana Shaw's last name was given after her beloved adoptive father who taught her to stand up, talk, and walk. He fed her first food and healed her first wound. He also stayed awake with her all night when she was sick or just needed the comfort of a mother or father. For Daviana, Jay was both her mother and father. Even today, through all the obstacles she found her birth parents back in her life, yet she still considers Jay her parent.

Daviana ran to Jay and said, "Bapu, I am so scared of him. I hear him calling my name in my sleep and even in my awakening state. I am scared he will hurt me and it's just too much pain. The chains cut into my skin Bapu, and it hurts so much. Samar told me to be brave and make sure I shoot Nimar if he enters, but I can never take a life. I too am a doctor who will only save lives and a lawyer who will defend all innocent victims to my last breath."

Tears flowed from everyone's eyes as the ghost of Lucy the nurse came and stood next to Daviana. Lucy tried to touch her, but her fingers just could not touch Daviana. She realized this has been happening more recently and maybe this was just the way things would be.

Jay touched his daughter's hair, and he kissed her on both of her cheeks. He wiped away her tears and with a napkin helped her blow her nose.

He laughed out loud as he said, "Oh baby girl still can't blow her nose properly. Come on, let it all out. I'm here."

Watching them both, I realized how I was lucky too. My baby girl had the best father in the world. Karma was good as I too had the best son in the world. Dave was listening to Daviana, and I realized she was not in any form to trust or marry anyone at this time. She needed to heal from inside out. Our survivor of this diary is also our healer.

Dave went and held both Jay and Daviana in his arms as he said, "Daviana, you are a fighter. You must never stop fighting for yourself. That is how you alone will save so many lives. Jay, you need to heal and stop blaming yourself for Daviana's marriage to Samar. You too are a victim who had no say. Samar was a good man. His family was just horrendous."

Edward walked to Daviana and Jay as he wanted to say something but stopped midway as he saw something that frightened him beyond what words could say. He became silent and kept watching over Daviana. He wanted to say something but could not. We were all going to testify in the hospital retreat through a two-way closed-circuit television to protect the victims. I knew the victims all felt better to have a nice bed and hot meals served in their hotel rooms in the retreat. The retreat had a view of the hospital, the lighthouse, and the beach.

The FBI agents arrived to take everyone's testimony. They had taken with them the recovered living and breathing bodies that we all took for dead. The victims were global. Each one had been brought to the hospital with false promises. Some came for treatment plans to treat false illnesses. Some were drugged and were sex slaves who were brought for their organs while others were brought here from their poor families who sold them for money. All the victims were testifying of their free will.

Edward was their biggest witness as he had given his recorded testimony to me in front of all the recovered victims and the FBI agents. He did this yesterday before Jacobus and his family left for the Netherlands. Edward worried if anything went wrong or happened to him, then these dangerous criminals would be left to roam the world freely.

Edward covered Daviana and said, "No one touches my granddaughter. It's all my fault. My blind faith in cultural honor and my fear of Charlotte Amanda ruined my life, my daughter's life, and my granddaughter's life. No more shall you win Charlotte Amanda. Even in death, I will say that I was wrong to say forced marriages are better. For me, it was better as you were evil, and I realized our relationship was infatuation. I was wrong to fear you and wrong as I kept quiet about your underworld criminal businesses. I will avenge your crimes even in death. Oh yes, you all wanted to have a thirteenth dead body in this hospital. I will volunteer as the thirteenth ghost and will never allow your dreams of making my granddaughter the thirteenth ghost come true."

Suddenly, I saw Edward fall to the ground as Dave held Daviana and moved her to the ground and laid on top of her. I held Viana and laid on top of her as I watched Jay lay on top of Lucy the child who just came into the courtyard with a police escort and her father Samar.

Everyone standing in the courtyard by the wishing well of the hospital grounds heard gunshots and ran in all directions. Lucy the ghost nurse and the eleven other ghosts all appeared at the top of the hospital tower. They joined hands and a lightning bolt went from there to another tower nearby, where the gunshots were coming from.

An elderly woman came out and stood in front of Edward screaming, "What did she have that I didn't? Revenge got the better of me as all my life I wanted to ruin and break up all marriages. I sold young girls so they could never become a wife. I sold human organs so these women and men could never live happily together. I didn't want anyone to be happy if I couldn't be happy."

Edward smiled as he saw his very weak, elderly, and fragile wife, Devi, walk toward him. She had the most beautiful eyes which even without any makeup always looked like they were lined with kohl. Her lips always seemed like they had red lipstick on. She said nothing but just watched her husband and dropped tears that fell on him. He caught her tears in his hands.

He said, "Devi, please forgive me. It was my responsibility to save Daviana as the bullet was coming toward her. She suffered because of my wrongdoings. Maybe my death will make up for some of my wrong. My dear, remember love is not always in union but in separation too. I will cross over into the other world and wait for you there. In our next life, we can rise like the phoenix and be reborn together. I will wait for you. Please take your time as you have so much more time to live and catch up on for your missed time. Arranged marriage for us worked as I found you, yet for others, I've learned, it's forced marriage when they don't agree to one another."

He was coughing and laid on Devi's lap. She held him and smiled.

She watched Charlotte Amanda and said, "I have kindness. I have respect. I have empathy. I have honor. I have good moral values. My life taught me to value a person's character as you can never separate a person from his or her character, be it good or bad. I believe in karma and justice. You imprisoned and separated me from my husband, yet I am still alive. My love story never ended, even in separation. I will not cry for my husband as aside from karma, I also believe in reincarnation. Until we meet again my beloved husband, we shall smile and be happy. Love flourishes not just in unions but in separation too if your heart belongs to one another. Sleep well, my beloved."

The police crowded the courtyard and the hospital as all the entry and exit ways were closed off. The police gave us some privacy as they knew an elderly husband was bidding his last farewell to his beloved elderly wife.

Edward said, "Devi, do talk with the younger generations about forced marriages, how it's wrong. Talk to them about how sex and organ trafficking must stop. Please donate my money in spreading this message and help spread this message before you come and join me. Let all know to live a moral life, not a corrupt one. Live life to the fullest, but don't take a life to extend your life. Call this foundation 'Ghostly Justice.'"

Everything stopped. The sounds of bullets, the screams, and the cries all stopped. Suddenly there was peace, and nothing could be heard.

Ambulances came and turned off their lights. Police sirens were no more crying for attention. Two bodies laid on the hospital courtyard. Edward's body was covered with family and friends crying and hovering over him. One hundred yards away was another cold and bloodied dead body of an elderly woman who spent all her living life trying to prove to the man who dumped her that he couldn't dump her. To her dying breath, she fought a losing game. She was so bitter, cold, wicked, and angry. After losing the man she was fatally attracted to, revenge became her new fatal attraction.

She had nothing left in this world to glorify her. Forever she would be known as the sex trafficker and the organ trafficker. She proved it's not always women who enter forced marriages or relationships, but men do too.

The cleaning crew came and finished their job. Samar was standing there with his head bent and arms raised as he closed his eyes and shot his mother when she had aimed to shoot Daviana. Nimar was not found anywhere during the intense search. Helicopters flew all over, but it was as if he vanished in thin air.

It was believed Charlotte Amanda waited for Edward and wanted to kill Daviana to punish him. She wanted Edward all for herself, but Edward refused even in death to be with her. His body was given to his wife for cremation and Charlotte Amanda's body was taken in police custody in a police van.

Jacobus called me as he reached the Netherlands. They were informed on the plane about the incidents.

Jacobus said, "It's all good. Life has a way of dealing with itself in its own way. In a short period of time, Nimar will be caught. Without any money or his evil mother, he too will be lost. Tell Daviana that Nimar can't do anything as all the evidence will guarantee him a lifelong prison sentence. Also, the thirty people who were almost dead and kept on the thirteenth floor will all testify and have been taken into the Witness Protection Program."

After a few horrific and eventful days, we finally returned home. The police came to our small cottage which was filled with family. A detective who went to school with Dave came into our cottage. He smiled seeing everyone, and all his memories flooded back.

Detective Claudio Agosto said, "Dave, first I will say it feels like I have a school paper I must finish writing and need help from your dad. I am blessed he was there for you and all of us who needed him."

Dave hugged the tall and muscular guy and welcomed him to our table to have a meal with us. Claudio took a plate and helped himself to coffee.

He said, "We have the final report from all the agencies. They informed us eleven victims of MacNider Hospital had willingly given written permission to do a test on them. It was part of a survey they all participated in. They were manipulated by Charlotte Amanda and Nimar. The victims were told they were being given a vitamin supplement in an injection for longevity and research to help the sick. Lucy, however, was a personal target by Nimar and Charlotte Amanda who blamed Lucy for stealing Samar from them. I also received proof the hospital had written warnings given to all employees not to participate in any tests not being provided by the hospital or supported by the hospital. This protected the hospital from any lawsuits but it's sad to see what people will go through to have an extra amount of energy. These days, some high-end apartment complexes also provide this kind of rejuvenation therapy which could be dangerous if not prescribed by your primary care physician."

He stopped to sip his coffee. I wondered how he slowly sipped his coffee. Dave and I rush to gobble our coffee down, like medicine. Dave was watching me, and I knew he was having the same thought.

Claudio then said, "There were more dead bodies than the twelve famous ghosts of MacNider Hospital. A spiritual guru who advises us has said, the dead will return to the places they lived or visited while living. So that proves why only twelve ghosts are roaming around the hospital."

We never told him about Edward also joining the twelve as we tried to keep the identities of our twelve a secret. I had heard Charlotte Amanda before her death publicly told everyone about the twelve ghosts, as she tried to blame everything on them. I just hoped her ghost would not return to our hospital as her body was taken far away from our hospital grounds.

No one in family even spoke about the possibility of her return as a ghost. We all avoided taking her name on our lips. The detective left as we all settled down and tried to have our normal quiet life return. Daviana and Viana moved into the guest quarters. Jay bought a house nearby as he was now raising Lucy.

The court finally gave him full custody of her. Originally, Viana and I agreed to raise baby Lucy and still will be involved, however, Jay was the perfect father to do this all over again as he raised Daviana. Now in his empty chest, he placed baby Lucy there perfectly. We all agreed to raise her as a joint family with Jay being the father figure. This was also agreed and approved by our ghost nurse Lucy and Agent Samar's wish. Jay worked for Jacobus in his science laboratory nearby, which kept him busy aside from raising a very active child, who we all helped as that's what families do.

Devi chose to stay with Jay as she said, "I love my daughter and my son-in-law David. Yet I know Jay is my son whom I never had. Also at this age, I don't know how long I have but I will stay close to baby Lucy. Jay proved to this world you don't have to be biologically related to be a son or a father, as the world will see how he is the father of Daviana and now Lucy. Also, biologically you can be what your Creator has created you. Just proudly be yourself. He is the most perfect son this old mother can have."

I sat on the porch of my cottage as Dave came in with two cups of coffee and said, "Dad, I have started the foundation for Devi. It's called 'Ghostly Justice' to help raise money for all who are victims of forced marriages, sex trafficking, and organ trafficking."

I sipped coffee with my son and watched the roses in our garden, smelling the amazing fragrance. I told him after all this nightmare, I was blessed to be able to represent a company that touched my inner soul. In honor of my daughter Daviana, I will with honor and just, represent all the victims who need a lawyer to prove them as the innocent. I want to bring justice to all the unjustly murdered victims whom I call the heroes, as you will forever remember them through this diary, *The Haunting Of MacNider Hospital*.

THE HAUNTING OF MACNIDER HOSPITAL

Dead bodies piled up.

All the living friends,

Relatives known,

And unknown,

Flee the eerie place

In fear

The dead will rise.

Yet when

There is no one,

When everyone

Runs and hides

In fear,

The dead shall

Convince all

Not to fear them,

Or run away

From them

As they breathe no more,

But fear

The reason,

The cause, and

ANN MARIE RUBY

Find the solution

To

THE HAUNTING OF MACNIDER HOSPITAL.

CONCLUSION:

Promises Given, Promises Kept

"Love grows
In union,
Or in
Separation
If only
And only when
The lovers say
To each other,
'Promises
Given,
Promises
Kept.'"

Love stories are written through dreams and are promises kept throughout the years, even when the path separates true lovers. I kept within my inner chest the promise I had given to my beloved wife years ago. After our wedding night, Hell had broken loose. Viana was taken away from me by her father, who believed different race, religion, and color could never unite. A very rich and honorable Indian family man had only agreed to let Viana marry a man of Indian heritage.

His regret and lesson learned happened after all the sufferings had occurred. Yet forgiveness and healing began after he passed away. I did wish all families around the globe could begin the forgiveness and healing period before the death of family members.

No reason was given. No answers were sent to me as to why my beloved wife left me with a broken heart. My eyes were overflowing with hidden tears, and I was shaken beyond understanding. Yes, I had forgiven her as I loved her more than I could ever hate her. The small cottage we bought to raise our small family had a white picket fence, a wraparound porch, and a huge floor-to-ceiling stone fireplace. The small warm kitchen Viana herself had designed was left empty.

She had said, "David, just know my heart only beats your name. Eternally, I shall be yours. Even if another man shows up as my husband, do know this body will never allow another man to touch me if there is life in my body. At this time, I must go as I can't share the reason of my departure, but know in life or in death, I treasure you and your love more than my own life, not more than yours. Promise me, you will always be mine."

She had left after that one conversation. I didn't stop her. All her clothes remained in the master bedroom as they still are there even today. All her shoes, jewelry, her bathing towels, and her slippers, everything remained intact.

Devi and Jay walked around the house as Devi said to Viana and me, "I feel like everything happened because of me. I walked into a story where my husband wasn't in love with me. He had to learn to fall in love with me. He broke up a love story that was made in Heaven. Today, I pray I can with my hands bless this love story to be complete. Not just in one life but in all rebirths, may you two always be together. I pray may you two also find a temple of love made for you in Heaven above. I also pray may no one come in between twin flames. May they always find one another."

Jay sat down and tried to feed his newly adopted daughter Lucy. She was a happy child and kept Jay on his feet. As she ran away from him giggling and tried to give him a hard time, he patiently ran after her.

After feeding his daughter, Jay came and gave me a hug. He said, "I never thought of Viana as my wife because we never married. We never shared a bedroom. Before she was kidnapped and called to be dead, I told her I would love her like a brother. I don't have the organs to have sex, but I do have the organs which can innocently love and take care of family and friends."

Dave walked in as he brought the coffee pot and served breakfast on the kitchen table. We had toast, pastries, cinnamon buns, eggs, potato tarts, and freshly squeezed orange juice. I enjoyed his obsession over cooking and volunteered to be his taster.

Dave laughed and poured me my coffee as he said, "Dad we, I mean Daviana, Devi, Jay, baby Lucy, and I have all decided to give you and Viana a small wedding reception, to renew your vows. You can't say anything as after all these years, your wife has come home. I must do this for you two."

It was a magical night as I wished upon a star for my Viana and my Daviana to find their beloved twin flames. All my life, I waited for my beloved and always believed in free will, true love, and blessings from our families. My wish was granted.

On this night, Viana and I had a very small wedding at the hospital inner courtyard, so that the thirteen ghosts of MacNider Hospital could attend. Yes, there he was, Edward, the new ghost of MacNider Hospital. He looked young and very happy to wait his time out for his beloved wife Devi, who had no interest in going anytime soon. We even had the Kasteel Vrederic family members attend the wedding as a special and blessed surprise.

Viana said, "For so many years, I waited to be in my husband's arms. I wanted the world to accept our love story and honor it, as I am alive today because I had the love of my husband in my soul. I will take my wedding vows only with David over and over again."

Dave hugged Viana and he kissed her on both cheeks. He then got down on one knee as he said to Viana, "I would like to ask for your daughter's hand in marriage if you and Dad will both bless us. Yes, I have asked Daviana, and she can tell you about her reply."

I saw my son and winked at him worried what was going on. He winked back and reassured me everything was just all right.

Daviana laughed and said, "Actually, I asked Dave when he was going to pop the question. He was so shocked.

He started to laugh and said he was waiting all his life for me to take the first step."

The whole crowd burst into laughter. I hugged both of my children and blessed them as did Viana. The wedding celebration was going to be small, but flowers filled the wedding venue as they were specially brought from the Netherlands.

The sweet flower-filled, long-awaited wedding is now forever framed in my heart. We served cake and dinner in to-go packets to all the employees of the hospital, the patients, and their family members. I loved how Jacobus went with his brothers from room to room and gave everyone special dinner and gifts as goody bags from the two happily married and blessed couples.

Devi gave away Viana and did not cry but laughed and said, "I give away my daughter to the love of her life, who never left even though time moved past them. He kept his love alive through the storms of life. I must say if any woman receives even ten percent of the love David has for Viana, she will call herself the luckiest bride on Earth or Heavens above."

When Jay had earlier given away Daviana, he cried and hugged her like a father does when he knows his daughter is going away to her in-laws. He kissed her and hugged baby Lucy who walked with him.

A father's love today became the everlasting guiding light not shining from the earthly lighthouses but from my soul to my daughter's, as it guided my child back to me. On my daughter's wedding day, I thought to myself, would she ever know how much I loved her and will love her until my last breath? Love is not always holding on to and being there with her yet true love is when you can let go for love and still live, breathe, and love till the last breath. Sweetheart, this father will never ask for any rights but will love you with all my being as in love there is no condition nor is there any documentation needed. It's just heart to heart.

Strangely, she was looking at me and made a heart sign and blew a kiss. I knew she too knew this bond and love we share is connected through our souls. A father's love for his daughter is never lost as it's sealed through love. I realized the battle of my life just brought me back my family. Today, for love through love and with faith to seal it, I have my complete family back.

As everything ended and nightfall approached, Dave told me, "Dad, even though I'm a married man, I have no plans on moving out. Remember, we are getting old in this house together. Daviana and I both discussed how she missed out on having both of you, so now she would like to have both of you. You know Dad, I always felt terrible when people would say I don't look at all like you. Now, I'm happy because I know my children will look just like you. It is said babies look like the person the father and mother love the most. We both love you the most."

In the middle of the wedding, I had received a call from a police officer who said, "David MacNider, we want to inform you that there have been sightings of Nimar Kapoor near the hospital grounds. Not to worry as we have increased our security. Also, you had said there was a new hand of a ghost before Edward died. Were you all able to find out who the hand belonged to? The hand that came out and kept saying it belonged to the thirteenth ghost. You don't have to answer now, but I thought I should remind you as you had asked me to find out if any other victims were missing."

Jacobus, Dave, and I decided not to talk about the ghost hand with anyone for now. I thought about the hand for a while and remembered seeing the ring, my family ring, which was on a finger. Theunis knew whom the hand belonged to as we had privately discussed.

Theunis had said to me, "This hand is the helping hand of your family member, the MacNider grandmother.

She had died in her house where you later built this hospital. She lost her hand because of a terminal illness. Your grandmother was a very positive person, so she lends a helping hand to people when and where they need a helping hand. She was and is looking after your lineage and all who help keep the hospital running. She wanted you to know. Remember, her spirit still roams around her land. People have said they still see her from time to time."

I told Dave, Jacobus, Erasmus, and all the Kasteel Vrederic family members. We all agreed not to share this news with the rest of my family.

Anadhi told all of us, "No bad omen today. Believe in only good things as when bad things do come, we just deal with them. Let's not ruin today with what if or what not. Everything will work out as I believe good things befall on all who believe in only good things."

Dawn broke open to our small cottage as throughout time we kept our wedding vows. When nothing was there to guide Viana and me, it was our blessed dreams that had guided us through all the troubles of life. These blessed dreams again brought and united two lovers who were standing on two parts of an ocean. Our dreams became our bridge of union.

As the foundation created by Devi was growing, we shared our personal diaries with all. So, anyone who needs a guiding lighthouse can be guided by our life stories. I have opened the very personal pages of my personal diary. Nothing is hidden or left out as then whoever so chooses can be guided through our stories of this one life.

As a family, we fight all sex traffickers, all organ traffickers, and have shared our stories so no one is forced to marry against their will or wishes. To all of you and my beloved wife, daughter, and my beloved son, I will say the promises I had given all of you I have kept through this diary. In this household, we all say, promises given, promises kept.

I am David MacNider, and this is my personal diary. I call this diary *The Haunting Of MacNider Hospital*.

P.S. I heard Dr. Samar Kapoor, the CIA agent, is traveling around the globe hunting down criminals no one else can catch because they can't see them. It is also rumored his nurse ghost bride has been traveling with him at various times. Maybe you can follow up on them when you open their upcoming diary which I heard they called, *The Spy And His Ghostly Wife*.

PROMISES GIVEN, PROMISES KEPT

For you, I am.

For me, you are.

Promises made

At the wedding altar

Which come from

Two minds,

Two bodies,

And two souls,

Will last

And be blessed,

As the vows are

Tied with

The wedding vows

Through the

Seven lives

Across the bridge

Of life

And death,

As twin flames

Who belong to

One another,

Never separate

Through time,

Through land, and

Through ocean,

As they are tied

In an

Eternal knot

Through

PROMISES GIVEN, PROMISES KEPT.

ANN MARIE RUBY

MESSAGE FROM THE AUTHOR

"Always for
The others,
Forced
Into
Unconsented marriages,
Forced to
Sell body parts,
Yet when will it ever be
About me,
The
Individual,
And
My choice?"

Are you still scared of hospitals where the living wait to be healed? Are you still scared of ghosts? What about the morgues where the dead rest in peace or lack of peace? Sometimes in the hospital, the candle flames diminish as hope fades away. It's then we find the blessed hands of physicians and their team members who cover the burning candles to prevent hope from fading until the storms of life leave. As we traveled through MacNider Hospital and in union, solved some murders, got acquainted with some ghosts, and caught some international and local criminals, don't fear hospitals anymore but know there is a friend there for you too.

Why did I write this book? To entertain people in a safe and controlled environment where you can explore fear, romance, social awareness, and family drama through fictional characters who make the realm of this book into reality. Aside from entertainment, I always focus on inspiration through hope. Hope weaved with faith is spread throughout all of my fictional and nonfictional books. Just open the pages and catch the glimmer of hope.

In this book, I introduced you to the victims of some forced crimes not usually talked about in the public. A message from all the victims of these crimes to the assailants is although our individual voices may be too low for you to hear, our combined voices will raise tsunamis and drown all the assailants out.

Through the mystery of MacNider Hospital, we learned to take control of our own fate. David the diarist welcomed you through his diary to Montauk, a place everyone calls the end of the world, to solve a mystery that had begun years ago. Through this suspenseful, psychological, and romantic thriller, you have now awakened your inner humanity. Please join forces with me and help all victims of these crimes if you so see them.

What do you call a person who takes control of others to put himself or herself above everyone else? I call it superiority complex, or megalomania. Do you ever think your verbal or physical torture could give pain to the others? A friend of mine told me she can't compare her pain with the pain of others. When she is hurt, she knows she must take painkillers, yet when another person is hurt, she says "Oh, it will pass."

Today, I want to raise an issue that is like a braided bread. A few issues were braided to talk about a certain group of affected people who go unnoticed and unheard. It's like my friend had honestly said, "If it doesn't affect us, why should we even care?" Yet, I do care, as all humans feel and ache. Even though another person's pain doesn't touch me physically, it still touches me emotionally. I care as a human with humanity.

I am blessed to have had your company as we journeyed together through the world of forced marriages and organ trafficking within a Gothic book. The story took place within a hospital where the dead had risen. The criminals were hidden within the walls. The heroines Viana, Daviana, and Lucy were the victims, and the heroes David and Dave own the hospital where everything took place. We laughed, we cried, we had goosebumps, and we even had shivers down the spine. I believe the inner soul heals when we the individuals feel our emotions. It's my way of healing through words of wisdom.

Did you know human embarrassment keeps these topics hidden under the bed as the victims are suffering on top of a stranger's bed? Just think, maybe one of your neighbors at this specific moment is being forced into a horrible crime against his or her will. What will you do? Will you speak up for your neighbor?

Manipulating people into forced marriages or to sell their body organs with or without their consent is a crime. Since forced marriage is a crime, enforcers of forced marriages are in my eyes, criminals. Taking control of whom you should marry, or coercing to sell your body parts in order to save another life, are both psychological tortures and emotional manipulations.

Calling someone crazy if they don't agree with you, is manipulation. I ask you the name callers, did you ever think, who is the crazy one? Those forcing their ways on an innocent, or the one being forced? Today, a lot of traffickers are being caught. What about the participants for whom these traffickers are blooming their businesses? All participants who contribute to blossom illegal businesses should also share the same punishment.

At times, the victims are forced to enter the corners of life they didn't choose. With no voice but fear of what the others would say, some enter groups and societies where they live a life not in freedom but in a cage. They lose their wings to ever fly again freely.

According to the International Labour Organization, in 2021, around 28 million people were forced into labor and 22 million people were placed into forced marriages. Amongst those forced into labor, around 23% were sex workers. Did you know Global Financial Integrity estimates 10% of all organ transplants are illegally transplanted? Some are the body parts trafficked from sex workers and forced marriage victims.

Yes, even in this day and age, we are still forced into marriages, forced to practice religions, or even forced to go places or stay at home, not by choice but through simple manipulation. It seems impossible to believe but numbers speak for themselves. Everyone wishes to be happily married to their twin flame, yet when we see a married couple walking together or separately doing their own things, we don't realize a lot of these people are unhappy.

What about a person selling his body parts to feed his family? Do we even ask or see if we could be there for him? Or do we just keep walking on our own path? Even my friends have told me for my own safety, not to pry but just mind my own business.

Nonconsensual and forced marriages give birth to emotional and physical distress, where a prisoner must find a way out. Marriages are made in Heaven, where the home you build through this wedded bliss becomes a temple. Nothing is forced as everything is chosen by two individuals, when they become from two to one, united through holy matrimony.

Yet what happens when this wedded bliss starts with force and dishonesty? What happens when two bodies don't unite out of love but under pressure to save a family's honor and grace? Elders advise us to adjust ourselves with the situation as love comes after marriage and you learn to live with one another.

It is true, arranged marriages have worked for centuries as they are and shall remain a way of life. An arranged marriage and a forced arranged marriage are different. Around the globe, under societal pressures, there are so many men and women who are forced into arranged marriages neither one wants to be in. These couples never wanted to be in a relationship, but for the honor of their family, they agreed to the marriage.

In this Gothic paranormal thriller, I walked through two major issues, forced marriages and organ trafficking. As the storyline continued, I touched upon other issues affecting members of our society. All of these issues are psychological torture and human rights violations. These violations cause an avalanche of illegal crimes as one act of illegal action rolls out so many more.

I have the pen in my hands, so even if in the real world, abusers get their way out, here they must be found guilty of the crimes they are committing. I unbraid complex issues which can't be solved in one day. Talking about the issues, however, will open the doors to finding the solutions.

In my books, you won't call a victim a prostitute. You won't accuse a forced marriage victim of taking the vows willingly. You won't point fingers to dead organ trafficking victims and say they knew they were sharing their organ parts. Even if the victims can't speak for themselves, the pages of my book will speak for them.

Through this mystery, I want people to believe in love and in themselves all over again. It matters not if you are in love for a day or must wait for eternity, love and lovers will unite. Where there is one half of the twin flame, the other half will be pulled like a magnet to make this heart complete. Only when you believe in true love, your true love will find you. So, believe in love.

My message is say no to forced marriages. I want everyone to be aware if they are tricked into being victims. Say no to all forms of physical abuse. If you want to get a tattoo, then go and choose one. Don't carry the marks of abuse on your body like a tattoo when those marks were not chosen by you. Say no to the people who call you crazy when you choose to take a different path from them.

I would encourage all humans to live this one life to your own heart's desires, not how the others want but how you want to live it. Don't live life in fear. Live with joy and happiness. It's your life and the decision how to live it should be yours. If through this journey, mistakes are made by your own footsteps, then your mistakes will be guidance left for the future generations to learn from. Make your own mistakes. Don't become another person's mistake.

If we could gather up the men, women, and children who have committed suicide as a result of human manipulation, and ask them to share their stories, I guess we would only have sad stories to share. Tears would make a river even in the desert. You are not wrong for wanting something different for yourself. Your wings are not broken as they are damaged from fighting the storm all by yourself. I want to hug all of you who are in a forced marriage, who are being physically or emotionally tortured, and tell you that you are loved and are special.

Like my four beautiful and graceful women, Devi, Viana, Daviana, and Lucy, may you too have someone out there who is waiting for you. Maybe he is a friend, a brother, or a beloved. It is never too late to have a new friend. Choose a friend like David, Dave, or maybe if you are lucky, the family members of Kasteel Vrederic will become your true friends. Just open the pages of my *Kasteel Vrederic* book series.

I would rather wait and dream about my twin flame than be in a forced marriage. If no one comes, then I will still have my sweet dreams to comfort me, not the physical and emotional pain to deal with. If someone calls me crazy for choosing to live my life my way, so be it. Dreaming of a happily ever after is far better than being forced into an abusive marriage any day, anytime.

I want to bring hope back to you, the lonely bird flying in the rough storm all by yourself. Never give up seeking your twin flame. This book is your key to hope, love, and everlasting happiness that break open the lock where you are being held a prisoner. Keep the window of hope open and believe in love.

Tonight, dream a little and keep the window to your inner heart open for your twin flame will arrive, breaking open all the obstacles of this world, to profess eternal love only to you. Like you, your twin flame has saved all of his or her love only for you. Tonight, respect yourself, love yourself, and honor yourself as you are the real treasure you have been searching for your whole life.

I treasure all of you, as I have written this book for you, the one who was psychologically, emotionally, and physically tortured, tormented, and manipulated by the others. Wipe off the tears and stand up against the strong winds, high waves, or burning fires, as I am through this book standing up for all of you.

Also, just one piece of advice, don't fear the dead who have departed this world. Fear the living predators who take innocent lives. Now, don't be petrified by a hospital, a ghost, or the dead. Come and enjoy the message of this book, spread the message, and inspire others to read this book.

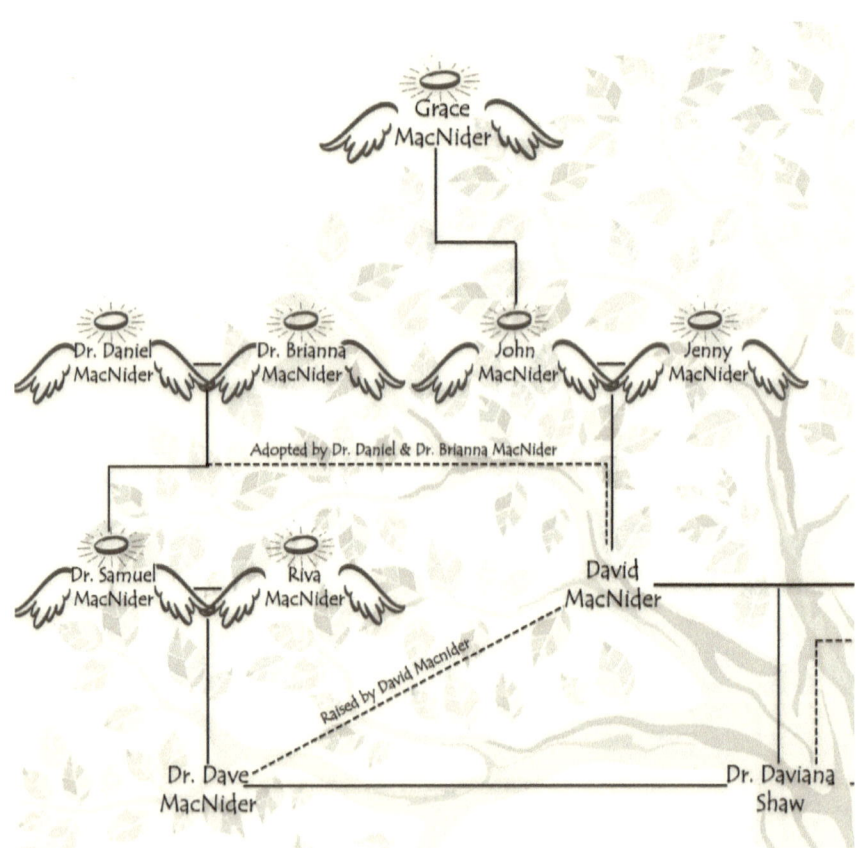

MacNider

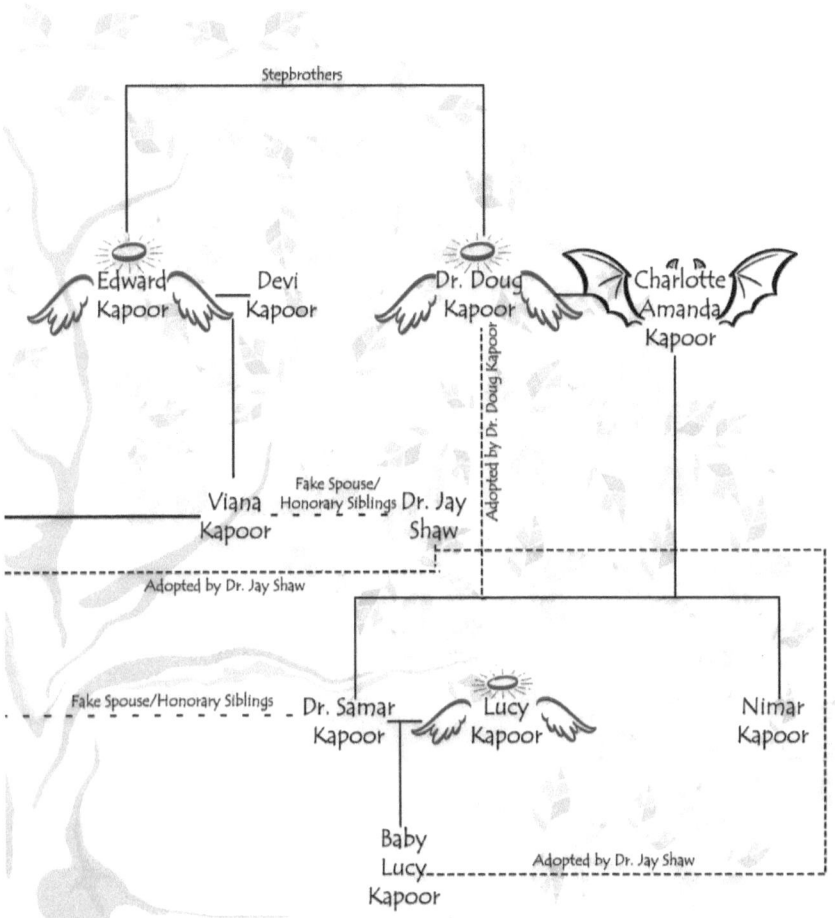

Family Tree

INHABITANTS OF
THE HAUNTING OF
MACNIDER HOSPITAL

David MacNider   Co-owner of MacNider Hospital and David's Retreat. Attorney. Husband of Viana Kapoor, father figure of Dr. David "Dave" MacNider, and biological father of Daviana Shaw.

Dr. David "Dave" MacNider   Co-owner of MacNider Hospital and David's Retreat. Medical doctor at MacNider Hospital. Son-like figure of David MacNider, and husband of Daviana Shaw.

Daviana Shaw   Medical doctor and attorney. Biological daughter of David MacNider and Viana Kapoor, adopted daughter of Dr. Jay Shaw, fake spouse/honorary sibling of Dr. Samar Kapoor, and wife of Dr. David "Dave" MacNider.

Viana Kapoor   Wife of David MacNider, mother of Daviana Shaw, and fake spouse/honorary sibling of Dr. Jay Shaw.

Dr. Jay Shaw   PhD. Fake spouse/honorary sibling of Viana Kapoor, adoptive father of Daviana Shaw, and guardian of baby Lucy Kapoor.

Charlotte Amanda Kapoor   Notorious international underworld trafficker, widow of Doug Kapoor, ex-lover of Edward Kapoor, and mother of Samar Kapoor and Nimar Kapoor.

Dr. Samar Kapoor   Medical doctor and CIA agent. Fake spouse/honorary sibling of Daviana Shaw, widower of Lucy Kapoor, father of baby Lucy Kapoor, adopted son of Doug Kapoor, biological son of Charlotte Amanda Kapoor, and brother of Nimar Kapoor.

Lucy Kapoor   Nurse at MacNider Hospital. Wife of Dr. Samar Kapoor, and mother of baby Lucy Kapoor. Ghost of MacNider Hospital.

Edward Kapoor   Husband of Devi Kapoor, father of Viana Kapoor, maternal grandfather of Daviana Shaw, and ex-lover of Charlotte Amanda Kapoor. Ghost of MacNider Hospital.

Devi Kapoor   Widow of Edward Kapoor, mother of Viana Kapoor, and maternal grandmother of Daviana Shaw.

Baby Lucy Kapoor   Biological daughter of Lucy Kapoor and Dr. Samar Kapoor, adopted by Dr. Jay Shaw.

Dr. Samuel MacNider   Adoptive brother of David MacNider, biological father of Dr. David "Dave" MacNider, and husband of Riva MacNider.

Riva MacNider   Wife of Dr. Samuel MacNider and biological mother of Dr. David "Dave" MacNider.

Grace MacNider   Paternal grandmother of David MacNider and former owner of the MacNider estate whose wish was to open the MacNider Hospital.

Dr. Daniel MacNider   Adoptive father of David MacNider and husband of Dr. Brianna MacNider.

Dr. Brianna MacNider   Adoptive mother of David MacNider and wife of Dr. Daniel MacNider.

John MacNider   Biological father of David MacNider and husband of Jenny MacNider.

Jenny MacNider Biological mother of David MacNider and wife of John MacNider.

Delilah Sommers Detective with the local law enforcement in Montauk, New York.

Claudio Agosto Detective with the local law enforcement in Montauk, New York.

Ahmed Operating room nurse. Ghost of MacNider Hospital.

Levi Operating room nurse. Ghost of MacNider Hospital.

Ms. Johnson Food service worker. Mother figure of Lucy Kapoor. Ghost of MacNider Hospital.

Dev Biomedical technician. Ghost of MacNider Hospital.

Jack Lab technician. Ghost of MacNider Hospital.

Nathan Medical assistant. Ghost of MacNider Hospital.

Nancy Patient service representative. Ghost of MacNider Hospital.

Mandy Hospital executive manager. Ghost of MacNider Hospital.

Wanda	Housekeeping. Ghost of MacNider Hospital.
Brandy	Housekeeping. Ghost of MacNider Hospital.
Paul	Housekeeping. Ghost of MacNider Hospital.

SPECIAL APPEARANCES FROM THE *KASTEEL VREDERIC* SERIES

Dr. Jacobus Vrederic van Phillip	Medical doctor with multiple specialties, and one-of-a-kind specialist in never-done-before transplant surgeries. Son of Erasmus van Phillip and Anadhi Newhouse van Phillip, cousin of Antonius van Phillip and Andries van Phillip, uncle of reincarnated Andries van Phillip and Griet Vrederic van Phillip, twin flame and husband of Dr. Margriete van Achthoven van Phillip, and father of Rietje Vrederic van Phillip. Reincarnated form of sixteenth and seventeenth-century Jacobus van Vrederic.
Dr. Margriete van Achthoven van Phillip	Medical doctor, cardiologist, and pediatric cardiovascular surgeon. Co-owner of Agatha and Marinda's Orphanage. Twin flame and wife of Dr. Jacobus Vrederic van Phillip, and mother of Rietje Vrederic van Phillip.

Reincarnated form of sixteenth and seventeenth-century Margriete van Wijck.

Anadhi Newhouse van Phillip   Author. Daughter of Dr. Andrew Newhouse and Dr. Gita Shankar Newhouse, granddaughter of Martin Newhouse and Miranda Newhouse, granddaughter of Hari Shankar and Parvati Shankar, twin flame and wife of Erasmus van Phillip, mother of Dr. Jacobus Vrederic van Phillip, aunt and adoptive mother of Antonius van Phillip and Andries van Phillip, grandmother of reincarnated Andries van Phillip, Griet Vrederic van Phillip, and Rietje Vrederic van Phillip. Reincarnated form of sixteenth-century Mahalt.

Erasmus van Phillip   World-renowned painter, and twenty-first-century owner of Kasteel Vrederic. Son of Greta van Phillip, descendant of the Van Vrederic family, twin flame and husband of Anadhi Newhouse van Phillip, father of Dr. Jacobus Vrederic van Phillip, uncle and adoptive father of Antonius van Phillip and Andries van Phillip, and grandfather of reincarnated Andries van Phillip, Griet Vrederic van Phillip, and Rietje Vrederic van Phillip.

Reincarnated form of sixteenth-century Johannes van Vrederic.

Antonius van Phillip World-renowned painter. Son of Petrus van Phillip and Giada Berlusconi van Phillip, nephew and adopted son of Erasmus van Phillip and Anadhi Newhouse van Phillip, twin brother of Andries van Phillip, cousin and adoptive brother of Dr. Jacobus Vrederic van Phillip, twin flame and husband of Katelijne Snaaijer van Phillip, and father of reincarnated Andries van Phillip and Griet Vrederic van Phillip.

Katelijne Snaaijer van Phillip Stepdaughter of Ghileyn Snaaijer, twin flame and wife of Antonius van Phillip, and mother of reincarnated Andries van Phillip and Griet Vrederic van Phillip.

Andries van Phillip Deceased world-renowned pianist, son of Petrus van Phillip and Giada Berlusconi van Phillip, nephew and adopted son of Erasmus van Phillip and Anadhi Newhouse van Phillip, twin brother of Antonius van Phillip, and cousin and adoptive brother of Dr. Jacobus Vrederic van Phillip. Now reincarnated son of Antonius van Phillip and Katelijne Snaaijer van Phillip, grandson of Erasmus van Phillip and Anadhi Newhouse van Phillip, nephew of Dr. Jacobus Vrederic van Phillip and Dr. Margriete van Achthoven van Phillip, brother of Griet Vrederic van Phillip, cousin of Rietje Vrederic van Phillip, twin flame and husband of Tara Bella, and adoptive father of Hana Bella van Phillip and Ahana Bella van Phillip.

Tara Bella van Phillip   Daughter of Sitara Bella and Marcello Esposito, twin flame and wife of Andries van Phillip, and adoptive mother of Hana Bella van Phillip and Ahana Bella van Phillip.

Griet Vrederic van Phillip   Daughter of Antonius van Phillip and Katelijne Snaaijer van Phillip, granddaughter of Erasmus van Phillip and Anadhi Newhouse van Phillip, niece of Dr. Jacobus Vrederic van Phillip and Dr. Margriete Achthoven, sister of Andries van Phillip, and cousin of Rietje Vrederic van Phillip. Reincarnated form of sixteenth-century Griet van Jacobus.

Rietje Vrederic van Phillip   Daughter of Dr. Jacobus Vrederic van Phillip and Dr. Margriete van Achthoven, granddaughter of Erasmus van Phillip and Anadhi Newhouse van Phillip, and cousin

of Andries van Phillip and Griet
Vrederic van Phillip.
Reincarnated form of sixteenth
and seventeenth-century
Margriete "Rietje" Jacobus
Peters.

Theunis Peters Adopted son of Aunt Marinda.
Adoptive brother of Alexander.
Biological son of Incubus and
Succubus. Reincarnated form of
sixteenth-century Theunis Peters.

Alexander van der Adopted son of Aunt Marinda.
Bijl Adoptive brother of Theunis.
Reincarnated form of sixteenth
and seventeenth-century Sir
Alexander van der Bijl. Cousin of
seventeenth-century Frederic van
der Bijl.

Ahana Bella van Biological daughter of Ahana
Phillip Roy, sister of Hana Bella van
Phillip, and adopted daughter of
Andries van Phillip and Tara
Bella van Phillip.

Hana Bella van Biological daughter of Ahana
Phillip Roy, sister of Ahana Bella van
Phillip, and adopted daughter of
Andries van Phillip and Tara
Bella van Phillip.

GLOSSARY

Get acquainted with some terms and places that were used in this book.

Bapu Respectful way of calling an older man such as one's father in India

CIA Central Intelligence Agency, a United States federal agency, gathers international intelligence and conducts undercover operations for national security

Cremation A method where a corpse is disposed through burning

Dreams Images that play out in the mind during sleep, explained in detail within Ann Marie Ruby's book *Spiritual Lighthouse: The Dream Diaries Of Ann Marie Ruby*

FBI Federal Bureau of Investigation, part of the United States Department of Justice, is a law enforcement agency that investigates domestic crimes and threats

Forced Marriage A marriage without consent, also a human rights violation

Ghost Spirit or soul of the deceased with apparitions in the transition after death

India Country officially called the Republic of India located in South Asia and one of the oldest civilizations on Earth with Hindi as one of its official languages

Kasteel Vrederic Family From the world of Ann Marie Ruby's *Kasteel Vrederic* book series

MacNider Hospital Fictional hospital in the fictional world of Ann Marie Ruby's book *The Haunting Of MacNider Hospital*

Maximum Security Prison The most violent and most dangerous inmates are housed here under a high level of security

Montauk A village located on the east end of the Long Island peninsula in the state of New York in the United States

Montauk Point Lighthouse Historic lighthouse, first lighthouse in the state of New

York, and the fourth oldest lighthouse in the United States

Morgue Place where the human corpse is stored until identified or claimed

Nana Term used to call maternal grandfather in India

The Netherlands Country in Northwestern Europe with territories in the Caribbean, and with Dutch as its official language

Organ Trafficking Serious international crime that involves harvesting human organs to sell illegally

Rakhi A thread or talisman that sisters tie around the wrist of their brothers during Raksha Bandhan

Raksha Bandhan Popular annual Hindu celebration honoring the eternal and pure bond of safety between brother and sister

The Old Lighthouse Fictional lighthouse in the fictional world of Ann Marie Ruby's book *The Haunting Of MacNider Hospital*

Winter Solstice   The shortest day and longest
night of the year in December
in the Northern Hemisphere

ABOUT THE AUTHOR

"Meet Ann Marie Ruby from California.
This is her story."

Ann Marie Ruby was born into a diplomatic family for which she had the privilege of traveling the world. This upbringing made the whole world her one family. She never saw a country as a foreign country yet as a neighbor who was there for her as she would be there for them. After all, isn't that what families do for one another?

Ann Marie became an author as she started to place her chosen words into the pages of her diaries. She knew she must collect all her thoughts and produce them into different diaries. Each diary became her different books.

Ann Marie's life goal is not to just write something but only what she believes in. So all her thoughts and words remained within the pages of her diaries until she realized it was time she must share them with you. Otherwise, she felt selfish and knew that was not her characteristic as she lives for everyone, not just for herself.

INTERNATIONAL #1 BESTSELLING AUTHOR:

Ann Marie became an international number-one bestselling author of twenty-seven books. Alongside being a

355

full-time author. She loves to write articles on her website where she can have a better connection with all of you. Ann Marie, a dream psychic, became a blogger and a humanitarian only because she believes in you and herself as a complete, honest, and open family.

PERSONAL:

Ann Marie is an American who grew up in Brisbane, Australia. She resided in the Washington, D.C. area, later settled in Seattle, Washington, and currently lives in California. In her spare time when she is not writing books, she loves to meditate, pray, listen to music, cook, and write blog posts.

BESTSELLING:

Ann Marie's books have placed her on top 100 bestselling charts in various countries including the Netherlands, United States, United Kingdom, Canada, and Germany. In 2020, she became a household name as her books began to consistently rank #1 on multiple bestselling charts. *The Netherlands: Land Of My Dreams* and *Everblooming: Through The Twelve Provinces Of The Netherlands*, both became overnight number-one bestsellers in the United States.

In 2020, *The Netherlands: Land Of My Dreams* also became a bestseller in the Netherlands and Canada, consistently becoming #1 on various lists and one of the top selling books on Amazon NL. *Everblooming: Through The Twelve Provinces Of The Netherlands* became #37 on the Netherlands top 100 bestselling Amazon books chart which includes all books from all genres. Ann Marie's other books have also made various top 100 bestselling lists and received multiple accolades including *Eternal Truth: The Tunnel Of Light* which was named as one of eight thought-provoking books by women.

ROMANCE FICTION:

Ann Marie's *Kasteel Vrederic* series was written in a diary fashion. She has always kept a diary herself, so she thought her characters too could keep a diary. All of their diaries became individual books yet collectively, they are a part of a family, the Kasteel Vrederic family.

OTHER BOOKS:

All of Ann Marie's nonfiction and fiction books are available globally. You can take a look at short descriptions about the books at the end of this book.

THE NETHERLANDS:

Ann Marie revealed why many of her books revolve around the Netherlands, sharing that as a dream psychic, she had seen the historical past of a country in her dreams and was later able to place a name to the country. This is described in detail in *Spiritual Lighthouse: The Dream Diaries Of Ann Marie Ruby* and *The Netherlands: Land Of My Dreams* where she also wrote about her plans to eventually move to the Netherlands.

Ann Marie has received letters on behalf of His Majesty King Willem-Alexander and Her Majesty Queen Máxima of the Netherlands after they received her books *The Netherlands: Land Of My Dreams* and *Everblooming: Through The Twelve Provinces Of The Netherlands.* Additionally, Ann Marie has received letters on behalf of His Excellency Mark Rutte, the Prime Minister of the Netherlands for her books.

WRITING:

Ann Marie also is acclaimed globally as one of the top voices in the spiritual space, however, she is recognized for her writing abilities published across many genres namely spirituality, lifestyle, inspirational quotations, poetry, fiction, romance, history, travel, social awareness, and more. Her writing style is hailed by critics and readers alike as making readers feel as though they have made a friend.

FOLLOW THE AUTHOR:

Now as you have found her book, why don't you and Ann Marie become friends? Join her and become a part of her global family. Ann Marie shall always give you books which you will read and then find yourself as a part of her book family.

For more information about Ann Marie Ruby, any one of her books, or to read her blog posts and articles, subscribe to her website, www.annmarieruby.com.

Follow Ann Marie Ruby on Twitter, Facebook, Instagram, Threads, and Pinterest:

@TheAnnMarieRuby

BOOKS BY THE AUTHOR

INSPIRATIONAL QUOTATIONS SERIES:

This series includes four books of original quotations and one omnibus edition.

Spiritual Travelers:
Life's Journey From The Past
To The Present
For The Future

Spiritual
Messages:
From A Bottle

Spiritual Journey:
Life's Eternal Blessings

Spiritual
Inspirations:
Sacred Words
Of Wisdom

Omnibus edition contains all four books of original quotations.

Spiritual Ark:
The Enchanted Journey Of Timeless
Quotations

SPIRITUAL SONGS COLLECTION:

This series includes three original spiritual prayer books.

SPIRITUAL SONGS: LETTERS FROM MY CHEST

When there was no hope, I found hope within these sacred words of prayers, I but call songs. Within this book, I have for you, 100 very sacred prayers.

SPIRITUAL SONGS II: BLESSINGS FROM A SACRED SOUL

Prayers are but the sacred doors to an individual's enlightenment. This book has 123 prayers for all humans with humanity.

SPIRITUAL SONGS III: THE RISING LOTUS

Unitedly let us rise out of the murky waters of Earth with hands held up toward the Heavenly skies, as we build a bridge of union between all the creation and the Creator through 41 prayers.

SPIRITUAL LIGHTHOUSE: THE DREAM DIARIES OF ANN MARIE RUBY

Do you believe in dreams? For within each individual dream, there is a hidden message and a miracle interlinked. Learn the spiritual, scientific, religious, and philosophical aspects of dreams. Walk with me as you travel through forty nights, through the pages of my book.

THE WORLD HATE CRISIS: THROUGH THE EYES OF A DREAM PSYCHIC

Humans have walked into an age where humanity now is being questioned as hate crimes have reached a catastrophic amount. Let us in union stop this crisis. Pick up my book and see if you too could join me in this fight.

ETERNAL TRUTH: THE TUNNEL OF LIGHT

Within this book, travel with me through the doors of birth, death, reincarnation, true soulmates and twin flames, dreams, miracles, and the end of time.

THE NETHERLANDS: LAND OF MY DREAMS

Oh the sacred travelers, be like the mystical river and journey through this blessed land through my book. Be the flying bird of wisdom and learn about a land I call, Heaven on Earth.

EVERBLOOMING: THROUGH THE TWELVE PROVINCES OF THE NETHERLANDS

Original poetry and hand-picked tales are bound together in this keepsake book. Come travel with me as I take you through the lives of the Dutch past.

LOVE LETTERS: THE TIMELESS TREASURE

Fifty original timeless treasured love poems are presented with individual illustrations describing each poem.

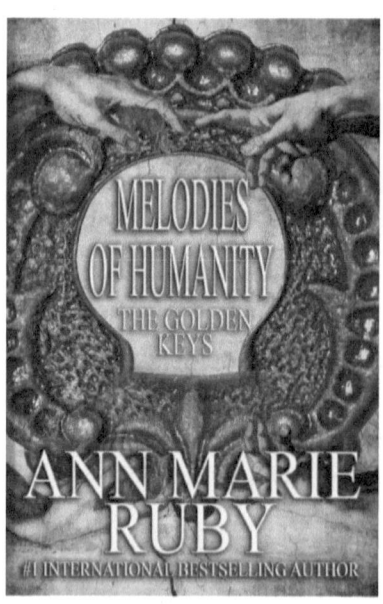

MELODIES OF HUMANITY: THE GOLDEN KEYS

Thirty-two poems retell the melodies of humanity, calling all humans to awaken their humanity through love, the golden keys everyone carries within their inner souls.

KASTEEL VREDERIC SERIES:

ETERNALLY BELOVED: I SHALL NEVER LET YOU GO

Travel time to the sixteenth century where Jacobus van Vrederic, a beloved lover and father, surmounts time and tide to find the vanished love of his life. On his pursuit, Jacobus discovers secrets that will alter his life evermore. He travels through the Eighty Years' War-ravaged country, the Netherlands as he takes the vow, even if separated by a breath, "Eternally beloved, I shall never let you go."

EVERMORE BELOVED: I SHALL NEVER LET YOU GO

Jacobus van Vrederic returns with the devoted spirits of Kasteel Vrederic. A knight and a seer also join him on a quest to find his lost evermore beloved. They journey through a war-ravaged country, the Netherlands, to stop another war which was brewing silently in his land, called the witch hunts. Time was his enemy as he must defeat time and tide to find his evermore beloved wife alive.

BE MY DESTINY: VOWS FROM THE BEYOND

Fighting their biggest enemy destiny, twin flames Erasmus van Phillip and Anadhi Newhouse are reborn over and over again only to lose the battle to destiny. Find out if through the helping hands of sacred spirits of the sixteenth century, these eternal twin flames are finally able to unite in the twenty-first century, as they say, "Reincarnation is a blessing if only you are mine."

HEART BEATS YOUR NAME: VOWS FROM THE BEYOND

While one is sleepless, the other twin flame is sleeping eternally. Now how does Antonius van Phillip awaken his twin flame Katelijne Snaaijer from beyond Earth, and solve a murder mystery, she is the only witness to yet also a victim of? Find out how the musical sound of heartbeats guide him to his sleeping beloved while he solves the mystery sleepless.

ENTRANCED BELOVED: I SHALL NEVER LET YOU GO

The pages of Margriete "Rietje" Jacobus Peters's love story from her diary slowly go missing from the library of Kasteel Vrederic. The twenty-first-century descendants fighting death and time must travel back in time to save their ancestors and their beloved Kasteel Vrederic. Traveling through the tunnel of light, the family of the twenty-first century must save the seventeenth-century twin flames. Rietje and her beloved twin flame Sir Alexander van der Bijl must create another paranormal, magical, historical, romantic diary for the dynasty to even exist.

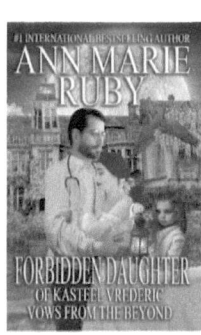

FORBIDDEN DAUGHTER OF KASTEEL VREDERIC: VOWS FROM THE BEYOND

Jacobus Vrederic van Phillip stopped pouring tears and burning himself with memories of passion to become a stone, so he could live with memories and not recreate new ones. The Vrederic family members realize the curse of past life's karma will come and meet them in this life and erase the only child who kept the dynasty going, the child known to all as the forbidden daughter of Kasteel Vrederic. The man who has sacrificed his life for all members of his family and society now must find a way to awaken his sleeping soul, recognize his twin flame, and bring back as the beloved daughter the only child he had rejected. To this world she was known as the forbidden daughter of Kasteel Vrederic.

THE IMMORTALITY SERUM: VOWS FROM THE BEYOND

Andries van Phillip, the famous pianist, gets calls from his dead twin flame Tara Bella in his dreams. All dressed in red, she roams around a burning castle trying to rescue all the people from within, without realizing she was the victim, not Andries. Now the paranormal family travels across the ocean as they fight Succubus the demoness, rescue the woman in red, and solve a murder mystery, all while they know before time ends, they must find the immortality serum.

WOMAN IN THE MIRROR: VOWS FROM THE BEYOND

An undying love story began in the sixteenth century, yet the evil eyes of Succubus wiped away the story of Kees and Marinda van Vrederic before it even had a chance. Voyage to Kasteel Vrederic where the paranormal family helps rewrite the unresolved love story of Kees and Marinda, even after their death. They must unravel the mystery behind the identity of the woman in the mirror, whom everyone seeks, before it is too late.

BRIDE OF THE IMMORTAL: VOWS FROM THE BEYOND

The ninth book in this series is coming soon.

BRIDE OF THE IMMORTAL: VOWS FROM THE BEYOND

SHATTERED WINGS: DIARY OF A CHILD BRIDE

Ahana Roy fought this unkind world to make room for her in this society, where she would not go to bed hungry. She was brought to the city of dreams where her dreams were shattered as she became a child bride. How will she fight the war of being a child bride in a city that has no idea of her existence? In her shattered dreams, she found a ghost sailor who promised to be with her, dead or alive. Following the advice of a dead sailor, Ahana wandered the streets of New York City looking for help. There she found the paranormal family of Kasteel Vrederic as her helping hands. This is the diary of child bride who said, "I had no chance in life as I was born with shattered wings."

THE BRIDE, THE GROOM, AND THE GHOST

Viviana Stella Vivour was separated from her beloved groom during the 1866 massacre in New Orleans, Louisiana. For over a century, she has been roaming the streets of "The Big Easy" as a ghost bride. Now in the twenty-first century, Viviana's spirit is transported to her reincarnated past-life groom Silas Coleridge Vivour's historic Victorian home by the Mississippi River. She is shattered to witness him facing forced retirement through ageism. Separated by a breath, Viviana and Silas come face-to-face with their past-life enemy who became a demon to separate them again. The twin flames find solace in ways they never expected as there appears Aurelius van Phillip, a mysterious young man, who can see Viviana and the demon.

THE HAUNTING OF MACNIDER HOSPITAL

MacNider Hospital of Montauk has become a crime scene, where twelve ubiquitous ghosts appear seeking revenge for their deaths, all revolving around a forced marriage victim charged with murder. The MacNider father and son duo must solve who is the victim and who is the slayer in this Gothic psychological thriller.

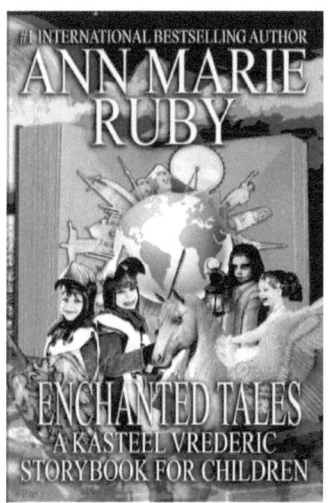

ENCHANTED TALES: A KASTEEL VREDERIC STORYBOOK FOR CHILDREN

Travel around the world in seven nights. Through enchanted tales you will meet and assist superheroes from the seven continents of this world. While there, you will learn about different cultures and landmarks. Keep your magical lanterns glowing as you help the girl with the lantern solve mysteries around the globe.

BROTHER BEAR AND THE FOUR INVESTIGATORS: A KASTEEL VREDERIC STORYBOOK FOR CHILDREN

Kasteel Vrederic's second storybook is coming soon.

Coming Soon

BROTHER BEAR AND THE FOUR INVESTIGATORS: A KASTEEL VREDERIC STORYBOOK FOR CHILDREN

www.ingramcontent.com/pod-product-compliance
Lightning Source LLC
Chambersburg PA
CBHW020258030726
47499CB00001B/256